THE
KILLING
CAROL

To: Susie
Merry
Christmas!

(signature)

THE KILLING CAROL

An
Anna Greenan Mystery

Jennifer Bee

LEVEL
BEST BOOKS

First published by Level Best Books 2021

This novel is entirely a work of fiction. The names, characters and incidents portrayed in it are the work of the author's imagination. Any resemblance to actual persons, living or dead, events or localities is entirely coincidental.

Jennifer Bee asserts the moral right to be identified as the author of this work.

Author Photo Credit: KJ Jugar

First edition

ISBN: 978-1-68512-040-5

Cover art by Level Best Designs

This book was professionally typeset on Reedsy.
Find out more at reedsy.com

For my family, especially my daughter—who taught me to be brave, my son—who taught me to persevere, my husband—who taught me how to sacrifice, and my parents—who taught me everything else.

Praise for THE KILLING CAROL

"Jennifer Bee's debut novel, *The Killing Carol*, opens with a satisfying bang. It delivers a clever mystery from the past filled with twists and intrigue. Bee uses the benign 'Twelve Days of Christmas' as the framework to carry disturbing clues—one dreaded day at a time. With a deft hand, she keeps the reader engaged and guessing. Well done!" — Leah Weiss, Bestselling author of *If the Creek Don't Rise* and *All the Little Hopes*

"*The Killing Carol* - A mystery/thriller with a satisfying romance and lots of twists and turns. The tension never lags. The song 'The Twelve Days of Christmas' becomes filled with menace as Anna receives one note a day with a twisted message." — Judi Lynn, *USA Today* bestselling author of *The Body in the Attic*

"In her debut novel *The Killing Carol*, Jennifer Bee does what all the best writers of mysteries and thrillers do. She makes the unbelievable believable and the believable unbelievable. Reading her novel, I felt I was re-entering the world of the immensely successful TV series *Mare of Easttown* with its blend of small town coziness and unrelenting, surprising, and dark mystery." — John Guzlowski, author of the Hank and Marvin Mysteries. Guzlowski's book of poems *Third Winter of War: Buchenwald* was nominated for the Pulitzer

"Jennifer Bee's *The Killing Carol* is not your usual Christmas story. Small town intimacy coupled with deep-rooted secrets gives this book the suspense and twists of a thriller with the hope and faith of a Christmas miracle tale. Jennifer Bee manages to turn 'The Twelve Days of Christmas' into something eerie without losing touch with the joy of the season." — Tina deBellegarde, Agatha-nominated author of *Winter Witness*, a Batavia-on-Hudson Mystery

Chapter One

December 26

Potrage, New York

Anna had always believed the most powerful words were the unspoken ones—those she wished she'd said and those that went without saying. As she stood in the middle of her living room, snow melting off her winter coat, she realized she was mistaken.

"On the first day of Christmas, my true love gave to me the reason your husband had to die."

The note was typed on heavyweight cotton paper. She read it over and over, careful not to touch the writing, as if touching the actual words would somehow diminish their potency.

Who would send me this? And why?

A hoax. Had to be. But her intuition interceded and she knew better than to doubt the hairs on her neck or the knot in her stomach. Someone sent this message, and more would come. One didn't pick the song "The Twelve Days of Christmas" and stop after the first day. That would be like cutting a dozen roses to put one in a vase.

No, more notes would be forthcoming. Anna was sure of it.

Could this be real? Her hands trembled. *No. Can't be. Can it? Please. No.* Her husband, Jake, had been dead for three years. The car accident couldn't be undone, and the finality of it still stole her breath.

Jake murdered? No. No way. It was an accident. Nothing more.

Her house felt as artificial as the unlit Christmas tree in the corner. The natural cherry dining table, the pillowed sofa—all of it felt placed like the setting of a play, and she couldn't help but feel like she had lost her script and forgotten her lines.

The home phone rang.

To her right sat the hand-painted writing desk her grandmother had left her. At that moment, the desk had the same effect on her as Nana once had; it grounded her. She stuffed the cryptic note in the overfull desk drawer and glanced at the caller ID. *Ryan.*

"Hey." Pinning the cordless between her ear and shoulder, she wiggled out of her wet coat. "I just walked in." Anna slung her winter coat over the desk chair and peeled off her hat. Static electricity crackled, no doubt leaving half her hair standing on end. Her hair, like her life, had a will of its own, a montage of dark twists and unruly curls.

"I figured. We're still on for tonight, right?" Ryan's question held a smile.

"Um… Ah…" She knew he'd ask. He always did. Ever since her husband passed away, his best friend checked in on her. At first, she was grateful for the company, but now… She didn't want to be an obligation. "I told you, I can't. I have my book study and—"

"You should see this letter I got."

Her breath caught. "What letter?" *Did he get the same Christmas note?*

"From the Better Business Bureau. In a nutshell, they said no."

She exhaled. "Well, try again. You can't take no for an answer."

"I never do. So, about tonight?"

"I can't. I told you. I'm hosting this month's book study. They'll be here in fifteen minutes."

Someone knocked.

"Shoot. Listen, I'll call you later. Someone's at my door."

"I'll hold. What if it's some weirdo?"

"In Potrage?" *The Christmas note. The reason your husband had to die.* "Ya know, hang on a sec." Anna peeked out the door's etched glass.

She should've known. *Ryan.*

As Anna opened the door, she couldn't hold back her grin. "What are you doing here?" Ryan tucked his cell phone in his jacket pocket and beamed. His disheveled, brown hair was peppered with gray, and an awful aqua tie poked out of the top of his beige sweater. "I'm taking your advice." Ryan kissed her cheek as he walked past. The musky scent of his cologne trailed behind him.

"What advice?" Anna shivered as she shut the door. It seemed almost too cold to snow, no matter what the weatherman claimed.

Ryan lifted his chin. "I'm not taking no for an answer."

Anna placed the cordless back in its cradle. "Well, you were right."

"I was?"

"Definitely a weirdo."

"See that." He winked. "You weren't serious about canceling tonight, right? I mean, I could go and sit by the phone and wait for you to come to your senses, but I thought I'd save you all that groveling and begging."

"No. You can stay. Although, it is *so* like me to call and beg a man for his company."

"With that hair of yours today, you might have to."

Anna laughed and tried to pat down her mop. Ryan had her, and he knew it. As hard as she tried to think of a quick retort, nothing came except, "Ya know."

Ryan pitched his brown leather jacket on the sofa back. "Hey, you didn't plug in your tree."

The glass ornaments rattled, and the artificial tree swayed as Ryan wormed beneath it. The white lights lit and glistened against the glittery silver garland. A ridiculous, fuzzy pink thing topped the tree—a wedding gift with no fathomable intended use. The tree topper had been Jake's idea.

Anna checked the thermostat and cranked it up. Sixty-six degrees, but the house seemed even colder than that. The furnace must be having trouble keeping up. Thank goodness for the fireplace.

Since half the book study was twice her age, she had to warm things up quick. If she was chilled, they'd be frozen. As she pulled back the fireplace's metal screen, the scraping sound made her cringe. Tiny puffs of soot floated upward as she tossed logs into the hearth.

Ryan stood behind her. "So, what can I do while you have your meeting?"

"You could attend. May even learn something."

"Oh, please." He twisted an old newspaper and handed it to her. "I cannot believe you guys are meeting the day after Christmas. Don't you ever take time off?"

Anna needed to look into getting a gas insert or one of those fireplaces where you just pushed a button and the flame came on. Someday. Since Jake died, she felt blessed when she could cover the essentials. "It's our Christmas party. We were supposed to have it weeks ago, but the weather's been wild. Storm after storm. Finally, with this snow stranding almost everyone, we agreed we'd bring our leftovers and hang out the day after Christmas."

Wedging the paper between two logs, she added the kindling and lit it. Anna closed the screen and stood. "We don't *officially* meet again for a few more weeks, but our group has always felt more like a family. It seems only right to spend some part of the holiday together." Anna moved toward her desk. She wanted to tell Ryan about the note. Get his take on things. "I've gotta talk to you about something. When I got home today—"

The doorbell clanged.

"Shoot. I'll tell you later." Anna waved him off and answered the door. "Why hello there, Daisy."

Daisy Peters stood about four feet and weighed about eighty pounds. Seventy-nine of it had to be spit and vinegar. "I didn't know if I should come. The weatherman's acting like the sky's falling." Expertly made up in a mink coat, Daisy sauntered in. "How was your Christmas, Anna?" Daisy hugged her—the cold radiating off of her.

"Fine, and yours?"

"Uneventful." As Daisy strolled past, her silver cane seemed more like an accessory rather than the necessity it had become. Some people made everything look easy. "Oh, you have a visitor. Hello, Ryan." She held out her hand.

Ryan kissed it and, in his best southern drawl, said, "Now, Miss Daaaisy."

Daisy nodded, and Ryan helped her out of her fur. "Well, good for you, Anna." She adjusted the gold brooch on her green blazer. "About time. Every woman needs a stinger in her beehive now and again."

Anna's mouth hung open. "No, he's not. It's not—"

Leave it to Daisy to say something grossly inappropriate and not even realize it. Or maybe she did and the nonchalance was part of her charm.

"Now, hush up, and let's get this party started. I don't know how long the weather will hold, and I hate driving in this stuff."

Ryan gestured toward the French doors separating the living room and den, one of the few room dividers in the open layout. "I'm gonna use your computer."

"Don't leave on my account. I'm too old for secrets." Daisy rested her cane on the edge of the dining table and scooted in her chair. "This town has too many and they require too much energy to keep. Oh shoot. Ryan, can you be a doll and grab the pasta salad and rolls out of my back seat? I didn't want to slip on my way in and spill 'em. Car's unlocked."

"Sure. Not a problem." Ryan headed out.

"Daisy, let me pull the cheesecake out of the freezer and get set up."

"Go ahead. Need any help?"

"Nope." Anna headed into the kitchen and flipped on the coffee pot. Her mouth watered as she placed the gourmet cheesecake on the cutting board to thaw. The group assigned her dessert and coffee, the best part of any dinner party.

Chatter emanated from the living room. Ryan must have returned with Daisy's dinner rolls and salad.

Daisy had come to her first book study shortly after Anna moved to town, six months after Daisy's son, Tommy, disappeared. Daisy had described her son as a runaway train. He'd served time for armed robbery and was wanted for questioning in a hit-and-run. When the Potrage police came to talk with him, Tommy was gone. No note, no explanation. Daisy apparently never heard from him again. That was more than three years ago.

Daisy must have wrangled with questions. Where is he? Will I see him again? Is he guilty? But ultimately, she had asked their group only one. Do you think he's

5

alive? Like life itself was somehow a victory, or maybe Daisy knew not to ask what she didn't want answered.

The coffee sputtered as it brewed; its rich aroma filled the kitchen. Anna stepped back into the great room and set the paper plates, plastic utensils, and Styrofoam cups on the dining table.

"Oh, before everyone gets here, I have something for you, my dear." Daisy pulled a white envelope from her blazer's pocket and set it on the table next to Anna. "Open it after I've left. Just a little something for Christmas."

"Oh, thank you. You didn't have to—"

"I wanted to. And thank you for the poinsettia you left on my doorstep." Daisy squeezed Anna's hand.

Anna sat, wide-eyed. "How'd you know it was me?"

"I have my sources." Daisy smirked.

The doorbell rang.

"I'll get it." Ryan spoke to someone in the doorway, but Anna couldn't process the words. The voices were frantic; the news not good.

In Anna's muddled mind, everything began to move in slow motion. The feeling of unease she'd come home to intensified. *The reason your husband had to die.* Anna's mouth was dry, her chest heavy.

She stared at the woman across the table. Daisy, once so full of vigor, now seemed somehow older and frail.

They shared a single glance.

A lifetime passed between them in that moment.

From the expressions playing out on Daisy's face, she knew what the news would be. Daisy knew, and Anna sat helpless and watched the very moment her sweet friend's heart shattered.

"Daisy." Gloria Lonnie rushed in and knelt beside the table, her auburn hair drenched. A trail of snow and ice followed her from the door. She took short, rapid breaths. "You need to come with me. It's Tommy. Oh Daisy…" Gloria wept.

Daisy held up her hand as if unwilling to hear anymore. She nodded once. A single tear slid down her cheek. Ryan helped her to her feet.

He held open her mink, and she slid it on.

With the dignity of royalty, she turned back. "We'll have to reschedule this get together." Daisy adjusted her cane.

Anna rose. Her whole body trembled.

"It seems..." Daisy raised her chin. "They have found my son."

Chapter Two

Anna flopped onto her sofa and stared at the fire. The flames moved in a rhythmic dance—the dance of the dead. Tiny flecks wafted up the chimney like sacrifices to God. Had Jake been one of those sacrifices? Murdered and somehow she never knew. Now, Tommy was gone too.

Ryan turned the last person away, effectively canceling the night's party. He walked over and took the seat beside her. "You're shaking." He reached for his jacket and draped it over her shoulders. His brown leather coat was warm and weighty with a rich, earthy scent.

Anna's heart panged for Daisy, knowing how unbearable the days and nights to come would be.

"You okay?" Ryan brushed a stray hair from her cheek. His hand felt soft and gentle.

Part of her wanted to fold into him, but she didn't want Ryan, just a place to hide.

Anna leaned against the sofa's armrest. "Do you know what happened?"

"Apparently, someone was struck and killed on the corner of Main and Route 15 near Kesterson's place. Looks like it's Tommy. Daisy has to give a positive I.D. before they say for sure, but..." Ryan shrugged. "Small-town cops, you know. The whole town knows before the family does."

Anna did know. She'd been there. Vince Adams, the officer who had come to her door, had taken her right to the scene of Jake's accident. She was living a nightmare while the whole town watched, like the next twisted phase of reality TV. "Believe me. I get it." This whole thing made no sense.

"The man's been hiding for three years and shows back up at Christmas time walking around town?"

Ryan pushed up the sleeves of his sweater. "Stranger still, I don't know if you recall, but the reason Tommy skipped town was a hit-and-run a few years ago."

"I remember. Details are fuzzy, but I know a boy he hung out with died."

"Darrell Hartman. A bunch of kids partying under the bridge. It was foggy. Some of the kids brought ATVs, some drove, Hartman walked. From what I heard, Hartman left early but never made it home." Ryan's hand swept across the back of his neck. "They found him roadside the next day. Hit-and-run. The tire treads matched Tommy's pickup. Potrage P.D. went to question him, and the rest, well…"

"Oh." Anna closed her eyes. "How sad."

"Tommy hitting Hartman was no accident."

"What? They were friends."

"They argued." Ryan loosened and slid off his necktie.

This seemed unbelievable. Tommy was trouble, but…

"That's how the cops pinned it on him so quickly. They went to question him before the lab work came back on the tires."

Anna shook her head. "Daisy never told me any of this."

"If he were your son, would you repeat it?"

"So, you think this hit-and-run was some sort of retaliation?"

"I don't know." Ryan forked a hand through his hair. "It's sad though. Right at the holidays too."

The reason your husband had to die. Could the note be connected? "Tell me about the night Jake died."

Ryan's face contorted in obvious confusion. "What? Why?"

"I wanna go over it." Anna closed her eyes, trying to squeeze out the image of Jake's car—the mangled, twisted metal, the still-smoldering fire that would have taken him even if the crash had not. The stench of burning rubber, gasoline, death.

"What does this have to do with Daisy and her son?" Ryan gestured toward the entryway.

"Nothing. Everything. I don't know."

"Jake died in an accident. You know this." Ryan sank back as if the weight of what had happened somehow fell upon him.

Anna spoke slowly. "Please, tell me again."

"It was tax time. He was going over my books. You remember how he got."

She remembered everything: Jake's smile, his laugh, his touch. There were times she thought she still saw him. Times when he seemed so close she swore he was in the house.

"Jake said he had to get home. I should've told him not to go. The roads were bad but …" Ryan's voice caught. He seemed entranced by the fire. "He hit black ice and…he…"

Anna's stomach churned. She couldn't bear to hear anymore. Wiping her damp cheek on her shoulder, she got up, knowing Ryan would need a minute. No matter how much she hurt, in a lot of ways, Ryan struggled even more. Hers was pain. His was guilt. He, too, longed for peace, haunted by the same ghost, for different reasons.

"The seat belt… If he'd. I wish he'd… I should've never insisted he come over." Ryan hung his head.

Anna walked over and pulled the cryptic note out of the desk drawer. "Do you think Jake could have been murdered?"

"What?" Ryan bolted upright. "Why would you even ask something like that?"

Anna clutched the paper. *Could it be connected to Daisy's son?* She had to tell Ryan. "When I came home today, this had been shoved against my front door."

Ryan took the paper. *"On the first day of Christmas, my true love gave to me the reason your husband had to die."* The color drained from his face. "Why didn't you tell me about this when I got here?"

"I tried, but then Daisy showed up. I didn't want her worrying…It's probably nothing." Anna shook her head. Maybe she shouldn't have showed him. "I'm sure it's nothing."

Ryan studied the message. "Did you call the police?"

"No. For what? To tell them I got a creepy note? It's not like someone's threatening me." Anna gestured toward the crinkled paper. "Realistically, what can they do? Jake's accident happened three years ago."

"You still should report it." Ryan passed her back the note, stood, and walked to the fireplace. He pulled back the metal screen and poked at the burning logs. The fire popped and cracked, and more sparks fluttered up. The scent of the burning wood filled the air.

"Sounds like the Potrage P.D. will be busy enough trying to figure out what happened to Tommy." Anna wandered to her back window. The swirling snow blocked the hills of the state park. "Listen, you should probably head out. It's really starting to come down out there." She turned and faced Ryan.

"I've got four-wheel drive." A picture of Jake, Ryan, and her sat on the mantle. Ryan picked it up.

Anna had memorized every pixel of that picture, every bead of her sleek, black dress, every laugh line on Jake's face, every paisley in Ryan's horrible tie. She was thirty-one. It was her fifth wedding anniversary. She'd just taken on a new job writing commercials in Rochester, and, earlier that afternoon, they had closed on this house.

They had been terrified, excited, but, most of all, they had been happy.

The house was forty-five minutes east of Buffalo, where they all grew up, but she and Jake had loved the house, and they'd live by Ryan again. After college, Ryan moved to Potrage to take over his father's business.

Now, three years later, Jake was dead, and Anna was alone. She'd often wondered if this house and its location were a part of some unspoken contingency plan. The town was small and safe, and Jake had to know Ryan would always look out for her. If Jake thought it, he never said it, and she questioned now more than ever what else went left unsaid between them.

Ryan ran a finger across the picture. "Besides, you really shouldn't be alone."

"I don't need a babysitter."

"I'm not babysitting." He regarded her with a mischievous grin. "Babysitters get paid. I'm your guest."

11

"No." Anna chuckled. "Guests get invited."

Ryan pointed toward the ceramic manger scene beside the Christmas tree. "The wise men weren't invited. They still showed up."

"The wise men brought gifts."

"Wise men always do."

Anna awoke the next morning to the scraping sounds of a snowplow. She rolled out of bed but didn't dare look at the clock. *It's way too early.*

Ryan hadn't headed out until almost midnight, and she doubted it was much past six.

An hour or so later, she managed to shower, dress, and meander downstairs. Freshly fallen snow twinkled in the budding daylight. Several more inches had fallen overnight. Finger-like streams of powder wafted across the freshly plowed roadway. Three feet of snow had already accumulated this week, and more was forecast.

Her cell phone chimed with the daily notification from the *Potrage News* App. Hopefully, it wasn't from the weather center.

Anna picked it up and gasped at the headline. *No. It can't be. There's no way.* She read it again just to be sure.

"Daisy Peters Dead."

Chapter Three

"Daisy Peters, 65, a lifelong Potrage resident, was found dead in her Vermont Street home late last night after identifying the remains of her only child, Thomas Peters. Thomas (Tommy), 23, was struck and killed by a car on Route 15 near Main Street shortly before four p.m. Thursday. Daisy was found five hours later. Foul play is not suspected in either case. Father Matthew Browning will host a joint service for Daisy and Thomas Peters December 29, at nine a.m. at Saint Andrew's Catholic Church. All are welcome to attend."

Anna scrolled through the online edition of the daily paper searching for any additional information, finding none. Someone had to know something.

She threw on her coat and went to dig out her driveway.

Twenty minutes later, Anna pulled her SUV into Ryan's General Store. The only place in town to get a hot meal, groceries, and live worms. Not to mention gossip. Loads of local gossip.

Cautiously, Anna made her way across the icy parking lot. Grace was never her strong suit, even in ideal conditions, let alone amidst Mother Nature's temper tantrum. Despite her best efforts, a gust of wind sent her sliding.

Finding her footing, Anna stepped up onto the salted walkway and opened the store's front door. The wind caught it and nearly yanked her arm from its socket.

Perhaps the universe is trying to tell me something. She, as usual, ignored it.

The store was packed. Anna wrestled the door closed, painfully aware the murmur of voices stopped when the spectacle of her grand entrance ended. Some patrons nodded, others smiled knowingly. Some asked if she was all right. She returned their pleasantries as she brushed the stray snowflakes off her coat sleeves. Eventually, everyone returned to their conversations.

The grill sizzled, and the coffee smelled fantastic.

"Anna." Ryan waved from behind the busy breakfast counter. "You okay? It's absolutely awful out there."

"Fine. Thanks." Anna's voice cracked, and her face burned. She cozied up to the counter, sitting on the only open barstool sandwiched between Vince Adams, the town's only full-time cop, and Father Matthew, the local priest.

Vince rose, mumbling into the walkie clipped to his shoulder. Young, early twenties, with a muscular build and clipper cut hair, Vince looked like a cop. Only in a town as small as Potrage could he have advanced so quickly. Although, when the only other cop in town also drove the school bus, what did you expect? "Ryan, cancel that." Vince tossed two bucks on the counter. "I gotta take this coffee to go."

"No problem." Ryan stepped out from behind the grill. "See ya."

Under his filthy apron, Ryan wore a white shirt and a tie featuring ugly, rabid-looking chickens.

Where'd he buy that? A glance toward the tie rack provided the answer.

"Hi. I'm glad you stopped by. You hear about Daisy?" Ryan flopped his order pad in front of her.

"I did. The *Potrage Daily* put out an article."

"It's unbelievable." Ryan tapped his pen on the counter. "Can I getcha breakfast? I've got a fantastic ham and cheese omelet."

Ham and cheese was her favorite. Ryan must have remembered.

"Sounds good. And some coffee." She peeled off her gloves and crammed them into her purse. The zipper barely closed, and, as a result, her red handbag looked more like a pregnant hotdog. Plus, it was so small she barely felt it. As a result, she left the darn thing all over town. No matter. She kept one credit card in it, and it was just about maxed out. If someone wanted to steal her identity, they could have it and all her unpaid bills too.

Ryan set down a cup of coffee in front of her.

"Thank you." Anna stirred in creamer.

The grill sizzled again as Ryan went back to cooking. "Yours will be up in a second, Father."

"Take your time." Father Matthew was a thirty-three-year-old Catholic priest with blond hair and blue eyes. The man must have heard one ear-piercing calling because he was definitely celibate by choice. "How are you this morning, Anna?" Father Matthew slid off his glasses and wiped them with a napkin.

"Okay." Anna sighed.

Father Matthew held his glasses to the light, wiped them again, and then slid them on. "No doubt as saddened as I am about our Miss Daisy."

Anna blew on the coffee. Steam wafted out of her mug. "I just can't believe it."

"Nor do I." Suspicion etched his tone.

Foul play isn't suspected in either case.

"I just saw her yesterday." There was something about a Catholic priest and confessions.

"Really? Was Daisy well?"

"She seemed fine. Obviously, until she heard about Tommy." Anna's chest ached from the memory.

"You were with her when she got the news?"

"Unfortunately."

Father Matthew sipped his coffee. "It's very sad. I always got a kick out of Daisy."

"Me too." Anna pictured Daisy in that fur that weighed as much as she did. "Do you know what happened? Was it a heart attack?"

"Well, I know what I've been told."

Twice now, Father Matthew said something that made her think, and she had a sneaking suspicion he might have stopped down to Ryan's store for the same reason she had.

"Apparently, she was taken to Nolles Hospital to identify her son. She did. Her girlfriend, Gloria, drove her home." Father Matthew set down his mug.

"Gloria Lonnie? She was the one who came to my house and delivered the news."

"Yep. A couple hours later, Gloria stopped by to check on her. Found Daisy face down in the living room. Dead. The county coroner said natural causes."

"That's awful." Anna sighed. "What do you know about her son coming back?"

"Tommy was—"

"Here you go." Ryan handed Father Matthew his pancakes and topped off his coffee.

"Thank you."

"No problem." Ryan winked at Anna and then went back to cooking.

She couldn't stop the smile lifting her lips as she stared into her coffee cup.

"Could you pass the syrup?" Father Matthew pointed at the syrup dispenser.

She did so.

"As I was saying, I guess Leo was driving up 15, hit some ice, lost control, and accidentally struck and killed Tommy."

"Leo Adams? Vince's younger brother?" Anna pointed to the recently vacated stool beside her, unable to suppress the shock. She hadn't meant to be so loud and glanced around to see if anyone overheard. No one seemed to notice. Or if they did, they were kind enough to pretend otherwise.

"The one and only." Father Matthew poured thick maple syrup on his pancake stack. The sweet aroma made Anna's stomach growl.

Anna didn't need to ask if charges were pending. The Adams were the wealthiest, most powerful family in town. They made up the police force, the judge, and the town physician, and their family business, a salt mine on the outskirts of town, employed three quarters of the community. No, there would be no charges.

"What was Tommy doing here? Did you hear why he came back?"

Father Matthew raised his brows and peered at her over the top of his wire-rimmed glasses. "I was told he came to see his mother for Christmas."

She shook her head. "So, after being in hiding for three years, he sneaks home to see his mother, and then what? Opts to walk through town for kicks?"

"I wish I knew." Father Matthew stuck a forkful of pancake in his mouth.

After breakfast, Anna headed home with a sinking suspicion the Christmas note was somehow connected to Daisy and Tommy. Next to nothing happened in Potrage. Now, two people were dead at the same time she started receiving cryptic messages. They had to be connected. But how?

The reason your husband had to die.

It didn't make sense. Jake died in an automobile accident. It had to be. But what if the note was right? Could her husband have been murdered?

Technically, the first day of Christmas was the day before yesterday, Christmas Day. When was the note shoved against her front door? Could it have been there since Christmas Day? Anna went to midnight Mass, but that was it. She had gone to the cemetery in the afternoon but went in and out through the garage. She always used the garage. In fact, the only reason she used the front door was because the garage door opener didn't work.

That opener rested in the cup holder beside her. Anna eased her truck into her driveway, hesitated, and then slid off its back.

The batteries were gone.

Her heart hammered. She bolted inside and called Ryan at the store.

"Ryan's General Store, this is Chris."

"Hi, this is Anna Greenan. Is Ryan busy?" Anna slid off her coat and pounded the snow off her shoes.

"He stepped out for a bit. Said he'd be back in a couple hours."

"Oh...Um..." *What? Where would he have gone?*

"Wanna leave a message?"

A cacophony of voices chattered in the background. The store sounded like it was still busy.

"No, I'll try him on his cell."

"Okay. Have a good day."

"You too."

Anna hung up and dialed Ryan's cell. Her call went straight to his voice mail.

Something bothered her, something more than just the note.

Chapter Four

The Messenger sat in the first pew as the priest blessed the ivory casket in the back, swinging the ball of frankincense, chanting prayers. The church smelled like flowers—flowers, frankincense, and myrrh. The stained-glass windows glowed, and tiny flecks of dust shimmered in the light like glitter falling from the rafters.

The parishioners rose so he did the same. They sang his favorite hymn about God calling us each by name. The Messenger choked back tears but stood silent, unwilling to bear false witness to the claims he no longer believed.

On the church's ceiling was a painting of God with His arms outstretched, as if He held the entire congregation in His hands.

How many more will slip through His fingers, or sometimes does He just let go?

The Messenger waited for an answer, knowing, once again, no answer would ever come. It didn't matter because, even if it came, no answer would ever be good enough.

To pray against reality was to have no faith, so he had said and repeated countless times. Today, standing here, silent, he realized he had been mistaken. Faith was, by definition, the belief reality could be changed. But his faith had left long ago when the power of evil triumphed again.

Potrage was miles away, but the far-reaching hand of its horror was in this church. Its victim sealed in the casket.

His sister let out a sob in the pew in front of him. Her frail frame shuddered with grief—a shell of who she once was. Her eyes were sunken and swollen. Her skin held a grayish hue.

He could offer no condolence. Some losses were too deep for words to reach. Nothing could, or would, change her new reality.

His niece, Valerie, had been only nine when it happened. She'd known evil, and The Messenger had sat quiet, in anguish—because of his job, in agony—because she was his family.

Now, it was too late. The cross Valerie carried had been too much, and he would forever have to live with the fact he had never lightened her load. He had tried many times, but she was a lost sheep no shepherd could find.

It mattered not if heaven existed, for Valerie had known hell and escaped.

Three years he choked on the silence. Three years he bore the burden of truth. Three years he watched his only niece unravel like a tightly wound string until now, when there was nothing left to hold onto.

He had been the one to spot her tied between the oak trees. Her long, strawberry-blonde hair spilled around her like a halo. She had broken her own wrist trying to wrangle free. She had said she'd begged them to let her go, to stop, and she had begged God to make them stop.

Why didn't God listen to me, she'd asked him. The question, so full of pain, sucked the air from his chest that afternoon, and every day ever since.

Why didn't God listen?

Chapter Five

After the sabotaged garage opener, Anna was positive she should have received another note by now. If her timetable was correct, these notes started Christmas Day—the first day of Christmas—the same day someone tampered with her garage door opener. Which meant yesterday, December 26, was the second day. No note. At least not one she had found...yet.

Sunlight glittered off her snow-covered lawn. The brightness was blinding. The brilliant backdrop made Anna's white mailbox appear dingy.

The mail. Of course! She never picked up yesterday's mail. She was so freaked out by the time she got inside, she had never even thought about grabbing the mail.

Anna slid on her shoes and bolted out, immediately regretting not tossing on a coat and boots. The wind ripped through her sweater, and her hands and face stung. She trudged through the wet snow up her long driveway. Yanking open the metal box, she grabbed the stack of mail and slogged back inside.

She flopped onto her desk chair, peeled off her soaked socks, and stuck her frozen feet into her fuzzy slippers. She leafed through the mail. The cold stuck to it like a stamp. Bill, bill, credit card offer, envelope. No return address. Postmarked Potrage. The mail didn't come until later. This was yesterday's mail. She tore open the envelope. Inside was the same heavyweight paper.

"On the second day of Christmas, my true love gave to me two sets of books and the reason your husband had to die."

When the phone rang, she jumped. Her fingertips tingled. "Hello."

"Hi." Ryan's voice sounded scratchy. "Just calling you back. Was out running errands. What's up?"

"Not much." Anna straightened up the writing desk in the entryway, sticking pens in the pencil drawer and the sticky note pad back into its holder. The paper with the Christmas lyric lay on the desktop.

"What? What's wrong? You got another note."

She sighed, holding the phone with her shoulder. "I did." Should she invite him over? "Do you wanna come here after work?"

"On my way."

"No. Not now, after work's fine."

"Sure. See you soon." Ryan hung up.

That's it? He didn't even ask what the note said. Maybe he's busy.

Less than ten minutes later, the doorbell rang. Anna peeked out as Ryan peeked in. Of course, he came right over. She should've known better.

"What's going on?" Ryan walked in. He untied his apron and slipped it over his head. "Where's the Christmas note?" He flung it over the back of the desk chair and must have spotted the Christmas lyric. Ryan picked it up. "Anna, this isn't funny."

"I'm not laughing. If those notes are right, then Jake was murdered. Two sets of books—Jake was an accountant."

Ryan's shoulders rose. "Maybe you should call the police now."

"I can't. What if Leo Adams is involved?" Anna walked over and tucked the desk chair in.

Ryan's apron slipped to the floor. She picked it up and draped it over the seat.

"That's insane."

"Hear me out. Daisy dies a few hours after her son, and there's no investigation?"

"You don't know that for sure." Ryan shook his head.

"The paper said foul play isn't suspected in either case."

"The newspaper could be wrong." Ryan began to pace.

"It was Leo Adams who ran Tommy over. How hard is our town's only full-time cop going to investigate if the case he's building is against his younger brother?"

Ryan wielded the Christmas lyric. "These notes have nothing to do with Daisy or her son."

"We don't know that. What I do know is the same time I find out Jake may have been murdered, two other people around town are dead. One hours after she left my house. Call me crazy, but this is Potrage. Things like this don't just happen here."

The doorbell chimed.

Someone pounded on the door. "Anna Greenan, it's the Potrage P.D.." Vince Adams' voice boomed.

"Speak of the devil." Anna pursed her lips, a warning to Ryan to keep his mouth shut, and opened the door.

Vince flashed his badge like they needed to see credentials. "Miss Greenan."

"Hi, Vince." Anna stepped aside. "Come in."

Vince ducked as he stepped through the doorway. He removed his police hat and pounded the snow from his boots. "I need to ask you some questions about Daisy Peters."

Ryan slid the Christmas note into his back pocket.

"Sure." Anna forced a smile and tried to relax.

Vince pulled out a small, green notebook. "Rumor has it, Miss Peters came by here yesterday. Is that right?"

"Yep. She came and dropped off my Christmas present."

"Which was?" Vince raised his eyebrows.

"Oh." Anna walked to the dining table and picked up the unopened card Daisy had given her. "I don't even know. I never opened it." Anna peeled open the envelope and slid out the Christmas card. She read it. *Oh my. No. Oh Lord...*A lump lodged in her throat. The photo stuck to her fingertips. Her pulse spiked.

"What is it?" Ryan stepped closer, concern etching his tone.

Anna glanced at him and choked out, "Money." Indeed, behind the Polaroid was a twenty-dollar bill.

Ryan stared at her, and she could tell her emotions were transparent.

Stay calm. Breathe. Anna plastered on a smile. "She gave me a card and twenty dollars." Anna turned her back to the boys and slipped the Polaroid into the front of her pants. Turning back, she made a show of returning the card to its envelope and placing the envelope on the table.

Vince's eyes narrowed. "What's that?"

"What's what?" Anna tried to keep her voice light and airy. Her stomach churned.

"You're jittery." Vince lowered his chin.

"It's not often you get a gift from the dead." Anna shrugged and fixated on the puddle forming beneath Vince's boots as the snow he'd dragged in melted. She'd need to towel it up before it leaked beneath the floorboards.

The radio on Vince's belt sounded. He shut it off or turned it down, Anna wasn't sure which. "So, she gave you cash?"

"Yes."

"What for?" Vince shifted his weight.

"For Christmas."

"Daisy gave you a Christmas gift which you never opened?" Vince gestured toward the table. "Until now, that is?"

Ryan squirmed behind him. Clearly, Vince's questions were making him nervous.

Anna didn't want to hide anything, but she also didn't want to inadvertently dive into a pool she wasn't prepared to swim in. She could handle the Potrage P.D.. "Yeah."

Vince looked up and waited.

Seconds ticked by.

Sweat dotted Anna's hairline. "We had just sat down when the doorbell rang. Gloria Lonnie rushed in and took Daisy out. I found out later her son was killed." *When your brother ran him over.*

"So you didn't finish your..." Vince thumbed through his notes. "Why was Daisy here?"

"Oh, a Christmas party, for our book club."

Vince glared at her. "And what did Daisy tell you about Tommy?"

"Yesterday?" Tension rode up Anna's spine and knotted between her shoulder blades.

Again, Vince waited. This time Anna allowed the silence to build. Clearly, this was more than a friendly house call. The questions were one thing. Vince's tone was another.

Ryan moved beside her. "Vince, what's up?"

Vince wrote something down. "Did Daisy tell either of you Tommy was back in town?"

Anna shook her head. "No."

"Definitely not," Ryan added.

"Ryan, is there anything you can think of that would help with the investigation?" Vince regarded them both.

"This morning's paper said the police didn't suspect foul play," Anna said.

Ryan cleared his throat.

She ignored him. "What investigation?"

"I have a tough time believing you didn't know." Vince stared at Anna as if gauging her response.

She didn't give him one.

"Turns out our Daisy was murdered." He glanced back at his notes. "Thing is, Anna, a few different people have reported you were snooping around Daisy's place earlier this week."

"I dropped off a poinsettia for Christmas." *Holy crap. Am I a suspect?*

"Did you ring the bell?" Vince asked.

"No." Anna crossed her arms. The Polaroid felt cold against her stomach. She moved, and it slid down her thigh. She squeezed her legs together. The Polaroid stopped its freefall on the inside of her left knee. "I set the plant on the porch and left."

"Was Daisy home at the time?"

"I think so."

"You think so." Vince regarded her. His eyes narrowed. "But you didn't ring the bell?"

"It was supposed to be a surprise." Anna smiled.

"I see. So, you left a plant outdoors, in the cold, for Christmas as a surprise?"

25

Anna forced a chuckle. "I will admit, I didn't think it through."

"Vince, I was here with Anna and Daisy last night. I didn't leave until midnight or so." Ryan stepped forward, shielding Anna with a shoulder.

Vince stared at Ryan. "I see. Well, I may have more questions as forensics comes back. What's a good phone number for you, Anna?"

She gave Vince her cell number, and he wrote it down.

Vince flipped the notebook closed and shoved it in his pocket. "If either of you should hear or recall anything, let me know." He put on his hat, turned, and left.

Ryan closed the door. "You should've told him about the notes."

The Polaroid stuck to her inner knee. "Are you kidding?"

"He treated you like a suspect, you know."

"If he thinks I can murder, then fraud isn't a stretch. He'll likely think I wrote the notes myself to throw him off or something." She reached up her pant leg, trying to get at the picture, to no avail.

She stood and wiggled her hips, in the hope it would slide down, to no avail. "I had nothing to do with Daisy's murder." Finally, she unzipped her pants and stuck her hand down her leg. "Forensics will show that."

"What are you doing?"

She looked up, her hand midway down her inner thigh. "Don't ask." She peeled off the Polaroid, positive a portion of her skin was still stuck to it.

"Nice." Ryan nodded, as she rezipped her pants, and feigned nonchalance. "What is it?"

"A picture." She studied the photo, stunned, staring at a stranger. A stranger and a ghost, and, in a way, he was both.

Jake stood arm in arm with Tommy Peters. It was as if she saw her husband for the first time—handsome with piercing green eyes and wavy dark hair. Millions of things every day made her think of him, but nothing before or after would haunt her like this.

In her hand, she held a tangible secret. His secret—Jake took to his grave. His secret—that may have dug it.

The picture was dated one week before Jake died. The writing of the date, precise, in the lower left-hand corner of the picture.

"What the hell?" Ryan snatched the picture from her. "Did you know Jake found Tommy?"

"No."

"Did you even know he went looking for him?"

"No." Anna shook her head.

"I'm not surprised. Apparently, there's a lot about Jake we didn't know." Ryan's words stung. The truth often did. Ryan walked to the back window and looked out. "Daisy just stuffed this picture in her Christmas card? With no explanation?"

"Yeah." Anna needed some time to digest all of this. Why would Daisy give her this? And she was very specific. *Don't open it until I'm gone,* like she *didn't want to answer any questions, which implies she knew I'd ask.*

How did Daisy get the picture? Had she known Tommy's whereabouts all along? Did Tommy give her the picture? And why?

Daisy clearly knew more than she'd said. Anna tried to recall their more recent conversations, but it was useless. She was too frazzled to remember anything. She could call Daisy's friend Gloria and see if Daisy told her anything about Tommy. When he got here, where he was hiding all this time, why he came back. But it seemed doubtful Gloria would know, and, even if she did, Anna doubted even more Gloria would tell her. No one liked to speak ill of the dead. Plus, now wasn't the time. Daisy and Tommy weren't even buried yet. This secret kept for three years—a few more days wouldn't matter.

"Anna." Ryan turned to face her. "I think you should come and stay with me. I know you don't want help, but you need it."

"No. I'll be fine. I don't want to deal with this now."

Ryan held the picture up. "I'm holding a picture of Jake and Tommy. If this handwritten date is true, Jake found Tommy, and then Jake died a week later. This one's not optional."

"Give me that." Anna stole the picture from Ryan and shoved it in the desk drawer. "Not optional? Everything is optional."

"Fine." Ryan crossed his arms. "What options do you think you have?"

"I can ignore it."

"For how long?"

"I can leave town."

"And go where?"

"I can destroy it. The notes, the picture, everything." But she knew even as she said it that it couldn't be done. You couldn't destroy the truth. It would find its own way out.

Deep down, Anna wanted to run, in part out of fear, in part out of frustration. She was being forced to dig for things she didn't want to uncover.

Ryan's cell rang. "Yeah," Ryan snarled into the phone. He appeared agitated.

Whatever. Let him be mad at me.

"What time is it?" Ryan's tone softened as he looked at his watch. "Oh, I didn't realize it was that late. No, no problem. I'm on my way." Ryan extended his arm so Anna could read the time too. Where had the day gone?

"Oh, I'll tell her. No problem. Leave it on the counter. Thanks." Ryan touched the phone's screen.

"What?" Anna expected him to tell her someone left another Christmas note. Today was December 27. She should have received one more verse.

"You left your purse at the store."

Shoot. "I'll take a ride over and get it."

Ryan regarded her and exhaled. The tension evaporated. "I'll drive. I'm parked behind you, and I've got to lock up in forty-five minutes anyways."

"Let me get my coat." Anna grabbed her fuzzy coat off the hook and slipped it on. She stuck her hands in her pockets, looking for her keys. For the first time since she moved to Potrage, she wanted to lock her doors.

Chapter Six

Their footsteps echoed as they entered the deserted store. Anna's red handbag sat on the counter. No need to check if anything was missing as there was nothing in it anybody would want. She browsed while Ryan finished closing up. By the endcaps—Frosted Flakes, spaghetti sauce, and canned corn were this week's featured sale items.

From behind the breakfast counter, Ryan called out, "I'll just be a few more minutes."

"Take your time."

Amazingly, the tie rack held a necktie even more obnoxious than the rabid-chicken one Ryan sported. Anna slid it off the hanger. For only four dollars and ninety-nine cents, you could own a lime green tie covered in sickly pigs with bulging eyes.

"Isn't that fantastic?" Ryan hollered. "I own that one too."

Shocker.

"Almost done." Ryan vanished into the kitchen.

Anna wandered to the dairy section and grabbed a gallon of milk. Condensation fogged the glass doors as a chill nibbled her hand.

The entry bell jangled. Someone stumbled in. Ryan must have heard it too because he reappeared in the kitchen doorway. He gave Anna a sideways glance. She understood the unspoken cue and stayed still.

"Hello, Leo," Ryan said, a little too loud. "Whatcha need?"

Leo Adams. Her heart cinched. *He ran over Tommy yesterday.* Anna could picture him with his gelled black hair in some type of dark clothing. Twenty-something going on sixteen.

"Beer," Leo slurred, emphasizing the last letter like a speech patient. A display tumbled, followed by a retching sound.

"Whoa." Ryan leapt over the counter.

Anna waited where she was, an easy decision. Even at this distance, she smelled the vomit and dry-heaved. Nuzzling her face in her sweater, she tried not to breathe through her nose. The fragrant aroma of her deodorant muffled everything else.

"Gimme some beer." Leo threw up again.

Ryan appeared behind the counter. He dialed the store's phone and set the receiver down.

Bet he dialed 9-1-1. Smart.

"Sure, Leo," Ryan said in a patronizing tone. "Be right back." Ryan strode into the refrigerated section and grabbed a twelve-pack.

"You can't sell him that," Anna hissed.

"Shh. Stay here." Ryan walked around the corner and out of sight. "Coors all right?"

Anna waited. The gallon of milk in her hand was getting heavy. Leo didn't answer.

Ryan kept talking. "Hey, I'm about to lock up. Why don't you stay awhile and we'll throw a few back?"

"Nah," Leo said.

"How'd ya get here?" Ryan asked. "Anybody out in the car with you?"

"How much I owe ya?"

"Nothin'."

"Huh?"

"Can't sell this and let you get behind that wheel. Hey—Umph."

A thump and then a groan. Aluminum cans rained onto the floor. More scuffling. Glass shattered.

Something moved to her right. Anna caught the men's reflection in the mirror mounted above the freezers. Broken glass spaghetti jars littered the floor. Cans mixed in with it. The two men punched, pushed, and shoved. Ryan crouched, driving his shoulder into Leo's abdomen, thrusting him into the cereal display. Boxes tumbled end-over-end as the shelves crashed.

Leo lay motionless. His feet poked out beneath a mountain of Frosted Flakes. The entire incident lasted only seconds, but the entry of the store was trashed.

Ryan got up, dusted off, and looked directly into the mirror. He was covered in spaghetti sauce. Sauce and vomit. Half his face, and most of his clothes, was reddish-orange.

There was a steady whoosh of a rolling aluminum can. Finally, it thudded against the wall.

Ryan walked behind the counter and spoke softly into the phone, relaying what had happened, but leaving out Leo's name. Small town politics. No need to put the Adams' name out across the police scanner. The town would know soon enough.

Anna reached into her overstuffed purse for a can of mace, intending to give it to Ryan after he hung up. Not that he'd need it now.

Her fingers grazed an envelope. She pulled it out. Note number three. Of course. She exhaled. Today was December 27—the third day of Christmas.

Ryan came around the corner and startled her. "Leo just hauled off and slugged me. I can't believe it." Ryan rubbed his chin. Tiny shards of broken glass shimmered in his hair.

"You okay?"

"Yeah. Fine. But you should go before the cops get here. You don't need any more problems with Vince." Ryan plucked the glass out one piece at a time.

The smell of uncooked sauce mixed with vomit made her gag. "You drove."

"My keys are sitting on the counter. I'll call you later." Ryan gestured toward the mess behind him. "I'm going to have to clean this up and deal with the police. I'll be a while."

She took one whiff and didn't argue.

Anna called the store, and Ryan's cell phone, over and over. Finally, at three a.m., she drifted to sleep.

The next morning misty streams of flakes swept across her yard. Ryan's truck sat parked in her driveway. *Oh man. The neighbors are gonna have a field day with this one.* Anna dialed Ryan's home and the store again. Both places, no answer. Odd. She showered, dressed, and went to make coffee.

The note she received yesterday sat on the desk.

"On the third day of Christmas, my true love gave to me three years ago, two sets of books, and the reason your husband had to die."

Whoever wrote these notes had been in Ryan's store yesterday, probably while she was there, but not necessarily since her purse had been there all day long.

How many people would know it was her purse? As nosy as people were out here, at least seventy-five percent. The exact same percentage that now knew Ryan's truck had spent the night. First, the purse got left, and then the truck spent the night. Gossip fodder for weeks.

At the store, Anna had sat between Vince and Father Matthew. She hadn't noticed either slide anything into her handbag, but she hadn't been watching for it either. She was no profiler but doubted a cop or a priest would be on any potential suspect list.

But you never knew.

Who else was there? Unfortunately, she didn't know the names of a lot of people around town. Time to start to focus on those around her. One thing seemed certain, the location or placement of each note couldn't have been pre-planned. No one knew she'd be at Ryan's shop yesterday. No one could've planned for her to leave her handbag. So, whoever authored these messages was confident they'd be close enough to her for twelve straight days that he or she could hand-deliver each message with ease. Anna shuddered, suddenly chilled from the inside out.

The doorbell rang. A giant bouquet of fresh flowers greeted her.

"Ms. Greenan?" the teenage delivery guy hidden behind the arrangement asked.

"Yep." Anna took the flowers from him. They were gorgeous and smelled incredible. Lilacs, snapdragons, roses, carnations. "Thanks." Her heart fluttered. She couldn't remember the last time she received flowers. Let alone by delivery. She grinned.

"Sign here, please." The young man held out a board, and she signed and noted the company name. FlowersAnytime.com. She didn't think her small town had a florist.

Closing the door with her hip, Anna set the flowers on her writing desk and peeled open the card. Her smile vanished.

"On the fourth day of Christmas, my true love gave to me four people murdered, three years ago, two sets of books, and the reason your husband had to die."

Chapter Seven

Anna had waited on hold for a FlowersAnytime.com representative for twenty-seven minutes and counting. She'd give them five more minutes. Never mind she'd said that five minutes ago. Now it was a matter of principle. Clearly, Flowers Anytime doubted her tenacity. Did they honestly think they could wait her out?

"Flowers Anytime, thanks for holding. This is Sherry. How can I help you?"

Finally. "Yes. I just received—" Call waiting beeped. *Shoot.* It could be Ryan. He might need his truck. He'd have to call back. "I just received a delivery, and I'd like to know who sent it."

"Delivery address?"

Anna told her.

"Let me place you on a brief hold while I check on that for you."

Before she could object, elevator music filled the line. The other line beeped again and Anna clicked over. "Hello." Dial tone. She had accidentally hung up. *Son-of-a-.*

Forty-five minutes later, Anna was no closer than when she started. The flowers were ordered from the website. However, Flowers Anytime had a policy of not revealing a *secret admirer* without a court order. She had a better shot of winning the Pulitzer than finding out her secret sender. No matter what she said, or did, she got nowhere.

Fine. She went into the den. If the truth wouldn't work, perhaps playing cupid would. Anna went to her computer and sent an email to the florist's customer service division.

> *Re: Sender of flowers*
>
> *My husband left me six months ago when I was pregnant. I gave birth to our first child three days ago and today was my first day home. I just received a basket from FlowersAnytime.com from a secret admirer. I'm hoping it's my husband.*
>
> *Under the circumstances, could someone please give me the last name of the person who placed the order? Thank you.*

Anna gave all pertinent information: her name, the date and time she received the bouquet, as well as her address. She reread her email. *Great. I sound like a guest on a talk show.* Trusting the customer service representative wouldn't read the creepy card that accompanied her arrangement, Anna clicked send and hoped for the best.

The Christmas notes were becoming more specific, and if she wasn't going to beat feet and get out of dodge, she needed to find out if there was any truth to the messages.

Anna searched the web for multiple murders three years ago. Strange that she would rather look into the deaths of strangers than her own husband's.

Her search yielded nothing. She started in Potrage and then branched out to other communities. No multiple homicides anywhere close by. Was Jake one of the four? Did they all happen around the same time, or were they spread out over many months? All in one community or four different communities? If the notes were true, could some of the murders be cloaked as accidents like Jake?

She needed more information. Four people murdered, three years ago, two sets of books. Two sets of books. Jake was an accountant. He had kept the books for everyone in Potrage, not to mention his many clients in Rochester and Buffalo. That was where she'd start.

When Jake passed, his staff cleaned out his office for her and put everything into storage. It seemed the time had come to go through all of it. Anna dialed Ryan's cell and store again. Still no answer. Something was up. Someone would definitely be at the shop by now. She had his truck, but she had stuff to do. Maybe she could stop at the store on her way to the storage garage.

Her computer chirped, announcing a new message.

> *Re: Sender of flowers.*
> *Ms. Greenan,*
> *There ain't no man worth it! Being pregnant is a beutiful thing. I can't give ypu the name of the guy that sent you the flowers but even if it is your man tell him to get lost.. Emily*

Well, so much for Plan B. Moving on to Plan C.

Anna typed.

> *Re: Emily in Customer Service*
> *Look. I lied. My husband didn't leave me. I threw him out. The scumbag got my best friend pregnant too. Now I got flowers with a threatening card, and I want to know if it's from the pig so I can tell my lawyer. Thanks, Anna*

Just when she thought she couldn't get any lower than a talk show guest, Anna discovered reality TV.

To her surprise, Emily's response was almost instant.

> *They ain't from your man. They from a woman. That's all I can say.*

Before she had time to react, the phone rang.

"Hello."

"Is this Anna Greenan?" an official sounding voice asked.

Her heart crashed against her ribs. "Yes." She had only one thought...

Ryan.

Chapter Eight

Anna clutched the phone. "Yes, I'm Anna Greenan."

"Hello, this is Kim, a nurse at the Nolles Hospital Emergency Room. Mr. Ryan Martin was brought in by ambulance last night."

Ambulance? What? "Is he okay?" Her eyes stung. *Please let him be okay. Please. Not again.*

"He's pretty banged up, but he'll be fine. He asked us to give you a call. Are you able to pick him up and drive him home?"

"Yeah. Sure. I'll be right over." Anna exhaled. "What happened?"

"There was a scuffle at his shop last night. I'm sure he'll tell you all about it when you get here. Do you know where we're located?"

"Fillmont." *Hospital? How did this happen?*

"Now, he's going to have to take it easy. The cast will come off in a few weeks."

Cast? "I'm on my way."

Fillmont was twenty minutes from her house. She got there in twelve. The antiseptic smell made her cringe. The nurse guided her through the Authorized Personnel Only door into the triage rooms. Ryan was perched on the twin bed with his back against the wall, a bandage on his right temple, and a cast on his right leg. "Oh my gosh! What happened?"

"I don't know." Ryan winced and slowly stood on his good leg. He wore a plain, white T-shirt and a pair of baggy gray sweatpants. Someone had graciously washed his hair and cleaned him up. A clear, plastic bag filled with last night's vomit-covered clothes rested on the visitor's chair alongside

Ryan's discharge paperwork.

Anna lifted the crutches and paperwork. *Discharge Instructions for Partial Ankle Fracture.* "You broke your ankle?"

"Not completely. I guess—"

"You ready?" A nurse appeared in the doorway with a wheelchair. She was the spitting image of Renée Zellweger, definitely Ryan's type: little, blonde, and cute.

Certainly not like me.

"Yep." Ryan smiled, turned, and folded into the wheelchair. "Where'd you park?"

"Right outside the doors." Anna led them down the hall and into the circular drive where she'd left her SUV. She opened the passenger side door and pushed the seat all the way back, wedging the crutches in the back seat.

The nurse helped Ryan into the SUV. The process took *much* longer than necessary. "There you go, sweetie." She patted Ryan's thigh.

"Thank you." Ryan ogled her.

"If you need anything, anything at all, just call me." The nurse winked at him. Dusting off her cornflower-blue scrubs, she raised her chin. "But I'm sure your girlfriend will take good care of you."

Anna smirked and waited for Ryan to give her some cheesy line about how they were really only friends and help sounded really, really good.

"Thank you." Ryan pulled his door closed. He looked at Anna. "What?"

Anna smirked, rolled her eyes, and pulled away from the curb. The nurse waved and Ryan blushed. Anna just laughed.

"She can't help it." Ryan clipped his seat belt. "She's only human."

"Yeah. Pity." Anna made a right out of the lot and a left onto Osiano Street. "So, what the heck happened?"

"Honestly, I'm not entirely sure. I heard you slip out the back door," Ryan fidgeted in the passenger's seat, adjusting the truck's heater to blow on their feet instead of their faces, "and I started cleaning up. I knew the police were on their way, and Leo wasn't moving. I was scooping up glass and, all of a sudden, I got blindsided by something heavy. It felt like a sledgehammer, and that was it. The next thing I know, I've got paramedics standing over me with smelling salt. I'm on a gurney and then in an ambulance."

"How long after I left?" She turned onto the two-lane country road. A picturesque countryside of snow-covered meadows and rolling hills surrounded them.

"Quick. Like maybe three minutes."

"Don't you have a bell on the door?"

"Yeah, but I was sweeping up glass, moving displays, cans were rolling. If it jingled, I didn't hear it."

"And you're sure it wasn't Leo?" Deer peeked up in the distant field as if waiting for an answer.

"All I know is the guy in the ambulance said we were both unconscious when he got there, and Vince said the exact same thing. They think someone came in to rob the shop but then ran out the back door when they heard the sirens. Thank God I called the police when I did." Ryan rubbed his forehead and slid off the bandage. "I've got such a headache."

"I bet." Anna shook her head. "You'll be sore for a while. What's with the cast?"

"My ankle was all bruised up last night. They took an X-ray, and I guess I partially fractured it. That's why they kept me overnight. The foot specialist wasn't in until this morning, and they wanted to make sure I didn't need surgery. Which, thankfully, as of now, I don't." Ryan adjusted the seat belt. "I'm sorry I bothered you, but I didn't know who else to call."

"No bother." The sign read Village of Potrage. "Where do you want me to take you?"

"I'll be fine at home."

Anna glanced at his cast. "You're not going to be able to drive." She already knew he wouldn't want to go to his father's. He got along fine with his dad. They had a lot in common since Ryan took over the store. It was his stepmom he had trouble with. His sister had moved away, and Anna didn't think he had any other family in the area. "Why don't you stay with me? You're going to need the help, and I could use the company."

"Really?" He smiled. "You don't mind?"

She shrugged. "Nope. I've got plenty of room."

When Anna finally pulled into her driveway, she could tell his thoughts were elsewhere. "Do you need me to take care of anything at the store?"

"No. I hope the stock boys got everything done so we can open tomorrow. The place was a disaster. I'd hate to lose two days of business."

"I'll take a ride over later." Anna walked around her truck and helped open the passenger door.

The winter wind whipped, and Anna didn't want the breeze to slap the door closed on Ryan's bad leg.

"I'll go with you." Ryan reached for his crutches and threaded them through the seats. "There is one other thing you can do."

"What's that?"

"Could you go get me some clothes and my laptop and feed the cat?" Ryan balanced on the crutches. "Thank God I left my gym bag in the break room, or I'd be going home in scrubs."

"Better than vomit." Once Ryan cleared the vehicle, Anna reached in and grabbed his filthy clothes from last night, along with the hospital paperwork.

"Agreed."

"I'll head over to your place and grab your stuff as soon I have you settled in." She was so relieved he was all right, she'd have done just about anything. She couldn't bear the thought of any more death—Jake, Daisy, Tommy.

Anna waited while Ryan crutched to the sofa and then made her way down the hall to the downstairs bedroom. It would need to be straightened up before he could stay in there.

Clutching the doorknob, she hesitated. It had been so long since she'd walked into her former master bedroom. She took a deep breath and swung open the door. The mustiness of the deserted space surrounded her. She couldn't make out the furniture in the dark but knew everything would need to be wiped down and scrubbed off.

No matter how much she cleaned, she could never wash away the memories. They were there, covered by a dusty film, but as real and solid as the furniture beneath. It was in this room she and Jake had spoken of a child never to be conceived, whispered of dreams never to be fulfilled, and fantasized about places they'd never get to visit. They had thought they had time. They had been mistaken. It was said the kitchen was the heart of a home, but Anna never agreed. The kitchen was the face the world saw. A house's heart was sealed behind the bedroom's door.

"Anna—"

Anna jumped, surprised Ryan stood behind her. How had she not heard the cluck of his crutches on the wood floor? "Sorry," she stammered. "I...I haven't been in here since Jake died."

"I can make it up the stairs. I don't want to—"

"No. This has a bathroom attached and everything. Go make yourself at home and give me a few minutes to fix it up." Anna walked in and pulled back the drapes. The sun glistening on the white snow blinded her. She squinted and opened the window to air out the room. Tiny flecks of glittery snow snuck in through the screen.

She stripped the bed, dusted the dressers, and wiped off the bathroom counters. If she kept moving, she wouldn't have to think. She wouldn't have to remember.

Anna walked to Jake's closet and paused. She took a deep breath. The knot in her stomach ballooned. Forcing herself to just do it, she slid the door open and took out a pair of loose sweats and a sweater for Ryan, and tossed them on the bed. Crinkled on the floor was some of Jake's dirty laundry. She picked up his dress shirt and held it to her face. It smelled like him. Still, after all this time, it smelled like him.

"Anna?" Ryan stood in the doorway. "You okay?"

Her vision blurred. She nodded and closed the closet door. "There are clothes on the bed. Jake's socks and underwear are in the top two drawers of the chest." Her voice cracked. She didn't dare meet Ryan's gaze. She'd cry if she did. "I'll take a ride and get some clothes and your laptop and feed the cat. Anything else?"

Ryan hobbled closer and touched her shoulder. "I can stay on the couch. You don't have to—"

"I do." Anna turned and fought to meet Ryan's stare. His face was a kaleidoscope of emotion. "I'm okay." She squeezed the words past the lump in her throat. "It'll be okay."

After they ate dinner, Anna headed over to Ryan's apartment. She hadn't been to his new place. Ryan's apartment was in the newly built complex behind the town car wash. The canary yellow building had white stairs to the upper level. Anna walked up the well-lit staircase in front of apartment three to apartment three B. Ryan's many keys jangled with every step.

Three B. Thankfully, Ryan had left on his front light. Now, which key was it? He'd said it had three letters on it. What three letters she couldn't remember, but how many keys had letters on them? Anna stood at the door and studied the pile. All of the keys, but one, had three letters. *Good. At least I narrowed it down.*

After five attempts, Anna found the correct key, unlocked the door, and found and flipped on the light switch in the living room. Ryan's apartment was more spacious and open than she expected. The main space held the sitting area, complete with a no-frills leather sofa accented by two chairs in an earth-tone fabric, and a drop-leaf table and chairs. The kitchen had dark cabinets with silver knobs matching the stainless-steel appliances. The dark, long hallway beside the kitchen presumably led to the bathroom and bedrooms.

The place smelled like furniture polish.

Something rubbed against her leg. An orange cat looked up expectantly and meowed. Anna reached down and ran her hand over its back as it nuzzled against her calf. She couldn't just leave it here. Picking up the cat food and unopened box of litter, she set both by the door. *How hard can taking care of a cat be?*

A creak.

Her stomach flipped. Could someone else be here? The thought sliced through her. Silence. Her pulse quickened. Had the sound come from Ryan's place or one of the apartments on either side of his?

"Hello," Anna called out. Her nerves, already raw, caught fire.

Ryan had been attacked at his store. What were they thinking? *I should've never come here alone.* Anna waited and listened. Nothing. Regardless, her heart thundered in her chest.

After several soundless seconds, Anna resolved to grab only what Ryan *absolutely* needed and get out of there.

Moving quickly, she raced into the bedroom, turning on lights as she went. Anna snatched the laptop off the nightstand. Ryan could wear Jake's old clothes.

The cat leapt onto the bedroom's utilitarian desk. Anna reached for the orange fuzzball but froze when she saw the papers. *Oh, God, no.*

Chapter Nine

Anna gripped the metal desk chair to steady herself. A New York State Department of Motor Vehicles Accident Report sat on top of Ryan's desk. Driver's name: Jake Greenan. *This is Jake's accident report*. License number. Address. Direction of travel. Accident diagrams.

Sifting through the rest of the papers, Anna found pictures of what was left of their car, first responder accounts, even copies of newspaper articles from that day. Anna didn't want to see this and shouldn't have looked, but now that she had, she couldn't stop.

Slowly, she took in everything. Questions flittered at the edge of her cognizance. The accident photos Anna pushed to the side. Not now. Not ever. The onslaught of information sickened her. More handwritten notes. Time of death, outdoor temperature, the exact position of the car, its trajectory, estimated speed, everything you would want to know but would never ask. Things you didn't want to know but now would never forget. Anna scanned the pages, scores of them. What was Ryan doing with this stuff? Where did he get it? Why now, more than three years after Jake died?

Mixed in the stack, she spotted a printed email. *Witness Baker insists deceased swerved to avoid hitting pedestrian. No collaborative evidence. Evan Cummings, Greyson County Sheriff.* Anna didn't remember a sheriff. She didn't remember a witness either. *Baker. Crazy Old Man Baker?*

Anna staggered into the kitchen, grabbed a brown paper bag, and swept all the papers into it. Would she tell Ryan she had them? Or wait and see if he mentioned anything?

How could he have done this? Dug up all this information behind her back. What was he looking for? Why? And for how long? Why was all this coming out now? The notes. This...creepiness. She pulled her coat tight across her chest, trying to cover herself.

Anna loaded her SUV and headed back home, trying desperately to push aside the images that had haunted her for so long and were now thrust back into her consciousness. A familiar stinging started behind her eyes. She forced the tears away. She had to be strong. Had to hold it together.

Beside her, the cat in the carrier cried. Anna didn't blame it one bit.

Ryan must have read her expression the second she walked in the front door.

"What's wrong?" He was sprawled out on her sofa, his long leg propped up on pillows.

Red-hot anger shot through her. Somehow seeing him infuriated her. "Nothing. You're all set." She somehow kept her voice calm. She needed time to digest all of this. "Got you some stuff and locked up your place."

Anna set the cat carrier down in the foyer and released the latch. The cat bolted under the chair. It had meowed the entire ride over. The more she tried to reassure it, the louder it complained. *Probably a male.*

"You brought my cat here?" Ryan leaned forward and clicked his tongue to call the kitty.

The cat didn't budge. Two yellow eyes peered out from under the club chair.

"I didn't have the heart to leave it all alone." The last word stuck as she struggled to look at him.

"He would have been fine for a few days with some fresh food and water. I could have had one of the guys at the shop look after him." Ryan patted his lap, trying to coax the cat out from under the chair, to no avail.

"It's fine. Wouldn't want the cat to think you're not...trustworthy." Anna let the barb lay between them.

"You sure you're okay?" Ryan swung his casted leg off the sofa. "You seem mad about something."

"Nope. Fine." Anna turned and went back out to the truck to get the cat food, litter, and the few toiletries she had grabbed from Ryan's bathroom.

She spotted the brown bag filled with Jake's accident info. Should she bring it in or leave it in her truck? She opted to bring it in with everything else and stuffed it under her writing desk.

"Seriously. Why are you upset? Did I do something?" Ryan's forehead creased in confusion. "I've just been laying here."

"Look it...ah... You're gonna have to wear Jake's clothes for the time being. I just grabbed the necessities for you." Anna started toward her upstairs bedroom, stopping at the base of the stairwell.

"That's fine. I'm okay with that if you are."

Anna looked at him. "It's fine."

Ryan's eyes scrunched up. "Where are you going?"

"I kind of just want to be left alone for a while." Anna continued upstairs. With his cast, Ryan couldn't follow.

Chapter Ten

The next morning, Anna got up and got ready for Daisy's funeral. She slipped into a plain, black pantsuit. The low-cut boots slid over her thin dress socks. Once standing, she wiggled her pant legs to make sure her loose-fitting fabric didn't catch in the boot cuffs. While not fancy, boots were the safest choice with the predicted snow and ice.

In the adjoining bath, Anna used a wide-toothed comb to curtail her dark curls, thankful for the frizz-stopping spray. The pink lipstick looked too harsh against her pale skin so she applied a gloss over the top to mute the shade. So far she had already wasted an extra ten minutes getting ready and counting. Although, she couldn't put off going downstairs forever.

It was strange to know there was someone else in the house. Even if it was someone she wasn't speaking to. Should she have stormed off like that last night? Probably not. In the sobering light of day, Anna wished she had talked to Ryan last night about the paperwork she found. It would've made facing him today that much easier. Instead, she stalked off to her bedroom while he knew full well she was fuming.

There might be a reasonable explanation why Ryan had all that information from Jake's accident. But still, he should have told her. Said something. She shouldn't have been blindsided, finding it like that.

It had taken months for Anna to stop dreaming about Jake. To stop seeing the wreckage each time she dozed off or hear the knock on the door that would forever upend her world.

Finally, life had started to feel…functional. Not normal. Nothing would ever be normal. Not good. Not bad. But at least she felt *something*. Then, to see all those papers strewn about like that...

Worst of all, Ryan knew that stuff was there and allowed her to stumble onto it. That just seemed cruel.

And why keep it all a secret?

Anna gave herself a final once-over and unplugged the blow-dryer. As good as it would get today. She walked back into her room and flopped on the edge of her bed, still unwilling to head downstairs. The click of Ryan's crutches echoed through the house.

"Good morning." Ryan's voice startled her.

Anna flinched. He hobbled into her bedroom.

"How'd you get up the steps?" She couldn't hide the shock.

"Slid up on my bum." Ryan looked at the floor. His brown hair was a tousled mess, his shirt and slacks—the same as he wore yesterday—wrinkled. The dark circles under his eyes showed his lack of sleep. "Anna, I found those papers you brought home. All Jake's accident stuff. I'm so sorry. I didn't mean for you to find that." Ryan hopped, turned, and sat on the opposite side of her bed. "With everything going on, I forgot I left those on my desk."

She had to know. "Why did you have that stuff? What were you looking for? And where did you get it all?"

"The notes." Ryan sighed and hung his head. "I wanted to know if those *stupid* Christmas notes could be true."

It really was the only plausible explanation. Wasn't it? What other reason could there be?

Anna exhaled.

For a while, neither of them spoke.

True, he should've told her, but maybe he tried and she never listened. She hadn't wanted to listen. She wanted to stick her head in the sand and let it all blow over, but the sand was suffocating. Avoiding reality was the route to madness, and if nothing else, she needed her sanity.

If she and Ryan didn't get moving, they would miss the funeral. "Are you coming to the service?"

"Of course. I can be ready in a flash." Ryan used the crutches for balance and slowly rose. "I am sorry. I should've told you."

"It's all right. I was just caught off guard." Anna smiled as a familiar warmth spread through her. She never could stay angry at him for long. "No more secrets."

Ryan didn't meet her gaze.

Chapter Eleven

L ate, as usual, Anna slipped into her pew at church, the very back row on the right. While there weren't assigned seats at Mass, everyone seemed to sit in the same spot each Sunday. Funerals, apparently, were no exception.

The organist was partway through the opening hymn.

The church smelled of funeral spices and flowers. Daisy's and Tommy's caskets were each draped in a white cloth in the center aisle. Fresh floral arrangements adorned the altar's oak steps. The church's stained-glass windows seemed to glow, backlit by the morning sun.

Lord, please take care of Daisy and Tommy.

Anna reached for the hymnal tucked in the wooden rack that hung off the back of the pew in front of her. As she opened the book, an envelope dropped onto the floor. Her name was typed across the front in the same font as that of the Christmas notes. Her pulse climbed as she bent down and picked it up.

The music stopped, the parishioners sat, and the morning's lecture stepped to the pulpit. "The first reading is a reading from the book of the prophet Isaiah."

Out of respect for the dead, Anna tried to hold off opening the envelope, but her reverence was no match for her curiosity. Trying to be as quiet as possible, Anna peeled it open. The tearing sounds somehow amplified in the silence of the congregation.

"On the fifth day of Christmas, my true love gave to me five golden rings."

They had to be here! In here. Right now. Watching. Anna scanned the sanctuary, but no one met her gaze. So many faces, names. *Who would do this? How can they sit in church and pray and act like this is normal?*

Ryan sat on the folding chair directly behind her. His broken leg extended out in front of him like an oversized baton. He mouthed, *what?*

Anna held up the paper for Ryan to see. Someone cleared their throat. She exhaled and faced front.

Whoever sent her these notes knew where she sat in church. They had to know of her close relationship with Daisy and that Anna would attend this service. They even guessed she'd sit in her usual spot.

Perspiration dotted her underarms and the small of her back. Anna studied the congregation, adding people to her suspect list, and then, mentally crossed each one off.

The voice of the lecture pierced through her thoughts. "Do not fear, for I am with you."

Anna closed her eyes and tried to let go of the anxiety coursing through her.

"I will strengthen you and help you," the lecture continued.

God, please help me. Please give me wisdom.

The service droned on, but Anna couldn't concentrate. She clutched the note. *Who is sending me these? Five golden rings? Rings? Marriage? Linkage? Circles?*

The pew shimmied as the person beside her stood. Anna did the same. A small but dedicated choir led the congregation from the back balcony in "Amazing Grace." Anna lip-synced the hymn and tried to force herself to stay focused. To stay calm. To think.

While this note was the same paper and font as the others, this message was different. For one thing, this clue was the exact same as the original Christmas carol lyric. Five golden rings. This note, however, left out the remainder of the song. It didn't mention the other verses: four people murdered, three years ago, two sets of books, and the reason that your husband had to die. All the other notes did. Why this change in format?

Possibly, because this envelope was left where anyone could find it. The verse, five golden rings, was meaningless without the context of the other mysterious lyrics.

Think. Think. Think.

Perhaps her perspective needed to change. What if the notes weren't as much something to be afraid of but a relay of information? Nothing more.

Maybe someone thought she knew something, or maybe she should know something, and, for whatever the reason, the writer couldn't tell her directly. She didn't want to be naive but also couldn't picture a single member of this congregation wanting to threaten her.

Maybe who's sending the notes isn't as important as why they're sending them. If someone wanted to harm her, why send notes? Especially over a series of days? Why create that kind of evidence trail?

Regardless, Anna couldn't let the unanswered questions consume her.

Father Matthew spoke of Daisy and Tommy, heaven and hell, life and death. All of it intertwined for eternity. "All Daisy wanted in life was to be reunited with Tommy. What she couldn't have in this life, by faith, we know she has in the next."

The priest's words gave Anna some peace. At least Daisy and Tommy were together.

Anna, too, had to have faith she would be okay, no matter the notes she received. They were just words on paper. Their only power was that which she gave them.

The service ended. The pallbearers carried the caskets out of the back of the church. Anna stuffed the cryptic note into her coat pocket, gathered her purse, and stepped into the outside aisle.

"Ready to head out?" Ryan pulled himself up on his crutches.

"I can take you, Ryan." John Adams patted Ryan's shoulder. Impeccably dressed in a designer suit, John's hair was a violent mixture of salt and pepper. The salt won.

Anna couldn't believe John showed up at this funeral. It was, after all, his son who had struck and killed Tommy days before.

Parishioner after parishioner glanced their way, but people with as much money as John always commanded attention.

"Thanks, but I'm all set." Balancing his crutches against the back wall,

Ryan donned his brown leather jacket.

"Really. No bother." John adjusted his sleek, black gloves. "I'm needed back at the salt mine. Your place is on the way."

"I'm staying with Anna." Ryan nodded toward her.

"I see." John sized her up.

Money could buy a lot of things, but there was no substitute for class.

John turned back to Ryan. "Very well, then. Thank you for your help with the—" he paused, clearly searching for careful phrasing "—unfortunate situation last night. It was appreciated. Did you get the envelope I sent over?"

"I did." Ryan's tone was all business. "It, too, was appreciated."

Chapter Twelve

"Let me guess," Anna started as soon as John Adams was out of earshot. "You're not pressing charges against Leo."

"Nope." Ryan hobbled out the church exit ahead of her.

Anna dipped her hand in the holy water and crossed herself. "And, in exchange, you took cash?"

"Pretty much."

The onslaught of cold air nipped at Anna's face and hands as she followed Ryan outside. "Are you crazy?"

Several people stopped and looked.

She lowered her voice. "That kid deserves to be in jail."

"Well, if he should cross you, you put him there." Ryan struggled down the icy handicap ramp to her left.

Anna took the steps, brushed past the sea of mourners, and headed to the confines of her SUV. Her coattails whipped like a flag in the winter wind. She started the ignition and turned up the vehicle's heat. The fan blew, but cold air poured out of the vents. The frigid steering wheel singed her hands.

The pallbearers hoisted the caskets into the side-by-side hearses. One family mourning two losses on the same day. *Heartbreaking.*

Ryan cautiously made his way across the snow-packed lot, enveloped by the sea of mourners heading to their vehicles. Eventually, he climbed in and closed the passenger door.

"I can't believe you're letting Leo off the hook like that." Anna ran a hand through her curly hair. How could Ryan *not* press charges after what Leo did? "You're a chicken."

"No. I'm a businessman. And the Adams' salt mine keeps me in business. We live in a small town. I'm not ruining a kid's life over one little incident. Everyone makes mistakes. Plus, he just ran over Tommy and is dealing with all of that. There's no need to make a bad situation worse."

"I don't think trashing your store and putting you in a cast constitutes a little thing." Anna blew on her hands to try to warm them.

"We don't know how I wound up in this cast."

That little ditty still made Anna wonder. Who had knocked Ryan out, and how did he break his ankle? Could it have happened during the fight with Leo and the adrenaline rush masked the pain?

"If Leo's not held accountable, he'll never learn a lesson."

"And I'm confident his father will take care of that." Ryan adjusted his seat belt. "John isn't going to let anyone wreck the family name."

Anna sighed. Ryan had a point. Small-town life had its pluses and its minuses. Crossing the town's most powerful family probably wouldn't be in Ryan's best interest, or the best interest of his business. "Maybe you're right."

"What was that?" A kilowatt smile flashed across his face. "Me right? As in you wrong?" Ryan clutched his chest.

Anna chuckled. "You're pushin' it."

"Fine." Tiny laugh lines etched his blue eyes. "This chicken accepts your apology."

"Okay." Anna held up a hand. "Sorry. I shouldn't have called you a chicken."

"No, a goat would've been more applicable."

"Goat?"

Ryan smirked. "Greatest of all time."

"At least we agree you're some kind of farm animal." Anna returned his smile.

The train of the immediate family's cars started the procession. "Did you wanna go to the cemetery?" Anna slid the gearshift to drive and filed into her place in the row.

"No, but if you want to, I will."

"I don't." With the frozen ground, the remainder of the ceremony would take place at the cemetery's mausoleum. Anna hadn't been there since Jake's funeral. She could still feel the chill of the pew under her black dress. See the glossy finish of his casket. Taste the salt of her tears. No, she didn't want to go to the cemetery. Not now. Not ever.

The procession moved slowly up the narrow side streets. Anna made a quick right and slipped out of line. The car in her rearview didn't follow.

"What was in the note you got?" Ryan's crutches clanked against the window. He lowered them against the door.

"Five golden rings. That's all it said."

"On your seat?"

"In the hymnal." The truck's heater finally roared to life, and the warm air began to thaw Anna's frozen toes. Boots or not, she should've worn thicker socks.

"Seems sort of sacrilegious, doesn't it? Leaving you a note in church?"

"I guess." Anna turned left onto Vermont Street. In the distance, her house sat nestled on a wooded acre. Her corner lot on Whispering Pines faced Vermont. "So odd...five golden rings. The only verse the same as the song. Maybe it's that much more significant."

"Well, that or the guy writing them is getting less creative."

"That reminds me. I called the flower company and found out the flowers, with the fourth note, were ordered by a woman."

"A woman? Really?" Ryan leaned forward. "That helps narrow things. A woman would—"

"All I know for sure is the credit card used to place the order had a woman's name. After thinking about it—it could be a stolen card. A wife, girlfriend, secretary." Anna's head felt like it was spinning. "I swear every time I think I've got a thread, it leads nowhere. Without a cardholder's name, it's useless."

"And you couldn't get that?" Ryan wiped the condensation from his window.

Anna shook her head. "I'm stuck on the verse two sets of books. I was gonna go over to the storage place and see what's there. I'm pretty sure Jake kept copies of everything."

"If any accountant would, it would be him. Let's go now."

"You up to it?" Anna glanced at him.

"Yeah." Ryan nodded. "I'll help. Better than lyin' around the house."

Ryan always had to be doing something, and being laid up had to be hard on him. His work ethic was one of the qualities Anna admired most. She made a U-turn and headed back toward town. The storage garages were near the salt mine, south down Route 39.

"Five golden rings is the same as the Christmas carol. It wouldn't make anyone suspicious. I mean, if someone besides you were to find it."

"Funny. I thought the same. Whoever's sending me the notes must go to our church and know where I sit."

"Sure seems like it. But then, maybe that's not true either, and that's what you're supposed to think. Did you look at any of the other hymnals? Did they all have an envelope, or was it just yours?"

"I...um...I didn't see any." *Shoot. I would have noticed, right? No, I didn't see this note until it flopped on the floor.* "You find out anything new about Jake's accident?"

Ryan shifted beside her. "Sure you wanna get into this?"

"I guess." Anna wasn't sure what Ryan was going to tell her, but she was past the point of surprise. "There was an email from a sheriff."

"Apparently, there was a sheriff at the scene."

"I don't remember one."

"Me neither. But it's significant because there's only one accident report that goes on file, and, in our area, the sheriff has jurisdiction over a town cop."

"So it should be his report on record?"

"Yeah, and it's not. Now, this guy and Vince could have been friends or known each other, or whatever, but I find it odd neither of us remember him."

"Did you call the sheriff's office and ask to talk to the officer that was at the scene?"

"Yeah, but the guy died a couple of months ago." Ryan picked up a quarter from her cup holder and fiddled with it.

"Murdered?"

"No. Cancer."

"Oh." Driving past the Adams' salt mine, Anna made a right into Jeremy's Storage Center and pulled up to garage number twenty-three. "Who was the email from then? The one I found?"

"Friend of his. Fellow officer. The guy remembered hearing about Jake's accident."

"What was the bit about Old Man Baker as a witness? Did he witness the crash?" Anna put the gear shift in park.

"Who knows?" Ryan shrugged. "Haven't seen him around town to ask."

"He's the guy on the bike that collects the cans, right?"

"Yup. Not exactly what I'd call a reliable source."

Anna didn't disagree. "I just don't understand why I was never notified there may have been a witness." Turning off the vehicle, she hopped out. The wind had finally calmed so it wasn't quite as cold as it had been. You knew you were in the throes of winter when thirty degrees, with no breeze, felt like a warm up.

Ryan's door closed.

"Why don't you wait until I get inside?" She flipped through the keys on her key ring.

"That's okay." Ryan climbed up onto the step beside her.

Anna inserted the key in the dangling lock. It didn't work. Anna made sure she had the right garage number. She did. She checked the key chain to make sure she had the right key. She did. *What the heck?* She tried again.

"What's up?" Ryan leaned over her shoulder.

"I think someone changed the lock."

Chapter Thirteen

"Wait here. I'll go ask." Anna inched her way across the empty parking lot to the main building. The sign read "Open," but the door was locked. "Open every day (except Sunday) ten to seven." Anna pounded on the door. A white, copy paper sign flapped against the window. Written in magic marker were the words "Closed for Daisy Peter's funeral." Small-town living struck again.

Ryan balanced on his crutch. "What?"

"Closed." Anna's boots crunched across the icy gravel as she made her way back to the truck.

"For the funeral?"

Anna nodded, too exasperated to speak.

Ryan opened his door. "We pass my apartment on the way to your place. Let's stop. Don't get me wrong. I love Jake, but I am not totally comfortable wearing another man's underwear."

Anna chuckled. "No problem."

Ryan packed a black duffel full of clothes. He chucked it over the apartment railing to the sidewalk. And then insisted on muscling it into her SUV and then into Anna's house. Apparently, it wasn't manly to have a lady carry your bag. Anna rolled her eyes, hoping the heavy bag didn't tip him over as he waited for her to unlock her front door.

The orange fluff ball greeted them in the entryway. It meowed all the time. Anna had no idea what its problem was but repeatedly reminded it that if it weren't for her, the cat would be rotting alone at Ryan's apartment. The cat didn't seem to care.

After he unpacked, Ryan settled into the sofa and propped his broken leg on the throw pillows. A playful grin swept across his face. "I know what we can do."

Anna was a little afraid of what would follow.

"Let's play—"

"No."

"Come on."

She shook her head as she tossed her coat over the desk chair.

"Please." Ryan folded his hands like he was praying.

Anna plugged in all her Christmas decorations. The glistening lights and shimmering garland helped brighten the dreary day. "I'd have a better shot at tug-of-war with a sumo wrestler."

Ryan narrowed his eyes and smirked. "You'd be more evenly matched."

"Ooooh." Despite herself, Anna laughed. "There are a lot of women who would take offense to that."

"I know, and you're not one of them." Ryan reached for the newspaper on the end table. "Besides, you know I think you're incredible looking."

Incredible looking? No, I didn't know that. Anna opened the entry hall closet and tugged the game off the high shelf. The tiles rattled in the box. *Incredible looking, did he really just say that?*

When she turned, Ryan's face was buried behind the newspaper. "All right, gimpy. Ya ready?"

"Gimpy. Good word." Ryan looked at her over the top of the fold. "But if I were you, I'd save my vocabulary for the board."

Anna set the game up on the cherry coffee table and pushed the table toward Ryan.

"May you get the X." She shook the box.

They each drew seven tiles.

Ryan picked up his last letter. "You jinxed me."

Anna smiled. His first word, X–rated, was an illegal one she let slide. The game went downhill from there.

Anna lost. She always did. Perhaps that was why Ryan liked to play Scrabble so much.

They ordered Chinese takeout, drank wine, and giggled.

"Do you think you could be in love with two people at once?" Ryan asked out of the blue. He acted half-lit. Not drunk, just feeling it a little.

The fire in the fireplace popped and crackled.

"Why?" Her chest ached. "Are you in love with two women?" *Do I want an answer to that?*

"No." Ryan took a gulp of wine. His deep-blue eyes bore into hers. Seconds passed. "I've always loved only one."

"Oh." *Is it hot in here?* Her face burned. She had to move. Anna folded up the containers of food and stacked them on top of the game box. "Why ask then?" *Wine. Need more wine.*

Ryan must have read her thoughts and refilled her glass. She couldn't look at him. She wasn't sure she wanted to.

"I just wondered if you think it would be possible for you to love two men instead of just one." Ryan spoke with a levity Anna didn't feel.

"For me to, or for anyone?"

Ryan didn't answer. They both knew she was stalling.

She slugged the Pinot. "Yes. I think it's possible."

Probable, but that might have just been the wine.

Chapter Fourteen

Her dreams were filled with a little girl not more than eight or nine. She had dark hair and eyes, and she wore a lime green dress with big white dots or flowers. Anna couldn't be sure which. Her pigtails, tied with yellow ribbons, flopped as she walked, and a teddy bear dangled at her side, its left ear torn. Tiny tufts of white stuffing slipped out the open stitches.

The girl smiled, and Anna felt like she'd known her all her life, although, somehow, she also knew they had never met. The child stepped closer and spoke to her in a language Anna didn't understand. For a moment, Anna felt hypnotized.

Anna had no concept of space or time, of where she was, or how long she stood staring at this child who spoke in the tongue of the angels.

Then, the little girl was gone.

Something had happened to her, although Anna wasn't sure what. She thought about what the child had said, trying to comprehend. This child whom she'd waited for all her life, that she'd never seen before and would never be at peace without. She thought of the language she spoke. It wasn't of this world—of this she was certain. Anna listened but heard only the beat of her own heart. Then, there it was, the voice of an angel.

In a moment of sudden clarity, Anna heard and understood. The little girl repeated it one more time as if just to be sure.

Softly, beneath a whisper, "Help me."

Shaken, Anna got out of bed and looked out the window. Part of her expected to see the little girl playing in the yard, the other part of her knew better. She wasn't sure which part she liked more.

Haunted. That was what she felt. Every hair on her body stood on end. This was more than a dream. She'd been served a summons, although she had no idea in what court she was supposed to appear and what judge would lay down her sentence.

Ryan was still asleep when Anna got downstairs, which was just as well. She didn't want to talk about what she had dreamt. She just wanted to forget it. But again, she knew better.

The past few days had been among the most stressful of her life, and her chalice of self-doubt runneth over. Daisy dead just hours after she left her house. Anna wasn't foolish enough to think she could have prevented it. No one had that power, but she still felt somehow connected to it. Responsible in some way.

This girl who she dreamt of needed her help. *How can I help the dead when I'm not much help to the living?* Was she dead? Anna wasn't sure. It didn't matter. She'd haunt her just the same.

"Anna." For the hundred and fiftieth time since Ryan came, she was surprised he stood behind her. "You okay?"

"Why?" She didn't bother to try to pretend. In some ways, she and Ryan were way beyond the petty games of guess what I'm thinking and then there were dozens of other games they'd still yet to play.

"I heard you crying in the middle of the night." Ryan stepped closer and put his hands on her shoulders.

"I had a nightmare."

"I thought I heard you whisper something, but then I thought there was no way I'd hear you all the way downstairs."

She turned and faced him. "What did you think I said?" Although, somehow, she already knew.

"Help me," Ryan whispered and then looked away.

Chapter Fifteen

The man sat on the mall's bench and waited. The young girl's mother leaned over and kissed the top of the child's head. It would be their last kiss. Did they sense it too?

Ashley. With her brown hair and matching eyes, the name suited her. Names often did.

Like Daisy. That old bat. *She loves me. She loves me not. She loves me. She loves me not.*

Just a few short days ago, from his car, he had watched as Gloria dropped Daisy off. Minutes passed, and he had waited and savored every moment like the sampling of a fine wine, or expensive dessert. He loved knowing what would happen and the wait for the culmination of his efforts. It was almost his favorite part. Almost.

Softly, he had closed his car door and had headed toward her house. He relished the crisp winter air, his favorite of all seasons. Five thirty and already dark. A stray branch skittered across the street. His footsteps echoed against the pavement, even and steady, like a metronome.

A pair of wicker rockers swayed on the porch, parted by a small, over-decorated Christmas tree. Was that Tommy's ghost rocking away? *Keep an open seat for your mother.*

The front door squeaked as he nudged it open. "Miss Daisy?"

She whimpered down the hall, no doubt weeping for her son. *Oh, Daisy, you'll see him soon enough.* He closed the door and locked it. The house stunk like the old. He hated that smell. It was, after all, death's precursor. No wonder today it seemed so much more intense.

Sweat prickled his brow. It had to be eighty degrees inside. Not surprising. Old ladies always had hot houses, as if thermostats and time were somehow connected; turn one up to turn the other back. If only it were that easy.

Queen Anne furniture covered in plastic cramped the small living room. The only light came from a brass floor lamp. Even the lampshade still had the plastic on it—that reminded him. He peeled the latex gloves from his pocket and wrangled them on, followed by a pair of leather gloves atop the latex, just to be safe. There would still be trace evidence, but that could be explained.

He followed the narrow hall toward the back of the house, careful to avoid the picture window. Of course, if anyone saw him, he'd say he had come because of Tommy.

Lies always went over best when laced with truth.

Yes, he had come because of Tommy. This was, after all, Tommy's fault. If he'd stayed away, then Daisy would be able to watch the ball drop this year like everybody else. Silence was costly, and it was time to collect.

Daisy lay face down on her bed. Her body racked with sobs. He stepped into the small bedroom. She stopped. She must have heard. Did she sense it? He often thought they did at the end.

She turned but showed no surprise to find him standing there. Streaks of mascara covered her face. Her short, wiry white hair was in disarray, and her always-immaculate clothes were a crumpled mess. Finally, the woman looked her age.

Apparently, reality proved a far better adversary than gravity.

In her expression, there was the flicker of recognition followed by disgust. Her eyes narrowed. *She knows what I've done and what is to come.*

He put his gloved forefinger to his lips and then pointed to her cane. She understood and slowly got to her feet. He guided her down the hall toward the bathroom. An accidental fall on a slippery floor. Perfect.

Daisy stopped and clutched her cane.

Swing, batter, batter, batter, swing.

But she didn't. Instead, she snarled at him through gritted teeth. "Go ahead and kill me. I don't care. You've taken everything from me. But I know what you did. Your secret's coming out, you filthy pig. Nine—"

"Shut up." Rage shot threw him. His hands bolted to her neck as he squeezed. "Shut up. Shut up." *Who does she think she is? How dare she not care?* He shook her like a throw rug. "Shut up. Shut up."

Daisy's cane crashed against the floor as her body went limp. So much for the accident.

He left her there—a useless heap on the hallway floor.

He had plucked Daisy's final petal just a few short days ago, and now he had his sights on a new flower. So fresh, so vibrant, like life itself radiated through her.

Ashley's mother stood at the soft pretzel counter. In her black leather jacket and turquoise satin pants, she looked like she belonged on a runway, not standing in a shopping mall. In her element, in the city.

Vanity always was his favorite sin.

Pretzel Boy—with his green, spikey hair—didn't take his gaze off of her. The man shifted his weight on the bench and grinned.

Pretzel Boy fawned over her like he'd never seen a woman before. Pervert. The earring in Pretzel Boy's nose must have pierced his brain and the green spikes were no doubt double-sided, but he didn't have time for Pretzel Boy. Today was Ashley's day. He clutched the paper bag. The present he bought for her swooshed inside.

While her mother blushed, Ashley wandered toward him. Her heart must have heard his call. Fate often spoke softly. She looked at him, her big eyes beaming with blinding trust.

He took a moment to gauge his surroundings. No one noticed him. They certainly weren't in the country anymore, where everyone knew everyone and you spoke to the guy next to you whether you knew him or not. No, this was the city. Things moved faster here. People didn't notice the people they slept with, let alone the people they shopped with. God, he loved the city. Its thousand sets of blind eyes made his job easy.

Ashley stepped closer, and he beamed. She recognized him. He knew she would. He'd made sure of it. The pet store was just a few doors up. He pointed at it, and she nodded. They walked side-by-side, her hand in his. A jolt of excitement shot through him.

He wouldn't be as stupid as last time. Experience was a powerful teacher, its lessons as vivid as any textbook's.

"It's cold outside, honey." Out of his bag, he pulled a girl's winter coat and hat. Baby blue. It matched the ribbons in her hair. "Why don't you put these on?" He held it open.

Ashley slid her arms into the coat's sleeves. "I thought we were going to the pet store."

"Yep. I just need to get some money out of my car."

He waited at the exit, conscious of the security camera. Certainly, Ashley wouldn't be recognized in her new coat and hat, but he might. He waited there, patiently, like a kid waiting for a snow day announcement. He knew it was coming, but didn't know when.

People entered. He couldn't wait much longer. What was Pretzel Boy doing? Telling her his life's story?

"Ow. You're hurting me," Ashley cried, and he realized he squeezed her hand too tightly as the anticipation ripped through him.

He softened his grip.

"I want Mommy."

He slung open the door.

There it was. Out of nowhere. He heard it, and it filled him. Worth the wait. Worth every second of the wait.

"Ashley!" Her mother screamed again.

This time they were already outside.

Chapter Sixteen

The next morning, Anna called the storage center.

"Jeremy's Storage, you've got Jeremy." The young man sounded like he should be the host of a soft rock radio station, not running a storage center.

"Hi, this is Anna Greenan. I rent unit twenty-three." Jeremy's Storage Center, Ryan's General Store, Sandy's Dry Cleaning, Potrage—clearly not originality's breeding ground.

"Yep. Saw you at the Peters' funerals." Jeremy sipped something. "Whatcha need?"

"Well…I was at the garage yesterday and can't get into my unit."

"Course not."

Of course not? What?

"You haven't been around," Jeremy cleared his throat, "but we had to change all the locks."

"What?"

"Yeah, while back. Got to be about two, maybe three years now. Right around the time you rented. We had somebody come through and bust all the locks on the units. I tried like hell to get ahold of you, but your husband had just passed, and you never called me back. So, I figured I better lock it up."

Anna tried to think back. She did vaguely remember the call but didn't recall anyone saying the lock had been cut. But back then they could've said her hair was on fire and she wouldn't have paid attention. "Was anything taken?"

68

"No. Not in any of the other units, and I did peek in yours. Everything seemed intact, so I threw on a lock and figured you'd stop out here sooner or later."

"Thanks." Rural America did have its advantages. "Can I stop down and get the new key?"

"Sure. Be here till ten tonight."

"I'll be there in a bit."

When Anna returned downstairs, the aroma of fresh coffee greeted her. Ryan sat on the couch, already dressed in a pair of khakis and a navy-blue sweater that matched his eyes. He lifted the remote and flipped off the mounted television.

"Hi, you're up early." With anyone else, she'd have felt silly walking around in flannel pajamas and slippers with bears on them, but, with Ryan, she could be herself.

"Not really." Ryan grinned.

One glance at the clock explained his smug face. It was almost ten-thirty. She must have been tired. Anna never slept this late. "I called the storage center."

"What'd they say?"

"Apparently, all the locks were cut right after I rented. Guess they tried to get ahold of me but I never called them back. They said nothing looked like it was taken. I thought I'd stop over there. You feel up to it?"

"Yeah. Go get ready. I'll take you out to lunch and then we'll head over."

"Sounds good." Anna walked past the den and noticed the computer on. Might as well check emails. Not that she ever got anything great, but she was due back at the advertising agency after the New Year, and it stood to reason someone might need to get ahold of her. Her office didn't have a lot of rules, but the no work-related emails going to your cell phone over vacation was the one she liked best. Business owners worked all the time, so they thought nothing of calling and emailing while their advertising agents were out on holiday.

In fact, if she worked in any other department, she'd never have gotten the time off. The week between Christmas and New Year's was big business for retail stores and advertising spending. Thankfully, all the ads she wrote were completed long before they aired.

"What are you doing?" Ryan asked. "I thought we had a date."

A date? Were they dating? They hadn't even kissed yet. That surely was a prerequisite.

Although, there was that one time...

They were eighteen, maybe nineteen, and Jake and Anna had just started dating. She made plans to meet Jake at the beach after her evening class. Anna had bought some cheap champagne, and Jake had promised to bring the pizza.

The pizza showed. Jake didn't. He had sent Ryan in his stay, or so she'd thought.

"What are you doing here?" She hopped off the hood of her beat-up, black Grand Am. The sand shifted beneath her feet, sliding into her sandals and in-between her toes.

"Jake got called in to work." Ryan trudged through the sand.

Seagulls squawked and hovered as the waves rolled in from the lake.

"So he sent you instead?" Anna smiled. She liked Ryan. In a lot of ways, he was like Jake, and the two of them were a riot when they got together. "Did you two think I wouldn't know the difference?"

"No, but I came bearing gifts." Ryan held up the pizza box. He set it on the hood and opened it. Stringy cheese stuck to the lid.

"So did I." Anna pulled out the brown paper bag with the champagne.

They spread a fleece blanket over the sand and picnicked. A couple of pieces of pizza and two glasses of champagne later, they were laughing like fools.

Ryan moved a little closer, and the conversation shifted. "So, you've been alone since your gram passed?"

"Yep." Anna nodded and forced a smile.

Ryan reached over and pushed a stray hair behind her ear. The gesture, an inane one, seemed somehow so intimate.

He leaned closer, and Anna's chest tightened. She closed her eyes. Goosebumps slid up her arms. He was so close. She couldn't breathe.

"Anna," he whispered.

She was going to whisper back but couldn't think. His warm breath grazed her cheek. In her ear.

A horn blared. They both jumped. A red sports car tore through the beach parking lot. "Go for it," someone screamed as the wheels screeched, and then they left as quickly as they came.

Ryan sat up. "Anna. I… I… I didn't mean to…" His face was crimson, and he spoke a mile a minute. "Oh, God. Oh, God. I'm so sorry. I know you're with Jake. He's my best—"

"Ryan." She had to stop him. "It's okay. It's fine. Nothing happened."

Ryan exhaled. "I should go."

It wasn't until years later, after Anna and Jake married, she found out Jake never knew Ryan had gone to the beach that night. Anna never told Jake about what happened. Neither did Ryan.

That was a long time ago.

"Anna, you okay?"

"Um." *Oh, yikes.* "Ah…um…" She gestured toward the den. "Did you leave the computer on?"

"Yeah. Sorry. Couldn't find my laptop."

"Bookshelf." Anna nodded toward the laptop. "But no big deal. Use whatever you want. I just wanted to check my email quick."

"Take your time."

Anna logged on and clicked on her mailbox. Thirty-five emails, but only one stopped her cold.

Re: The sixth day

"Ryan," she called into the living room.

"On the sixth day of Christmas, my true love gave to me six o'clock newscast, five golden rings, four people murdered, three years ago, two sets of books, and the reason your husband had to die."

By the time she finished reading, Ryan stood beside her. Without pause, Anna hit reply and typed.

"Who are you? Why are you sending me these notes? If you have something to

tell me, just say it. Let's meet."

Why she was offering to meet someone who was sending her cryptic notes she couldn't say, but it seemed more strategic than being combative. She didn't want to anger this person, but she wanted the notes to stop. And it seemed the only way to get the messages to stop was to learn whatever it was this person was trying to tell her, no matter how creepy and twisted these notes became.

"What are you—"

Anna clicked send before Ryan could stop her.

Moments later, her inbox showed one new message from Postmaster. *"This is an automatically generated Delivery Status Notification. Delivery to the following recipients failed."*

"Move." Ryan pushed on her shoulder to get her out of the chair, sat, and started typing.

"What are you doing?"

"I want to see where the original email came from." Ryan moved the mouse.

Anna had no idea what he was doing, or how he knew how to do it, but she wasn't going to complain or slow him down.

"How did they get your email?" Ryan glanced at her.

"This is my work email. It's published on the agency's website." Which meant whoever sent her these notes knew where she worked too. It figured.

"Go get ready." Ryan continued typing, his fingers flying across the keys. "I'll call you when I get something."

Anna forced herself to go upstairs to look for something to wear.

The notes plagued her, forever pulsating through her thoughts. *Six o'clock newscast.* What could be on the news tonight that would have to do with Jake being killed three years ago? The letters were like Pandora's Box. Once she opened them, she couldn't stop their momentum. Was the note referring to tonight's newscast or a newscast that aired three years ago? She didn't know. It might be nothing, but she'd tune in at six anyway.

After applying her makeup, Anna slid on a baby blue turtleneck sweater and navy-blue slacks, careful not to smudge her foundation on the shirt's collar. The color looked good on her, and the shirt and pants clung in just the right places. One glance in the mirror, and she nearly didn't recognize her reflection; she almost looked like herself again. Almost. Not the same happy-go-lucky girl of a few years ago, but a more seasoned version. As usual, her wild curls ran in a pattern as random as life's, but her eyes held a spark she hadn't seen in a long time.

"Anna?" Ryan called upstairs.

"Yep. Coming." Anna snatched up her purse and headed for the stairs. "Did you find something?"

"No. The email came from an untraceable remailer."

Shoot. "What does that mean?"

"Wow." Ryan stood at the foot of the steps.

"What's an untraceable remailer?" Anna saw his expression and took her time coming down the staircase.

"It's ah… You…um…" Ryan looked around. "What did you ask me?"

Anna laughed and couldn't hide her smile. *Still got it.* "I've never heard of a remailer. What is it?"

"Basically, whoever sent you this email first, sent it to a company. That company, in turn, replaced the original sender's email address with an untraceable one. Then, the company forwarded the email message on to you." Ryan shifted his weight from one foot to the other. His gaze bore into hers.

"Can we find out what the original email address was, or the IP address, or anything?"

"Not that I know of." Ryan smiled at her. "You look really pretty."

Anna looked at the stairway's carpet as heat flashed across her cheeks.

Chapter Seventeen

Anna eased her car up to the storage center office building. "You wait here. I'll be right back." She hopped out and left Ryan in the running truck.

Jeremy was seated at his desk, lost in a sea of paperwork. He looked up just as she opened the door. His brown eyes matched his skin, and his broad smile could have been seen two towns away. "Come in. Come in."

Anna always liked the man. "Hi, I'm here to—"

"I know. Glad you finally stopped by. Let me get that key for ya." Jeremy stood and dialed the lock on the wall safe behind him.

"Thanks." Anna glanced around the nautical-themed office. Photos of Jeremy fishing hung haphazardly all over the oak-paneled walls.

"Here." Jeremy handed her a single key with *Greenan* printed on the masking tape label. "What brings you in after all this time?"

Something about his question, or maybe the way he asked it, put Anna on edge. "One of Jake's clients is getting audited. Their new accountant needs some old information."

"Need help?" Jeremy's smile no longer reached his eyes.

"Nah, I brought Ryan with me. I'll be fine." Anna gestured toward the parking lot.

"Didn't realize you had somebody with you." Jeremy moved toward the window and peered out, moving the curtain. "Well, I'm here if you need me."

"Thanks. And thanks for taking care of my unit. Do I owe you anything for the new lock?"

"Nah." Jeremy brushed it off. "This one's on me."

She turned to leave.

"Hey, Anna." Jeremy quickly moved around her to hold open the door. "You take care of yourself, ya hear?"

"Thanks. You too." A chill rolled through her. It had nothing to do with the winter weather.

"Did you get the key?" Ryan asked when she climbed back into the driver's seat.

"Yep." Anna tossed the key in the cup holder and drove over to the row that held her unit. Should she tell him about the weird vibe Jeremy gave off? Nah. What was there to tell? Plus, she was on edge enough for them both.

Unlocking her unit, Anna heaved open the garage door and flicked the light switch. The fluorescent lights hummed, flickered, and then rolled to life. Box after box stood stacked floor to ceiling.

"Good God." Ryan followed her in. "This'll take forever."

There was something in this room they needed to find. She just didn't know what or even where to start.

On the sixth day of Christmas, my true love gave to me six o'clock newscast, five golden rings, four people murdered, three years ago, two sets of books, and the reason your husband had to die. Two sets of books. Here? Two sets? Or one set here and one set stashed someplace else? Did the three years ago refer to the two sets of books or the four people murdered? Or to Jake's death? She didn't know, but it didn't matter; she had to do something. Sitting at home would just make her crazy.

Jake's employees had done a nice job of organizing the space. The dates were marked on the front of each box. The farther back and higher stacked were the earlier years. The more recent the date—the easier to get to. The records went back a decade. Also, the boxes looked to be done alphabetically, and by area. Buffalo A-J, Rochester R-Z, Potrage E-J, etcetera.

Paper box lids rattled in the breeze. The unit wasn't heated. Anna rolled the overhead door closed to block the biting wind.

She began muscling things out of the way, trying to clear a place to sit. Ryan tried to help but, on one leg, was of little use. "The notes said three years ago." Anna piled one box on the next.

"Yeah."

"Then, let's start there."

"All right." Ryan opened the box to his left, Buffalo, A-J.

"I think we should start in Potrage."

"Okay." Ryan replaced the lid. "Any reason or just a hunch?"

"Both. The mailed note had a Potrage postmark. Other notes have been hand-delivered: in my purse, the hymnal at church. Plus, I don't think anyone outside of town would know enough about Jake and me to pull me into it. Not in this kind of personal way. I'm not on Facebook or Twitter, telegraphing my life. Jake had no use for social media either."

"Fair enough. Potrage it is."

Ryan used his crutch to balance his weight as he sat atop a small stack. He began sifting through the Potrage E-J box Anna had set on the floor beside him. Unable to locate the most recent A-D, Anna settled for Potrage K-P, and sat cross-legged on the floor. The concrete was uncomfortable and freezing. She removed her coat and slid it under her. Now her arms froze, but her bottom was comfier.

Slowly, methodically, they scoured through the papers. Tax forms, payroll, worker's compensation payments, phone bills, rent, you name it, Jake had it. His anal-retentive organization seemed like a God-send.

A rumble. Anna jumped. A jolt of adrenaline shot through her. "What was that?" She waited. Nothing.

"What?"

"Did you hear that?"

"No, I didn't hear anything." Ryan shook his head. "What'd it sound like?"

"Not sure. Maybe a car door." Anna strained to hear it again. Something. Anything. But all she heard was the buzz of the overhead lights.

Ryan reached for his crutches and moved to stand. "Want me to go check it out?"

"No, sit." Anna waved him off. "I'm sure it was nothing."

The more boxes she went through, the more positive she became they'd never find whatever they were supposed to. And, in truth, even if she were staring right at it, she probably wouldn't know it. This was a colossal waste of time.

A nearby church bell chimed. Five o'clock.

"You know." Ryan shifted on the boxes, the grimace clear on his face. "We're gonna need help. We don't even know what we're looking for. Any discrepancies would slip right by us."

"You're right. I was just thinking that."

"Let's go. After that latest note, you're gonna want to catch the six o'clock news. I'll give my accountant for the store a call. He's a friend of mine."

"You know, did you see A through D for Potrage from three years ago?" Anna double-checked but didn't see it anywhere.

"No."

"Odd, isn't it?"

"Do you have A through D for the prior years?" Ryan used the wall to help him stand up, adjusting the crutches under his arms.

"Yep. It's just the last year Jake completed that's missing."

"Well, then A through D in Potrage seems like a real good place for my guy to start."

Anna loaded a few of the A-D Potrage boxes in her SUV and dug a little deeper for the missing one. It definitely was gone. After she made sure she had her keys, she shut off the lights and locked up her unit.

Climbing in, she closed the truck door and yanked on her seat belt. Something wasn't right. The belt's usual tension was missing. The shoulder strap pulled free from the wall.

"What's the matter?"

"My seat belt's broken. It split at the seam where the belt meets the wall." The shoulder harness flapped against her hand.

"That's odd. It just snapped like that?"

"I guess…"

Anna never drove without a seat belt, especially after Jake died, because he hadn't worn one. She clipped what was left of the restraint and hoped the lap belt would be enough. Her thighs squished as she tugged the bottom part of the harness as tight as it would go.

"It's only five-fifteen." Ryan tapped the dashboard clock.

"So?" Anna couldn't keep the tension from her voice.

"We've got plenty of time to make it home before the six o'clock news. Why don't you take your time?"

Ryan must have been thinking about Jake's accident too. In all the years she'd known him, Jake always wore his seat belt. The man followed rules: speed limit, stop signs, seat belts. It never made sense. *Why the one time? But isn't that the way it goes?*

With the sun already set, Anna would've guessed it was much later than quarter after five—wintertime in the northeast. She pulled out onto Greenview Road and headed home. Headlights shown in her rearview. The truck behind her gained ground quickly. Too quickly. *The driver must not see me.* She made a fast right onto Short Pump Road to get out of their way.

The truck raced around the turn and closed the gap.

"Someone's behind us." Ryan shifted in his seat. "They're hauling it."

"I know." The rural road didn't have a shoulder to pull off on, and no one lived out here. Her pulse quickened. Every hair on her body stood on end. Anna gripped the wheel.

"They're going way too fast. You have to get out of the way."

"I know. But how?" She sped up.

"They must be drunk, or high, or something." Ryan sounded panicked.

Ice crunched under her vehicle's wheels. Her heart galloped in her chest. Headlights beamed larger in the rearview. Moving quicker. Closer. Too close. *Oh, God.* Anna wanted to stomp on the brakes and blare her horn, but they'd ram her.

A street sign came up quick and glowed green. She had to turn off but didn't want to skid on the ice.

"Slow down." Ryan reached for the roll bar.

"I can't."

One. Two. Thr—

A sharp right. Tires squealed. The force hurled her toward Ryan. *Don't tip. Don't tip.* The tires plopped down. The lap belt pulled tight across her groin as the SUV bounced. The free-floating shoulder strap and wall attachment whacked her chest, nearly knocking the wind out of her. They headed up the narrow, winding hill. Trees lined both sides of the street as darkness fell and swallowed what was left of the day.

Anna exhaled. Sweat dotted her hairline. "That was—" Headlights. In her rearview. Same truck. Still flying. "Oh no."

She pressed harder on the gas pedal.

"Don't!" Ryan yelled. As if on cue, a man stepped out of nowhere. Something flung into the road.

"Oh no!" Anna swung the wheel to the right.

"No!" Ryan grabbed the steering wheel, forcing it in the other direction. Anna slammed on the brakes to no avail. With the icy road, the truck flung like a beach ball in a hurricane. The backend slid out. Pain shot through her temple as her head whacked the window. Rocks pelted the SUV's frame. She had no control of the vehicle. Her thigh burned as she pressed as hard as she could on the useless brake. *No. No. No.* She squeezed her eyes shut and blocked out the spots. *God, help. Help, please.*

The truck skidded and skidded, whirled and whirled. Finally, it slid to a stop.

"Did I hit him?" Anna was unable to open her eyes. *I didn't. I couldn't have. I would have felt it. Heard it.*

"No." Ryan opened his door when she opened her eyes. If he stepped out, he would've fallen off a cliff. Ryan closed his door and looked out the back gate. The truck behind them was gone, and the man who had appeared out of thin air had vanished.

"Who and what was that?" Sweat trickled down Anna's side.

"I don't know... I...I didn't get a good look. It happened so fast."

The dark street was deserted. What had that man been doing out here? What had he pushed into her path? Was it deliberate or his kneejerk reaction to almost getting hit? "Hello." Anna opened her window and called into the darkness. "Anybody there? Are you hurt?"

No answer.

"Just get us out of here," Ryan said and Anna didn't disagree.

Her neck hurt and teeth ached. She had a knot between her shoulders. Reaching up to pat her head, she found a tender lump where her head had smacked the door.

As she drove home, every flash of light made her jump. More than once, she stopped for mailboxes and bales of hay she mistook for people.

"Did you see what kind of truck it was?" Ryan shifted in the seat beside her.

"No. All I know is it was big and a dark color."

"I wish I got a plate number or something. They're gonna kill someone, or get killed themselves. Idiots."

Anna pulled into her driveway, opened her driver's side door, and threw up.

Chapter Eighteen

"Good evening. Topping tonight's news at six, have you seen this child? Eight-year-old Ashley Grey was last seen yesterday at the Appleton Mall in Henrietta."

A recent picture of Ashley flashed across the screen. Her brown hair was tucked into butterfly barrettes as she posed in her navy-blue school uniform.

Anna sat up, fully expecting the missing child to be the little girl she dreamt of, and her eyes stung when she wasn't. *Thank you, God.* Anna had all she could handle today. Her head pounded.

"Anyone with any information is urged to contact the Henry Lake Police Department. With more on this story, we go live to reporter Stephanie Malhoon. Stephanie, what can you tell us?"

An attractive blonde filled the screen. She nodded at the camera. "Thanks, Irv. Ashley Grey of Pittstone was last seen here—" The screen flashed to the mall food court. A steady stream of shoppers strolled past. "—with her mother yesterday morning, shortly after the mall opened. Police are confirming tonight they're treating this case as an abduction and are calling on the public for any information. A toll-free hotline is being set up for anyone who may have seen anything that would help investigators. This is the..."

The news droned on, but Anna tuned out. She rested her aching head against the back of the sofa and exhaled.

"You okay?" Ryan picked up the television remote and turned down the volume.

"I can't watch anymore." Anna pushed herself up. "I'm going to take a bath."

"Go ahead." Ryan nodded. "I'll watch the news and holler if anything stands out."

"Call your accountant and see if he'll go through those files."

"Sure. We can meet him tomorrow."

"Have him come here." Tiny snowflakes flitted past her back window, glistening in the shallow light from the living room. "After almost getting run off the road, I'm not going to want to drive anywhere."

Ryan reached up to touch her hand. "You okay?"

No. Not at all. She forced a smile. "Yeah. I'm fine."

Sirens pierced the night silence. Anna yanked a pillow tight over her head. *Please let it stop.* Exhausted, but she couldn't sleep. The accident had freaked her out. Sore, tired, angry, she'd had enough. Vomiting in the driveway made her wonder if she'd suffered a slight concussion. Ryan wondered the same and insisted on waking her up every few hours after she refused to go to the E.R. Her pupils were the same size. She passed Ryan's follow-my-finger test and didn't want to incur medical expenses when there was no treatment to provide. A trip to the emergency room was a luxury she couldn't afford.

Anna had spent the night sifting through papers, the most important of which had probably been stolen, looking for clues to solve a mystery she didn't want to be a part of. And what did she get for it? Run off the road and a mind-splitting headache. Anna wrangled with whether or not to call the police and tell them her storage unit was broken into. She was pretty sure at least one box of papers had been stolen. Although, the police would inevitably ask when the break-in happened, and she would have to tell them three years ago, give or take a few weeks. The only lockup that would happen would be to her—in a padded room. No, she couldn't call the police. Plus, the police probably already knew about the break-in. Jeremy had to have filed a report to get insurance to pay for the damages. Anna had no way of being positive papers were stolen since she didn't have a master list of what was in the unit to begin with.

The phone clanged, but Anna didn't move. It wouldn't be good news. Not at this hour. Ryan must have answered. His muffled voice carried through the vent.

"Anna," Ryan called up the stairs a few minutes later.

"Hello." Anna picked up the receiver. Dial tone. She tossed off the blankets, threw on her slippers and thick robe, and headed downstairs.

Ryan stood at the base of the staircase. Half of his hair stood on end, the other half was matted flat against his head. He wore a pair of gray sweats and a white T-shirt.

"What's up?" She wasn't sure why she whispered. Everyone was awake.

"There's a fire."

"Here?"

"No." Ryan shook his head. "The storage center."

"Shoot." Anna ran down the remaining few stairs. "Who called?"

"Jeremy. I guess the fire started in, or around, your unit."

Anna didn't want to leave the rest of the boxes out in the car. "I'm going to go bring in those boxes." She slid on her boots and exchanged her bathrobe for a winter coat.

"Good idea." Ryan turned on the front porch lights and opened the door. Although he couldn't carry anything, he hobbled out with her anyway. "Jeremy said everything is lost."

"Not everything."

Hopefully, they had what they needed. And if not, there was nothing she could do about it now. Anna swung open her SUV's back gate and carried the huge, heavy boxes inside. The papers seemed to have multiplied like unwashed laundry.

Ryan closed the gate and followed her into the house. "What's that stench?"

She knew before she even looked. She had stepped in her own puke.

After Anna cleaned her boots and the front hall, she found Ryan sitting on the sofa. A fire flickered in the fireplace. The aroma of the cleaning solution had been replaced with burning wood. "Aren't you going to go back to bed?"

"Can't." Ryan shrugged. "I'm too awake now. Besides, it's almost five. I'm usually up by six."

"I can't sleep either."

"Wanna sit with me?" Ryan scooted over on the sofa and made room.

Anna flopped beside him, and he flung the fluffy, white blanket over her legs. Ryan put his arm around her, and she laid her head on his shoulder.

"I'm glad you're here." Anna spoke softly, barely able to squeeze the words out. Her heart ached.

"Anna." Ryan shook her shoulder. "Anna."

She ignored him until he pulled the blanket off of her. *Cruel man.*

"Anna!"

"What?" she snapped and then felt immediately guilty. She was curled up on the couch, a pillow beneath her head. She must've dozed off. Ryan had brought her a pillow and covered her up.

"Here." Ryan passed her a piping hot cup of coffee. "You missed the mechanic."

"What?"

"I called Greg and had him come by and fix your shoulder harness. This way you'll have a seat belt if you need to go out."

"Thanks." Anna sipped the coffee and set it on the end table. "Will Greg be able to do that?"

"He already did. You were asleep. The man's owned the repair service for the last fifteen years. I think he can fix anything. But my accountant is going to want to talk to us both, so you have to go get ready." Ryan folded the white blanket that once covered her. "He'll be here in about ten minutes."

"Oh no." No way a perfect stranger would see her in pajamas, no bra, and bear slippers.

Thankfully, Ryan's accountant ran late. The gravel of her stone driveway crunched just as Anna applied her lipstick. Ready. Just in time. Downstairs, she found Ryan waiting by the front door.

"There's something I forgot to tell you."

"What?" Anna peeked out the etched glass. A pink Cadillac parked in her driveway.

"My accountant has a second job." Ryan grinned. "He moonlights as an Elvis impersonator."

Chapter Nineteen

"Hey, thanks for coming on such short notice." Ryan stepped aside and let Elvis into the living room.

Dressed in a black leather jacket, jeans, and blue suede shoes, Ryan's accountant wore a gold The King medallion, which nicely complemented his pompadour and sideburns. "Thank you. Thank you very much."

Dear God, there is a hell, and Elvis is in it.

Ryan cleared his throat; his cue for Anna to close her gaping mouth and pull it together. "This is my friend, Anna." Ryan gestured toward her.

"How do you do? Name's Gary, but my friend's all call me The King. Elvis impersonator for eleven years." The King reached out.

"Nice to meet you." Anna shook his hand and bit her tongue.

"Golly. You're almost as pretty as Lisa Marie."

Anna smiled. "Thank you. May I take your coat?"

The King slid off his leather jacket and passed it to her. The heaviness of the coat surprised her, the stench of stale cigarettes emanating from it did not.

"Ryan tells me you're Catholic. Y'all pray to the saints. I'd love to have a talk to The Big One, you know." The King pointed heavenward.

"Jesus?" *I'm going to kill Ryan.* Anna draped the jacket over the writing desk's chair.

The King shook his head. "No, Honey. Elvis. The one and only."

Ryan beamed, clearly holding back his laughter.

"Hey, you know, I was gonna ask." The King adjusted his jeans. "One of you Catholic ladies gave me a crucifix. Ya know. The kind that still has Jesus hangin' on it, like He got stuck up there or somethin'. Well, one day, while I was gettin' ready for a show, Jesus fell off it. Craziest thing. Just fell right off. Whatcha think?"

He probably jumped.

"Does it mean something?" The King stared at her.

Anna shrugged her shoulders. "I'm sure it's nothing."

"Well, it's got me all shook up." He added a pelvic thrust.

Ryan is so dead.

"Oh, by the way." The King pulled an envelope from his back pocket. "Found this tucked under the windshield wiper of the SUV out there. Didn't want it to get blown away." He handed her an envelope.

Anna's stomach dropped as she opened the next note.

"On the seventh day of Christmas, my true love gave to me seven checks were written, six o'clock newscast, five golden rings, four people murdered, three years ago, two sets of books, and the reason your husband had to die."

She passed the heavyweight cotton paper to Ryan and let him explain the story to The King while she kept busy, tidying the already tidy house.

"Geez." The King finally broke character when Ryan finished. "That's one hell of a story. Where's the stuff you took from the storage garage?"

"In the den." Anna pointed toward the French doors. "I don't know if it'll help, but you never know."

"I got Ryan's account from Farrer, Gavinson, and Cash. Is that who bought your husband's client list after he passed?"

"Yes."

"So, they may have some copies of stuff. I'm going to start looking into this. Seven checks were written, huh?" The King shuttered as if a spider had crawled up his spine.

"That's what this note says." Ryan tossed the latest verse of the cryptic lyrics onto the writing desk.

"I don't get the two sets of books thing." The King's brow furrowed.

"Why?" Anna stopped cleaning.

"Well, whoever did this seems to have gone to a lot of trouble to hide whatever it is they're into. I doubt they'd keep a duplicate set of books. That's just asking to get caught."

Anna agreed. The King seemed like a nice guy when he was just being himself, and she wanted to ask why he spent so much time pretending to be someone he wasn't. Then again, there were lots of people who pretended to be someone they weren't; The King was just more honest about it than most.

"What's this going to cost me?" Not that it mattered, but Anna needed a rough idea. With the holidays just wrapping up, she had very little cash left for unexpected expenses, and her credit cards were nearly maxed.

"Ah. Don't worry about it." The King walked to the den and emerged carrying one of the boxes they'd taken from the storage unit. "Ryan's one of my favorite clients. I'm happy to help out."

She raced ahead to open the door for him. "No. I need to pay you." Anna was relieved but reluctant to take a handout.

"Twenty-five dollars." The King paused in the doorway and smiled. She knew she was getting off way too easy. "And you and Ryan come on out to one of my shows."

There had to be a catch. "You don't want me to be a groupie." Anna winked.

"No. Please. I've got tons of those."

Somehow, she knew he wasn't kidding.

Thankfully, The King took all the paperwork with him. Good. It felt like a load had been lifted.

"He's quite a character." Anna waved goodbye and then shut the door.

"Yeah, but you can't help but like him. And he'll take his time going through the stuff. He's meticulous."

"Well," Anna couldn't resist, "wise men say only fools rush in."

Ryan laughed.

"Thank you. Thank you very much." Her impersonation was lacking. But Ryan was an easy audience.

"What are we going to do tonight?" Ryan hobbled to the couch.

"Why?"

"It's New Year's Eve." Ryan leaned his crutches against the ottoman.

"I totally forgot." Was it already New Year's Eve? Where had the week gone?

Ryan grinned.

"What? Why do you have that look?"

He was up to something.

Ryan turned away and slipped something over his head. When he turned back, he shot her a toothy grin. A tie filled with giant, bloated, post-drug-use Elvis faces hung from around his neck. When Ryan squeezed it, Elvis' voice filled the living room. "Love me tender, love me true..."

"A little gift." Ryan wiggled. "From The King."

He wore that stupid tie all night.

In the kitchen, Anna covered the leftover pizza with plastic wrap.

"Would you hurry up?" Ryan shouted from the living room. "You're gonna miss it."

Anna never really liked New Year's Eve. It reminded her of loved ones lost and how fast time went by, but this year was different. She couldn't wait for the New Year since the end of this one had been so crappy. While she didn't know what would happen, she didn't think it could get much worse.

"Anna!"

The pizza balanced atop the milk and orange juice. She shut the fridge door before an avalanche of leftovers tumbled out.

Anna raced back into the living room as the glittery ball above Time Square began to descend.

"Ten. Nine. Eight." The television boomed.

She flopped beside Ryan on the sofa in the nick of time.

"Seven. Six. Five."

He slid his arm around her.

"Four. Three."

Butterflies fluttered in her stomach.

"Two. One. Happy New Year."

"Happy New Year." Ryan leaned over and kissed her. Gently. A soft peck between friends.

Her heart thumped, and her face burned. Then, Ryan hooked his finger under her chin, lifted it, and kissed her again. This time it was *not* a soft peck between friends. Breathless...she couldn't speak. Luckily, she didn't need to.

Chapter Twenty

Tension flooded the house after last night. Yes, it might have been just one not-so-little kiss, but it changed things; didn't it? Ryan fiddled and puttered with odds and ends and said little to her all morning. Anna didn't know what to say, or do, either. Should she acknowledge what happened or pretend it never had? She opted for the latter. They went to New Year's Day church service and acted like business as usual. Well, business as usual minus all normal eye contact and casual conversation.

"What's up with you today?" Anna finally mustered the courage to ask as she drove home after Mass. This standoff had to end. What was one incredible, magnificent, sexy smooch between friends?

"It's my dad's birthday." Ryan adjusted the SUV's vents.

Not the response she expected. "Oh…want me to run you to his place?" So, it wasn't her irresistible charm rendering Ryan speechless.

"No. He and the stepmother go to my sister's every year." Ryan looked out his window

Anna sensed he regretted bringing it up.

The stepmother, not *my* stepmother? "Did you send him a birthday card at least?"

Ryan shifted in his seat. "I wonder if The King has uncovered anything in those files."

"I'm sure he'd call if he did." Anna turned the wheel and pulled into Ryan's General Store's parking lot.

"What're you doing?" Ryan's eyes were as wide as his smile.

"I want to run in. You wanna check it out?" It had to be eating at Ryan that he couldn't work. This was undoubtedly the longest he'd gone without.

"Oh. Yeah. Absolutely." His enthusiasm overflowed. "Thank you."

Anna parked in an open spot near the door and allowed Ryan to take his time on his crutches.

The buzz of the Sunday breakfast crowd chatter reached a crescendo when Anna peeled open the heavy glass door. The familiar smell of bacon filled her nose, and her stomach growled. She held the door open for Ryan as he was treated to a hero's welcome: whistles, catcalls, fist bumps, and pats on the back. New Year's Day and the place was packed.

Anna vanished into the card section and let Ryan do his thing. No doubt, the man was in his element. She turned the corner and nearly plowed into Father Matthew.

"Oh. Goodness." Father Matthew adjusted the glasses she nearly knocked off his face. "I am sorry."

"My fault, Father. I shouldn't have been in such a hurry." Anna noticed his black scarf had fallen in the aisle. She picked it up and handed it to him.

"No problem. Thank you." Father Matthew took the scarf and draped it over his broad shoulders.

Anna had to smile. She would never get used to seeing a Catholic priest in his civvies, especially one as good looking as Father Matthew with his surfer boy, blond hair, and piercing blue eyes.

"Very nice homily today. I really enjoyed it."

"Thanks." His cheeks reddened.

"You here for breakfast?" Anna tried to keep the conversation light, hoping her compliment hadn't embarrassed him too badly.

"Not today. Just picking up some staples. You?"

"The same." Anna nodded.

"Hey, Father." Ryan hobbled around the corner. "Long time, no see."

"I didn't get a chance to ask you after Mass, how's the leg?" Father Matthew nodded toward Ryan's cast.

"The leg's fine. It's the rest of me that hurts." Ryan wiggled the crutches. "These things are brutal. My arms, ribs, you name it, it hurts. And the best part is I thought I was in shape."

"Don't we all." Father Matthew chuckled. "When I broke my—"

"I'll talk to you later, Father." Anna patted the priest's arm and then wove through the crowd, leaving him and Ryan to talk. She wanted to cash out before Ryan caught her.

No line at the checkout. Perfect.

The cashier rang her out. "That'll be two fifteen."

Anna peeled a five-dollar bill out of her wallet and handed it over.

"Hello, Anna."

The words sneered directly into her cheek sent a ripple of gooseflesh down her arms. Immediately intimidated, she turned; Leo Adams hovered over her. His black hair matched his ensemble. A sinister smirk swept across his lips. She wanted to smack him. How could he have the guts to shop here after what he did to Ryan and all the chaos he'd caused the other night?

"Miss." The cashier tapped the counter. "Miss."

Anna turned back.

The cashier handed Anna the change. "Have a nice day."

"Yeah. Thanks." Anna took the cash, turned, and glared at Leo.

He didn't seem to notice.

All good things came to an end, and, although Anna's vacation wasn't great, anything beat going to work. She didn't share Ryan's passion.

Anna couldn't think of anything she had pressing due at the office, but that didn't surprise her. She had a nine a.m., which pretty much guaranteed she'd remember something she needed at about quarter to. Far too late to get it done but soon enough to squelch all plausible deniability.

New Year's Day. It didn't feel any different than any other day. Not that it ever did, but she always expected some change. Some little nuance in the universe that said a new page had turned.

Today was also the eighth day of Christmas, and she'd gone all day without getting a note. One would come; they always did. Each note brought with it a new bought of anxiety, but each day that anxiety lessened. Anyone who wanted to harm her would've done it already. The notes might have been designed to freak her out, but instead, they ticked her off. She wouldn't walk around like a victim, curled up and fretting over words on paper—no matter how menacing those words might be.

She'd been so busy racing around all week long she never took a moment to consider each individual clue. Was the business a blessing, or a curse?

"Hey, Anna," Ryan called up the stairs. "What're you doin'?"

"Laying out my clothes for work tomorrow." Anna tossed the dress pants on her chair on top of her lavender shirt. She'd iron both in the morning.

"Excited to get back, huh? Don't blame you."

"Every day's a day closer to retirement." Anna came around the corner and bounded down the stairs.

"You know what your problem is?" Ryan asked when she reached the living room.

"I'm not sure I want to know. But go ahead, what?"

"You just haven't figured out what you want to do yet." Ryan sat on the sofa. "When you're where you're supposed to be, work feels a lot less like work and a lot more like play."

"I hope you're right." Anna flopped onto the club chair. "You know, I've been thinking about those notes."

"Me too." Ryan propped his broken leg up on the coffee table.

The cat skirted out from under it and hopped up next to Ryan to wind itself into a large, orange ball.

"Was there anything on the news the other night? You never said."

"No." Ryan gently stroked the cat's back. It softly purred but stayed curled up like a Swiss cake roll.

"Well, I don't know what the lyric regarding the six o'clock news was about, but the four people murdered has really been weighing on me. I think I figured out why."

"Why?"

"I might have figured out the four." Anna counted on her fingers. "Daisy, Daisy's son Tommy, Tommy's friend Darrell Hartman, who Tommy supposedly killed years ago, which caused Tommy to leave town, and Jake. Up until a week ago, I thought Jake was killed in an accident."

"And now?" Ryan sat up and waited.

"Now, I'm not so sure. But whatever the genesis of all this was, it started three years ago, because that's when Tommy left the party and supposedly struck and killed Darrell. And then Jake died a few months after that."

Ryan sat back and ran a hand over his chin. "The notes did say three years ago."

"Exactly." Anna nodded. "But the part that's eating at me is Leo Adams. He supposedly accidentally struck and killed Tommy a few days ago. Leo has got to be tied into this. It's just too big a leap for it to be anything else."

"You mean before he came into my shop drunk and high and knocked me around?"

"You knocked each other around, the way I remember it, but yeah." Anna felt guilty bringing up Leo.

Ryan had been a trooper with the whole broken ankle thing, but it had to hurt and had to be driving him nuts. If her mentioning Leo bothered him, Ryan didn't show it.

"So, whatever happened involves Hartman, Tommy, and Leo. The three musketeers." Ryan adjusted himself on the sofa. The cat trilled and then scurried away, clearly ticked at being awoken. "You were new to town, but those three hung out all the time. The question is, what could the three of them have done?"

"Or witnessed."

"What made you think of this?"

"I saw Leo at your shop this morning. He was behind me in the checkout line."

Her purse sat on the writing desk in the front foyer. She wanted to give Ryan what she had bought. The yellow plastic bag poked out of her handbag's front pocket, which meant Ryan could see it too. Anna got up, walked over, and pulled it out.

The moment her hands touched the bag, white dots blurred her vision. Sweat prickled her hairline. She felt woozy. Hot. So hot. Her legs went limp, and she folded like all life escaped her.

She knew she was falling but couldn't stop herself. It was as if she had no control over her body.

Then the darkness overtook her.

Chapter Twenty-One

Anna's pulse jackhammered against her neck. *What is this? Where am I?* She lay on her back with her right cheek jammed against something hard and cold. Anna couldn't move, as if something heavy pressed against her and pinned her in place.

Movement. Beside her. Anna wanted to look away but couldn't move her head.

She saw her! The little girl she dreamt of. The child's teddy bear, with its torn ear, laid lifeless on the ground too far for the child to reach. Why? Why couldn't she reach it? Then Anna saw the ropes.

Oh, Lord, no! The little girl was tied in eight places—two per limb. Terror stole Anna's breath.

Slowly, the girl turned her face toward Anna.

Anna wanted to run to her, to free her, but couldn't move, couldn't breathe. Speckles of blood from the child's wrists stained the lace cuffs of her shirtsleeve. The ropes had rubbed her skin raw. Her hair, a tangled mess. The child struggled to speak, her mouth moving without forming words.

Trails of tears trickled down Anna's cheeks, but somehow, the child's eyes were dry.

"Help me," the little girl finally whispered, her voice weak and other-worldly.

"Anna," she heard, but the voice was no longer the child's. This voice was strong and loud. "Anna!" Someone screamed her name.

The child faded away like a camera lens zooming out. The harder Anna struggled to get to her, the farther away the image moved. Until, finally, it blurred and then was gone.

Movement around her, although Anna didn't want to be a part of it. She wanted to be with that child, to save her, to help her.

"Anna!" a voice screamed, and Anna forced open her heavy eyelids.

She awoke lying on her back. The ceiling fan whirled above her. Her head ached, and her vision blurred. She must have passed out.

Ryan hovered above her, red-faced, a vein bulging on his forehead. "Are you okay?"

Pounding. Loud pounding everywhere. Her eyes felt so heavy; she couldn't keep them open. People all around her. Talking and moving. They asked her something, but she couldn't answer, couldn't understand. Maybe it mattered. Maybe it didn't. She was just so tired.

"What happened?" Anna sat up in the hospital bed. The monitor next to her chirped as the graph bounced in rhythm with her heartbeat.

"You fainted." Ryan ran a hand through his graying hair. "You went to the table, pulled out a bag, and then just fell."

"Oh." That explained her monster headache and the gigantic lump on the back of her head.

"You scared the living crap out of me." Ryan shook his head.

"Sorry." That poor little girl. Anna could still picture her. She couldn't get her out of her head. *Please God. Please help me help her.*

"I'm just glad you're all right." Ryan leaned forward and sighed.

How could this happen? She'd never fainted before. Never. "What did the doctors say?"

"Don't know. Your blood pressure was really low when the paramedics got there. The nurse said they want you to stay awhile."

"No." Anna pushed herself up. "My insurance is terrible, and—"

Ryan held up a hand. "Just for a little bit. They just want to keep an eye on you."

She had to tell Ryan about the little girl. She couldn't keep it a secret.

"They had to pry this bag out of your hand. I hope you don't mind. I opened it." Ryan pulled out the card. "Happy Birthday Dad?"

"In case you wanted to start this year off a little different." Anna shrugged. At the time the card seemed like a good idea...now...maybe she had overstepped.

"There was—"

"Wait. Listen. I have to tell you something." The words tumbled out. "When I blacked out, I saw a little girl. This isn't the first time I've seen her. I dreamt of her once before, but—"

"What do you mean? You dreamt of her before?" Ryan's face scrunched.

"In a dream, but not a dream. It was more intense than a dream." How could she describe this in a way that doesn't make her sound insane?

"What are you—?"

Anna plowed on not willing to allow him to stop her momentum. His questions would have to wait. He had to know. She had to tell him. "This child needed my help. Needs my help. I don't know if this is the past, present, or future. But she was tied with rope to poles or stakes or something. I don't recall. I just remember eight different attachments."

Ryan's complexion lost all color.

Anna thought for a moment he would pass out. "It was horrible I—"

"Anna. Stop." He looked past her. "There was..."

Anna waited. And waited. His gaze stayed fixed on something behind her. She glanced over her shoulder but found nothing but an empty wall. She looked back at him. "Was what? There was what? Answer me." The monitor's beeps quickened.

"A note." Ryan slid it out. The paper rattled as his hands trembled. "I found another note."

"What does it say?"

He seemed in a trance. "I already read it."

"What. Does. It. Say. Ryan?"

Ryan looked at her, his eyes wide with terror. "On the eighth day of Christmas, my true love gave to me eight ties a-binding."

Chapter Twenty-Two

Anna had no idea being haunted could be contagious, although Ryan had been profoundly infected. If the man said two words since their return home, that was pushing it. Anna busied herself wiping down the kitchen counters. The outdoorsy smell of the pine cleaner comforted her. A deer peeked around the oak tree in her backyard as soft snowflakes floated from the winter sky.

While she cleaned, Anna repeatedly tried to recall the image of the little girl and her surroundings, but the harder she tried, the fuzzier it became. Had she witnessed a flashback or a premonition?

Please, Lord, let me help her.

Anna wrung out the dish towel and hung it over the sink.

The Christmas carol plagued her thoughts. The messages had to be related to the child. But—more importantly—how could she prove the connection?

Ryan was on the right track when he mentioned the three amigos: Daisy's son Tommy and his friends Darrell and Leo Adams. She needed to talk to Leo—the only one left alive. He knew something. Had to. Did he kill Darrell and Tommy? Why would anyone murder their two closest friends?

Regardless, going to the Potrage police no longer appeared a viable option. Vince Adams, the town's cop, might be a great guy, but family was family, and she couldn't take any chances. She doubted Vince would ever investigate his brother, Leo, or even take her theory seriously. Not without proof. The notes could be too easily written off as a joke. Without some kind of substantiation, the cryptic messages were no more than a spooky Christmas carol.

What could she really tell the police about the little girl? She had a dream? A sighting when she blacked out? No, she'd sound desperate, or crazy, or both.

Could Jake have been murdered?

Old Man Baker's name had been mentioned in Jake's accident reports. She wasn't sure what made her think of Mr. Baker, but she needed to know if he remembered any details about the night her husband died. Jake's accident fit somehow into all of this, but she needed more information to uncover the link.

Learning the truth might be the only way to help the child who haunted her.

After talking with her boss, Anna left a voice mail for the office receptionist to reschedule Monday's appointments to later in the week. She took tomorrow off, but she had to get back. Her clients needed commercials, and she didn't trust anyone else to write them. For so many of her colleagues, it was just a job, but she understood. Some of these businesses had very little and the money they did have they were spending to get customers in the door. If she put everything on the line, she'd want someone who cared to create the ad, not someone who just did it to get it done. Anna didn't always love her job, but she cared about her clients. Plus, despite a dull headache, Anna was feeling remarkably well. It had to be the adrenaline.

She decided to devote today and tomorrow to these notes. She wished she had confirmation she was on the right track, but until then, she had to trust her gut instinct. Her gut insisted these notes involved this little girl. Confirmation or not.

Her husband, Jake, somehow tied into this, yet never said a thing. How could you not tell your wife something like this—whatever *this* was? How could Jake have kept secret finding Tommy when Tommy's mother sat in their living room each week? Unless Daisy knew.

Jake. Daisy. Involved in this. Her hair stood up on end. "Ryan!"

"What?"

"Call Elvis." Anna burst into the living room.

Ryan peered over the newspaper. "For what?"

She flung open the French doors to the den. "Tell him I've got some more books for him to go through." She tugged open the bottom drawer of the lateral file and pulled out years of her personal tax returns—finding the years when Jake had been alive. She knew Jake found Tommy Peters because Daisy gave her a dated Polaroid of the two of them together.

Anna carried the stack to the living room and set it on the writing desk in the hall. She yanked open the desk's drawer, where she'd stuffed the Polaroid Daisy had stuck in her Christmas card. *Thank God I kept it.* She'd been so taken aback at the image of her husband with Daisy's missing son that she never thought to look at it for clues. *Where are they?* The photo was taken in November. If Jake wore shorts, that would tell her something. The winter Jake died was one of the coldest on record. The snow came in on Halloween and stayed until almost Mother's Day.

Jake wore a thin Izod jacket and a pair of khaki pants. Tommy dressed similarly. Nothing in the blurred background provided any clues. The only semi-solid information she had was the handwritten date inscribed on the bottom.

"What are you doing?" Ryan struggled to stand and hobbled toward her.

"Call The King and tell him to come pick up my personal books as well. There has to be some record of this trip. Jake wrote off everything." Anna held up the Polaroid. "Also, instead of flying blind, let's give him a direction. We've agreed that Leo Adams is somehow involved in this. Jake did the books for the Adams' personal finances as well as the books on their family business—the salt mine. Tell The King to start there."

"Okay. Why this sudden urgency?" Ryan stepped closer and took the photo from her.

"I have to help her."

Ryan seemed to know better than to ask whom.

Chapter Twenty-Three

The doctor didn't want her to drive, but she saw no other option. Ryan's leg remained in a cast, and daylight faded fast. She didn't want to waste any time, not without knowing whether or not this all connected to the little girl. "Hey, I'm going to take a ride." Anna grabbed her keys out of the dish.

"What? Where to?" Ryan stood. "I thought the doctor told you to take it easy."

"It's not far. I wanna talk to Old Man Baker. I'd like to ask him if he remembers anything about Jake's accident. Maybe there's some connection I missed." The keys jangled as Anna wiggled into her boots. "Mr. Baker lives five minutes from here."

"Less than that." Ryan slipped his brown leather jacket over his blue sweater. He adjusted the sleeves. "I'll go with you."

Old Man Baker lived in the mobile home park just up Powers Road. Most people in Potrage referred to the park as The Farm. In fact, when Anna told people she lived off Vermont near Powers, they used the nickname as a frame of reference. How far up the road from The Farm?

Living in the proverbial fishbowl would finally work to her advantage since she had no idea of Mr. Baker's actual address, but someone would know. They'd also know his schedule, if he had children, maybe even his shoe size.

Ryan stayed quiet during the ride there. Maybe he was scared. Probably. But it didn't matter. Anna was scared too, but she had to help that little girl.

The trailers came up on her right, and Anna eased into the first row and parked beside the bank of mailboxes.

"Wait here." Anna shut the door but left the truck and its heater running. As she walked into the wind, it bit her cheeks and burned her eyes. She stuffed her hands in her pockets, nestled her face into her jacket collar, and trudged forward. She checked the grouping of twenty or so mailboxes for last names but found none.

Ryan opened his door. "No names?"

She looked toward her truck and shook her head. "No."

Ryan turned off the engine and joined her. He must have sensed she wasn't giving up.

The park had a simple layout: four rows of homes about five mobiles deep.

"Are you going to go door to door?" Ryan must have read her mind.

"That's exactly what I'm thinking." Anna started toward the closest home, a pale blue model with a white front porch. Children's toys littered the yard—all covered in a dusting of snow. A red tricycle, with turned handlebars, resembled the kind she rode when she was little. It certainly looked old enough to have been hers. Anna walked up the shoveled gravel.

Sudden, frantic barking stopped her cold. A gigantic dog bounded around the corner. The hair on its back stood on end as it halted. The dog lowered its head, ready to pounce, as its pink tongue slid in and out through its teeth. The deep growl lashed through her.

"Anna." Ryan cautioned. "No sudden moves."

Gravel crunched behind her, and the dog barked wildly. It lunged at her.

"Buster!" A little boy screamed. "Get over here."

The dog turned tail and headed into the nearby trailer. The little boy stepped onto his porch. Barefoot, he wore jeans two inches too short and a green sweatshirt three sizes too big. "She wouldn't have hurt ya. She's a sweet puppy."

Anna exhaled the breath she'd been holding. "I'll have to take your word for it. Is your mom home?"

"Nope." The little boy stuck his hands in his pockets and swayed back and forth. His curly mop of dark hair bounced with every movement. How could he stand there without socks and shoes? His feet had to be freezing.

"Who's there?" A man's voice boomed. "Who you talkin' to?"

"Nobody." The boy waved goodbye and then vanished before Anna could wave back.

"Put this freakin' dog out," the man yelled.

Anna and Ryan scampered, racing back to the truck, distance their only ally against the hound. Anna drove to the last row of homes, parking beside a white mobile that was accented with colorful hanging lights and a wooden cutout of a lady bent over a flower bed. "I hope they're not snowbirds." Anna stepped around the front of her truck.

"I wouldn't blame them if they were. This weather is brutal." Ryan joined her in the driveway.

Before Anna could knock, the door opened.

"Can I help you?" The elderly man wore polyester pants held up high with a black leather belt and a white T-shirt that had been through the wash too many times to wear in public, but too few times to toss away.

"I'm looking for O—" Anna caught her mistake before she made it. The nickname Old Man Baker might not be well received though she meant nothing derogatory by it. "For Mr. Baker."

"And you are?" A television blared behind him as he stepped onto his porch.

"Hey, Bill." Ryan moved around her. "How are ya?"

Bill lurched over the railing and extended a hand. "Ryan, how the heck are you? What're you doin' here?"

"We're lookin' for Ol' Man Baker." Ryan shook the man's hand. "You know where he's hidin' out these days?"

Bill pointed like he was hitching a ride. "Two rows over, brown trailer, third or fourth one in."

"Thanks." Ryan stepped back.

"Got yourself a lady friend, I see?" Bill nodded at Anna and hinged over the railing again. "Bill Barton."

"Anna Greenan." Anna stepped forward and shook his extended hand. "Nice to meet you."

"Likewise." Bill pointed toward Ryan. "You best take good care of this guy.

Can't get a decent omelet in this town without him."

She smiled. "Will do."

Old Man Baker's place was brown with yellow trim. Far better kept than she had expected for a man who made his living collecting cans. It had been months since she'd seen him riding his bike around town. Probably the cold weather, although that never stopped him in years past.

Anna knocked on his door and sensed Ryan move closer behind her. No answer. She tried again. Nothing. Ryan used one of his crutches to press the bell.

The door opened a smidge. Anna blinked.

What? No. How?

She couldn't believe who she saw.

Chapter Twenty-Four

Her throat seized shut, suppressing the scream. *He's the one. From the other night. He stepped into the road.*

Old Man Baker glanced at her, at Ryan, and then slammed the door shut.

"Hey." Ryan climbed onto the porch and hammered on the door. "Hey. Open up."

Anna stood frozen. Unable to believe it. She would've never recognized him. Old Man Baker's hair always neat and trim was now scraggly with a beard, but the face was the same. Those eyes that burned into hers. The same look of horror as she almost killed him and he almost killed her. The night her seat belt had been tampered with at the storage garage.

Ryan continued to whack the door as a handful of neighbors stepped out onto their porches.

"Ryan." Anna touched his shoulder. "People are staring at you."

"Let them!" Ryan rapped on the door. "Open up."

"Ryan!"

He stopped. "He was in the road. Remember? After we left the storage garage. You nearly drove us off a cliff to avoid killing him. I didn't recognize him that night."

"I know. Neither did I, but if you don't calm down, someone is going to call the cops."

Ryan refused to stop. He climbed off the porch and circled the trailer, pounding on its windows with his crutch. No sane person would open their door now. Anna wasn't sure what he was trying to accomplish, other than taking days' worth of frustration, and uncertainty, out on an innocent mobile home. "Baker. We need to talk to you. Open the freakin' door."

Gravel crunched, and the bystanders vanished. The patrol car's lights flashed, and the siren chirped once. Vince lowered the automatic window and leaned toward the passenger seat. "Problem here?"

That was fast. Vince must have been in the area. There was something about the man that went right through her, just like his brother.

Ryan lumbered toward the patrol car. "Yeah, I do."

Anna could tell he was going to be belligerent.

"This jerkoff stole from me."

What? Anna didn't say anything and hoped her wide eyes hadn't given them away. Vince glared at her as if trying to gauge whether or not Ryan was telling the truth. She gave him a shy smile.

Vince stepped out of the car. He took his time coming around. His grandiose air made her insane, and it was intensified by his six-foot-four frame and family name. "What happened?"

"Well, for about six months, inventory's been off. Small things. Loaf of bread here, can of this there. I never made too much out of it until I caught one of the stock boys stealing some beer. When I called him to the carpet, he said Old Man Baker takes stuff all the time, and he thought I knew." Ryan adjusted his crutch. No doubt his broken ankle ached from his escapades.

Vince looked down his nose at Ryan. "And you didn't know?" Vince's eyes narrowed. He towered over Ryan.

"No. But you know what? I don't give a crap. Just tell that man I better never see him around my place again." Ryan glanced at Anna and motioned toward her SUV. "Let's go. I'm done here."

Anna followed across the snowy yard, happy to be away from Vince and his prying eyes. How Ryan advanced so quickly on crutches, she had no idea, but she had to pick up her pace to keep up.

"Hey," Vince called from behind them. "What was this stock boy's name?"

"Doesn't matter." Ryan kept going.

"Does to me," Vince said. "If he's thinking about drinking underage, I want to know about it."

Ryan turned. "Barnes. Jason Barnes. Talk to him about it. It'll scare the living snot out of him."

"Will do." A car door shut. Anna didn't dare turn around to make sure it was Vince. She didn't want to press their luck.

When they got back to the vehicle, Anna looked at Ryan. "That was a heck of a story."

"It was true." Ryan closed his door. "The best ones always are."

"So, Old Man Baker was stealing from you?" Anna stuck her key in the ignition.

"God, no. I told him he could come in and take whatever he needed and, from time to time, he took a thing or two. He never abused it. I never minded." Ryan tugged his seat belt into place. "But, I did bust Jason Barnes trying to steal a case of beer, and he did use Baker as his excuse, and I did play dumb and say I didn't know a thing about it. I mean, God, it's been months since I've seen Mr. Baker. Months."

"You didn't tell Vince about the Christmas notes."

"You aren't willing to do that, right?"

"I didn't disagree with your decision." But Anna could tell he disagreed with hers.

"Eventually, you're going to need help." Ryan cranked up the truck's heat and held his hands in front of the vents.

"I've got help." Anna beamed, trying to lighten the mood. "I've got you."

"You need *professional* help."

"Tell me about it," she joked, but Ryan didn't laugh. "What now?"

"Well, we have to see Baker now. He witnessed something in Jake's accident and, conveniently, nearly caused one with the two of us. Let's give it an hour and come back. He doesn't have a car so he's not likely to go anywhere."

Anna made a three-point turn back toward Powers Road. A patrol car was tucked against the tree line beside Old Man Baker's street. Vince ran radar or interference; Anna just couldn't be sure which.

Chapter Twenty-Five

Anna and Ryan circled back to Old Man Baker's place a little after six. Gentle snowflakes glistened against the SUV's headlights. A red glow filled her rearview as Anna parked. Her brake lights illuminated the exhaust against the night sky.

"Let's go." A familiar chime filled the interior as Ryan opened his door.

Anna removed her keys from the ignition and followed him onto the front porch. Ryan tapped softly on the door and waited. No answer. A silhouette moved inside behind the sheers. Ryan rapped a little louder. This time, the door opened and Ryan jammed his crutch in the entryway, ensuring they couldn't be locked out.

To Anna's surprise, Old Man Baker shooed them in. Mr. Baker peered out the open door and closed and locked it.

"Hi. Hi. Ryan." Mr. Baker's left eye twitched.

Anna could tell he wasn't quite right. Not drunk or on drugs, just off. He talked really fast, and she was pretty sure it had little to do with the fact he seemed nervous. Although, she could tell by his rapid hand movements he was terrified. "What are ya, what are ya, what are ya doin' here?"

"Came by earlier." Ryan spoke in a soothing tone as he balanced against the door. "But you locked me out."

"Yep. Yep. I know. Yep. Locked you out. Yep." Old Man Baker tucked his long hair behind his ear and unrolled and re-rolled his flannel shirt sleeves.

The home had an open, modern layout. Anna stood in the foyer, which led to the white kitchen. Over her right shoulder, the living room had an enormous wall-mounted, flat-screen, stylish end tables, and an apartment-sized sofa with a coordinating chair. A hallway led to what had to be the bedrooms and bath.

Ryan caught Anna's attention and mouthed the word, *wow*. She nodded.

"This is a *really* nice place." Anna unzipped her jacket as perspiration dotted her hairline. The dramatic difference between the winter air and Baker's warm home was stifling.

"Yeah. Nice. Yeah." Old Man Baker flopped onto his sofa.

"Haven't seen you around." Ryan hobbled into the living room. "Who's buying your groceries now?"

"I know you." Old Man Baker started rocking. His long hair flung in his face, and his gaze stayed fixed on the floor. "I know you." He rocked a little faster. "You the widow." He kept rocking. "I know you."

Ryan raised his brows. Anna shrugged and took a seat in the club chair across from Mr. Baker.

"Listen." Ryan lowered himself onto the other side of the couch. He pointed at his cast. "This is why we're here."

Not exactly true, but she had to give Ryan credit for his improvisation. Old Man Baker would never know Ryan broke his ankle at his shop and not the night they skated off the road to avoid colliding with him.

Old Man Baker looked away and rocked. Anna's stomach churned from the incessant motion.

"We almost had an accident the other night." Ryan peeled off his jacket.

"Yep. You the widow." Old Man Baker nodded toward her. "I know you. You the widow."

The more he said it, the more it hurt. That was, after all, how people thought of her. The widow. She saw it in their eyes. Those who met her gaze. Most looked away.

"We're not talking about her. We're talking about me." Ryan scooted closer. "The other night, you stepped in the road."

"Yep. Accident." Mr. Baker stopped rocking and stared at Ryan. Confusion clouded his face. "Someone in the road."

"You were in the road." Ryan pointed at Baker's chest.

Baker nodded. "Someone in the road."

"*You* were in the road." Ryan leaned forward. His cheeks turned rosy as he raked a hand through his hair. "Why were you in the road?"

"Someone in the road." Old Man Baker swiveled and stared down the hall. Seconds ticked by.

Ryan clenched his fists.

Anna thought he might lose it. "I'm the widow." It was the only thing that came to mind.

Old Man Baker turned and gazed through her, as if seeing something from another world, another time. "He drove into that wall."

Oh my. Jake. He had to mean Jake. Her heart buckled as any peace it once held crumbled. Her eyes stung.

Baker nodded at her. "Someone in the road."

"Why?" Anna barely squeezed the word out. The vise grip in her chest intensified.

"Not crazy." Baker began rocking again. "Not crazy. Someone in the road."

"I know you're not crazy." Anna scooted closer. She had to hear. She had to know. "What happened? Please tell me what happened." She could hardly choke it back. "He was my husband." The tender whisper tore her heart in two. *He was my husband.* Warm tears pooled and slipped down her cheeks.

Old Man Baker stopped. His eyes glistened with a flash of recognition.

He remembers. Oh, God, let him remember. She had to know now. She needed the truth; she needed its sanctuary. "Please, please. Tell me what you saw."

"I know you." Old Man Baker smiled, a wild, wicked grin. "You the widow." He went back to rocking. Any recollection appeared to have vanished.

Anna sagged against the chair back and exhaled.

Pointless.

They would never know what happened. She had an idea and would have to live with that. It would take a miracle to unlock the mind of a madman, and if they tried much longer, Old Man Baker wouldn't be the only one the town called crazy.

Ryan's tone softened. "Why were you in the road? Did someone tell you to stand in the road?"

What? What was Ryan talking about?

"Not crazy." Baker rocked faster.

"Were you in the road the night Jake died too?" Ryan inched closer to Mr. Baker.

Could that be what happened? Had Jake swerved to avoid hitting someone, or something?

"Not crazy. I not crazy." Baker's head whipped back and forth. His hair flinging in frantic sweeps.

"Why didn't you let us come inside earlier?" Ryan leaned forward.

Old Man Baker rocked and rocked.

"Were you scared?" Ryan inched closer.

"Yep. Scared. Yep."

"Why are you scared?" Ryan reached out to touch the man's shoulder but must have thought better of it. He pulled his hand back. "Who are you afraid of?"

"Not crazy. No go. Not crazy. No go."

"Go where?" Anna couldn't make sense of any of this.

"Not crazy."

"Who's giving you money?" Ryan's question caught Anna off guard in part because of its directness, in part because she wanted the answer but never thought to ask.

"The church," Baker replied. "The church give me money."

"What church?" Ryan glanced at Anna as if to make sure she heard.

"Your church." Old Man Baker stopped moving and looked at Anna with wide eyes as if she just got there. "I know you. You the widow."

Chapter Twenty-Six

The man glared at Ashley. Tied, gagged. Lying on the dilapidated cabin's rotting floor. He really had no use for her. She seemed dirty to him now, and, no matter how many times he washed her, she still looked filthy. Trash. That was what she was. Trash and a problem. The incessant news coverage of her disappearance from the Appleton Mall made taking her out impossible. What now?

Now, he needed more.

He had a thirst he just couldn't quench. Ashley moaned, and he shoved a blue and white striped pillow under her head. She struggled a smile beneath the ratty denim gag, but he knew the truth. She hated him, and that was just fine. Her soft brown hair was a matted mess. He should've combed it after he had shampooed it. Now, he'd never get those snarls out.

Traces of blood streaked the corners of her mouth. If she didn't scream, the gag wouldn't have to be so tight. She had done that to herself.

Other than her face—with its puffy, cried-out eyes, she seemed fine. Scared. Kept peeing on the floor like a sick pet, but that would subside, especially now that dehydration started to set in. He got up and walked away. So filthy she made him sick.

Why would she think I would rape her? Does she think I'm an animal or something?

All he wanted were some pictures. Some *special* photos of her. She liked posing. He could tell, even though she cried her fake alligator tears. *Filthy.* At least he'd make some good coin off 'em. Photoshop the bull crap tears away for some. Other buyers would love those shots. To each his own.

Jeremy at the storage center needed to be spoken to. Jeremy and his incessant whining about the fire. He should've been told. What for? It wouldn't have changed anything. Besides, insurance would cover the damages. The source was legit. Electrical. And the only units destroyed were Anna's and the one beside hers. Jeremy should know better than to question him. The only reason the storage garage had been able to stay in business was the generous "donations" he'd thrown Jeremy's way since Anna had rented.

Finally, the favor had been repaid. He'd cut her lock and taken what he needed years ago. There was nothing left she'd want. Nothing that would tie anything to him. Not that she'd ever suspect him anyway. Brilliant. He had to admit it. He was brilliant.

She had mentioned to Jeremy something about an old account being audited. Was that the truth? He didn't know. Cunning woman. He'd have to be careful.

She survived the near-miss with Old Man Baker. Survived it but didn't report it. That—in and of itself—seemed noteworthy. Why not involve the police? Didn't she draw the parallels between her "accident" and her husband's, or were the similarities enough to intimidate her? He hoped so, although he doubted it. Maybe Ryan cautioned her.

Ryan and she were becoming quite close. Living together? Living in sin? So delicious, he almost salivated. Anna had stayed so isolated, but now... Not since she moved Ryan in.

He might be on to something. Perhaps it worked to his advantage that Ryan wasn't killed when he attacked him at the store. Destiny never ceased to amaze him.

Ashley's breathing slowed. Almost asleep. He had thought she was the one. The right height, the right age, but no, she wasn't.

He knew he would find her. He had to find her.

There was one among the masses that would save him. Give him redemption, but every time he thought he had her, he was mistaken. In the meantime, at least he'd make some money.

Ashley couldn't be blamed. She was just a normal eight-year-old. Nothing special, just like Valerie from so many years ago. No. One would come. He knew, and he would be ready.

He had no idea what she looked like or sounded like or felt like, but every part of him understood he would know her when the time was right. He had to wait. He had to be patient.

For now, he had Ashley. She would do, but she'd never quench his thirst.

Chapter Twenty-Seven

The next morning Anna drove through the mammoth iron gates of the American Salt Company. She couldn't put off confronting Leo any longer.

Mountains of salt unearthed from the mines encircled the parking area. Overhead was a labyrinth of interwoven enormous, industrial tubing. In the distance, bulldozers transferred salt from one hill to the other. The mounds—so massive—the giant machinery looked more like Matchbox trucks in an overfilled sandbox.

The closer Anna got to the corporate headquarters, the louder the milieu noises became. Mechanical sounds drowned out her truck's engine and rattled the steering column. Eventually, she found a parking spot and scooted into the corporate office building.

The outside cacophony of machines fell silent the moment the heavy, glass door closed behind her.

What would she say to Leo when she saw him? Anna had no idea. Whatever she decided, it probably wouldn't be well received. Nothing accusatory ever was.

A Christmas tree rivaling Rockefeller Center's sat in the middle of the atrium surrounded by a dozen colorful flags, one flag for each location of American Salt Company. Sunlight beat through the spectacular windowed dome above, like thunder through a silent sky. The enormity of the space intimidated her. Perhaps that was part of its design.

Her boots squeaked as she walked; the echo reverberated through the quiet building.

Anna stepped up to the mahogany desk. "Good morning."

"Hiya." The secretary smacked her gum and passed Anna a clipboard. "Sign in, please. What can I do for ya?"

Black hair. Red lips. A display of cleavage. Betty Boop had to have been hired by a man. The gum smacking alone would grate on any woman's nerves.

"I'm looking for Leo Adams." Anna handed her back the clipboard. "It's my understanding he works out of this office."

"You sure he ain't over in Perry?" Princess blew a bubble. It popped, and she sucked it back in.

"I'm sure." Anna tucked her keys into her handbag.

"Oh, you mean John's boy." She laughed. "I get it now. Duh. We all call him Stretch 'cause he's so darn tall." Another bubble. It popped. "He's not here."

"When will he be back?"

"His truck's scheduled for another pickup in about an hour."

"Oh, he's not in the office anymore?" *Odd his father owns the place and he's out driving a truck.*

"Not since I've been here." The receptionist shook her head.

"How long is that?"

The woman leaned forward, one of her colossal breasts almost played peek-a-boobie. "I've been *with* John for three years."

Anna understood implicitly. "I see." She wanted to ask if John's wife knew, but it probably wouldn't earn her any brownie points. "So, Leo will be back here in an hour then?"

"Looks like it." The secretary started clicking keys on her keyboard. "You can come back then. He always stops in the building to grab coffee and whatnot." She stopped typing and waited. "Or I can relay a message, I guess."

"No. No message... I'll stop back."

Anna opted to head over to Village Park and wait, away from the salt mine's noisy chaos. An hour didn't seem that long.

Children's laughter filled the air. Today had to be their last day of Christmas vacation, or did they call it winter break now? God forbid anyone should be offended.

It felt good to be out and about this morning. The sun shone bright, and the temperature had risen to a balmy thirty-three degrees. Anna pulled into the park's packed lot.

Ryan had called three times in the last half hour. She felt guilty not answering. It was nice to have him around, but the novelty had worn off. She had grown accustomed to being alone and found it hard to have someone else constantly in her space. Hard, but not impossible.

Life was funny like that. You adapted to the very things you never thought you could. For her, that thing was living alone.

Now Ryan lived with her, albeit temporarily. If she had only known years ago that they'd end up like this...Doing this dance: two steps forward, three steps back. It didn't start now. No. The music was just louder, or maybe no one danced between them anymore.

Her cell phone rang and she thought it might be him calling again. She snuck out before he woke up. Ryan shouldn't be involved in this. The Adams had the means, and the power, to ruin people in this town, and Anna didn't want Ryan or his business to be a casualty of her personal war.

She picked up the phone and glanced at the caller ID, Saint Andrew's Church. "Hello."

"Hello, this is Dora from Saint Andrew's."

"Hi, Dora. Thanks for returning my call."

"Father Matthew asked me to." Dora bristled, and Anna tried not to read into the fact she wasn't calling on her own accord. "I have what you asked for. Catholic Charities does have a small stipend set up for various members of our parish community to help with necessities."

Stylish furnishings and name-brand clothing probably didn't qualify as necessities. "A small stipend?"

"Yes. Do you have a pen?"

"Give me a second." Anna fished through the glove box and then under the seats. She found oodles of garbage, but no pen. She picked up a napkin, opened her purse, and pulled out her eyeliner. As good a pen as any. "Go ahead."

The caller gave her the number for Catholic Charities, and Anna jotted it down. Why? She wasn't sure. She had no intention of calling. Catholic Charities didn't provide Old Man Baker with the kind of cash he had. The fine furnishings alone were in the thousands.

"Thank you. Have a good day." Anna hung up.

A car pulled in beside hers. A young mother got out, opened her car's back door, and unbuckled a car seat. The little boy looked about four, adorable in his snowsuit, mittens, and fuzzy hat. A royal blue Michelin man. The woman carried him to the curb and set him down, and they walked hand in hand toward the hill. The little boy dragged his snow tube on a string behind him. Anna's eyes burned.

I would have been a good mom.

Anna wished she and Jake hadn't waited to have a baby. At least she'd have had something left. That might be selfish, but at least it was real. Now, at almost thirty-five, it was probably too late. When Jake died, she buried the hope of having a family along with him. Times like this she mourned for them both. Would she ever stop missing him? Would she ever be whole again?

Anna stared at the snow-covered hills and listened to the laughter. She watched snowball fights and wanted to get out and play too, but she had no one to play with, and that hurt even more.

Something glistened to her left, and she turned her attention to the little girl walking up the sidewalk. The child wore hot pink, mirrored sunglasses that matched her coat and furry hat. Instead of a scarf, she wore a fuchsia boa.

If Anna had had a daughter, she'd be just like this little girl. Total spunk.

The little girl passed the front of her truck. She pulled an old-fashioned sled—the wooden kind with the red metal rudders. Upon the sled sat a teddy bear having a tea party.

Oh my. No!

Anna sat up, unable to turn away. She hadn't recognized the little girl, but she did recognize the bear with the stuffing poking out its ear.

Chapter Twenty-Eight

The man sat at the park and watched the kids sledding and wished he could sled along with them. He wanted to be able to let go and be free. To run and laugh, but he couldn't. It was too late for him. His life had become this meaningless existence. Trolling for something, or someone, he might never find.

Ashley would be dead soon, and he didn't know how he felt about that. He had never killed a child before. It was easy to kill an adult, like good ol' Daisy, but a child seemed somehow a deeper transgression.

A more mortal sin.

They had talked for the first time today. Ashley lived in a green house with white shutters and a white porch, and her daddy left when she was only five, which was just as well because he and mommy fought all the time anyway and...

If he didn't kill her, Ashley might even kill herself. That was what Valerie did. He found out about it. Of course, he did. Would it change things? Did it matter?

His gaze was drawn back to the park to a little girl towing a wooden sled with red rudders.

His heart cinched. She was beautiful and dramatic and exciting. A long, feathery boa wrapped around her neck. He stared at her, hypnotized.

A jolt shot threw him.

Awakened him.

There was nothing in the world he could ever want more. Nothing he'd ever want again. She seemed the culmination of all his futile searches.

His sanctuary.

He knew he'd recognize the one when he saw her, and this time he was sure of it. This time it was different. This time his conscience fell silent.

Many men had shared they knew the moment they met their wife. They knew this woman would be the one they'd spend the rest of their life with.

Now, he too knew what destiny sounded like. It rang in his deaf ears, and he could hear nothing else.

The child stopped and peered in his direction. *Can she feel it too? Does she know?* Warmth flooded through him. Her spirit called to his, and he longed to be with her. He wouldn't rest while they were apart.

It was time. He nodded and headed toward her.

Chapter Twenty-Nine

Anna bolted toward the little girl, bobbing and weaving through the stream of people. The child's parents had to be close by. Anna didn't want to scare them, but at least they'd have a forewarning. Maybe she was wrong; maybe what she saw for this child could be prevented. The child's parents would think Anna had gone mad, and that was fine. She'd rather be locked up than have any child suffer the way this little girl would.

"Um…sweetie…please. Stop." Anna leapt onto the sidewalk. "Hey, honey." Anna heard the swish of a snowsuit as a little boy tore in front of her, almost knocking her down.

"Aaron!" His mother screamed and then said to Anna, "I'm sorry."

"It's okay." Anna paused and let the mom go by.

The little girl sat in the shelter. Her neon pink snowsuit provided a sharp contrast to the weather-worn wooden bench. The child placed a teacup in front of her bear and poured an imaginary liquid from a plastic kettle. All the while she chattered animatedly.

"Anna?" Somewhere behind her a voice called out. Anna kept moving, racing toward the child.

This time the voice spoke with more force. Stern, deep. "Anna!"

Someone grabbed and held her arm.

"Ow." Anna whirled around.

"You lookin' for me?" Leo towered above her in his American Salt uniform. Salt stains left a cloudy pattern on the left breast pocket. Leo had to be at least six foot three, and his spiky, black hair added another inch. His breath reeked of alcohol. His chiseled face had a scar from his left eye down to his chin.

Her stomach churned. She looked into his wild, brown eyes and knew him to be capable of anything.

Oh no.

His grip on her arm intensified.

"Ow. Stop it. You're hurting me." Anna wrangled free.

"I asked you a question...You lookin' for me?"

"Ah...yeah, but..." Anna glanced back at the shelter. The little girl was gone! Panic reached up from the pit of her stomach. *Not now. I don't have time for this now. I have to help her.* "Listen, now's not a good time." *Where is she? God, help. Where'd she go?*

Anna shielded her eyes from the sun. The entire park lay in front of her. The child had to be here. There was only this giant sledding hill and a bunch of picnic tables. Where could she have gone? And so quickly? Anna's heart thumped. The footprints in the snowscape blurred together. Too many people tugged too many sleds.

"Now..." Leo stepped closer, no more than a thread separated them, "... seems like a fine time to me." Anger radiated from him.

Leo had no concept of consequences. You could see it in his eyes, in his stance. Probably because very few people in this town had the guts to hold him accountable, Anna included.

Her pulse raced. *I should have never gone to see Leo without Ryan. What was I thinking?*

"What. Do. You. Want?" Leo clenched his fists, and Anna thought he might pummel her. In broad daylight. With so many witnesses. He didn't seem to care. He would get answers one way or another.

"To ask you some questions." She should have planned better. Did she honestly think she could wing this? Her gaze swept over the park again, her thoughts bouncing from Leo to the little girl.

"About?"

His sharply pronounced question galvanized her focus. "My husband." Jake was the first thing to come to mind. Always was, always would be.

Leo stared at her. "What about him?"

"The reason he had to die." Anna spit the words at him, choking back tears, suffocating the rage. All this time she had thought Jake passed as part of some unseen divine plan, comforting herself with the lies like only the good die young, and other nonsensical crap. But Jake's goodness hadn't killed him; it was whatever *this* was. This coded secret linking his past to her present.

A sly grin formed on Leo's lips. "I guess Jake died because he was stupid."

"Is that why Tommy died too?" *Crap. Too late to turn back now.* "And Daisy. And your friend Darrell." Darn it. She had to be crazy, but she couldn't hold back. Something within her had snapped. A pent-up fury poured out.

"You know," Leo looked toward the sledding hill, "you really shouldn't be asking questions if you're not ready for the answers."

Anna squared her shoulders and lifted her chin. "I am ready."

"Is Ryan?" His tone conveyed danger for her, for Ryan. "He had quite an accident at his store the other night."

Anna could tell by Leo's playful smile he enjoyed this.

"The man's lucky to be alive."

How dare he? "It looked like he cleaned your clock pretty good."

Leo stepped back, eyes wide. "I didn't realize Ryan was..." He seemed to search for the word. "*Entertaining* at the store that night."

Me and my mouth. What did she just do? "Ryan told me he knocked you out."

"Did he now?" Leo sneered. "You should've stuck around at the store that night, Anna. That's when it got really interesting. Obviously, you missed the best part of the show. The true surprise." Leo stepped back, seeming to disengage.

"Listen, I didn't want to meet you to talk about Ryan. I want to talk about my husband."

"Aaaaaand."

The courage she once mustered slipped from her grasp. Each moment took another portion. "And the reason that he had to die."

Leo shook his head. "I already answered you. Your husband was stupid."

Cold bitterness swept over her. "Why do you say that?"

"He didn't wear his seat belt." Leo laughed, a humorless laugh, and brushed a stray snowflake off his sleeve.

"What about Tommy? You, and he, and Darrell used to all hang out. Why are they dead?"

"You're asking the wrong person." Leo again seemed to stare past her at the sledding hill. "The wrong person and the wrong questions."

"What are the right questions?"

"Now, I can't tell you that." Leo looked at her. His gaze drilled into hers. "It would take all the fun out of it."

"Well, who should I ask then? At least tell me that." Anna's voice betrayed her. She hated the desperation in it, but she needed answers. She needed to know.

"You tell me something." Leo ran his hand through her hair and then traced her cheek.

She winced.

"Why are you asking all of this now?"

"How do you know I haven't been asking all along?" Should she tell him about the "Twelve Days of Christmas" notes? Maybe then he would tell her what she needed to know. What harm could it do?

"Because her body's not even cold yet." Leo started to walk away.

"Whose body?" Anna chased after him. "Daisy?"

He turned and lunged at her. Anna's scalp burned as he held a fist full of her hair. His hand grabbed her neck. *Oh, God.* He inclined her head toward his. His warm, wet breath filled her mouth as his lips drew near. They must look like two lovers in a passionate embrace.

"Listen." His lips brushed against her ear.

Goosebumps rose on her arms. The word went through her. She could taste his cologne. Her gag reflex kicked in. Bile rose on her throat.

"Leave it be. Let her go."

"Let what be? Let who go?"

He squeezed her neck harder, and a searing pain shot up to her inner ear.

"I'm not telling you again. Let. It. Go. It'll be better for everyone." Leo released her.

She exhaled and coughed, clutching her neck. The inside of her throat felt raw, and her fingertips and toes prickled. She glanced around, waiting for anyone to ask if she was okay. A witness. Just one. But no one seemed to notice. Leo winked and walked away. Her heart thwacked against her ribs. She stood motionless as Leo climbed into his American Salt dump truck. The rage that had boiled up in him vanished as if it had never been, and he waved like they were two old friends who met for a walk in the park. Almost like he was two different people in one body. Nothing he did, or said, could have terrified her more.

Chapter Thirty

Anna remained too shaken to drive. Warm air pumped out the truck's vents, but it didn't help the chill rolling through her. Kids' chatter filled the winter air. Misshapen snowmen stood erect, like rock formations, across the flat land by the picnic spot. Some parents pulled sleds, while others chatted at the base of the hill. No one even so much as glanced in her direction.

Scum ball, Leo. She hated him, but she hated the fact she was so terrified of him even more.

Anna noticed her eyes were slightly bloodshot. She angled the rearview mirror toward her neck. It still throbbed at the exact spot where his hand bit into it. Faint red lines were all that remained. Lines that would fade, even though the memory of how she'd gotten them would not.

Leo's words echoed in her head. "Her body's not even cold yet. Leave it be. Let her die." *Who?* She doubted he meant Daisy. Leo Adams was insane, Anna was sure of it. Insane, but speaking truth. She was even surer of that. "It would be better for everyone."

The little girl with the pink boa was long gone, but she existed, and she was safe…for now. Maybe this child was just symbolic. Maybe all of this had nothing to do with her but dealt with a different child.

Anna's cell phone rang. A welcome distraction. "Hello."

"Hey, Anna." Kathy, her saving grace at work, the only other sane person in the ad agency's creative department.

"Hi. What's up?" Anna forced out the words, keeping them light and airy.

"You okay? Your voice sounds scratchy."

Anna cleared her throat. "Yeah. Just a little hoarse." Her neck burned.

"Rumor around here is you fainted."

Leave it to Kathy to know all the work gossip. "Yep. I still don't know what happened. Felt fine, and the next thing I know I'm lying on the hallway floor surrounded by paramedics. But I'm okay, and I'll be back in tomorrow. How are things there?"

"Who's at your house?" Kathy blurted.

The question shot through Anna. "What?" She gripped the phone.

"I called there a few minutes ago, and some guy answered and acted like he lived there."

Ryan. Anna exhaled, smiled, and sank back against her seat. It had been all of ten minutes since she thought of him. Funny how that seemed the new normal. When had that happened?

"Is there something you forgot to tell me?" Kathy assumed her usual quizzical tone. Secrets never lasted long and would not be tolerated between them.

Anna should've known better.

"I don't see you for ten days, you get a boyfriend, and move him in?"

"No. Definitely not." Anna ran her hands over the steering wheel, not really wanting to get into it. She wasn't sure how this would go over. Kathy was a great friend—a great friend unafraid to voice her opinion. The true mark of loyalty.

"Is everything okay?" The concern in Kathy's tone was unmistakable.

"Yeah. Fine. Why?"

"A fax came for you. Actually, that's why I'm calling." Kathy exhaled. "I can...uh...leave it on your desk." There was an unusual hitch in her tone. "But you should probably—"

"What does it say?"

"It's freaky. Want me to read it?"

A fax? Almost no one faxed anymore. Although, her work phone, fax number, and email were all on the company website. A simple find for anyone who took the time to check the agency's contact page. "Now, we both know you already read it. So, *yes*, please read me *my* fax." Anna leaned over and sifted through the glove box for a scrap of paper and pen in case she needed to jot something down. No luck. She checked the center console. Nothing. Finally, she unzipped her purse and pulled out her eyeliner and a fast-food receipt.

Instead of reading, Kathy sang. "On the ninth day of Christmas, my true love gave to me nine-year-old girl, eight ties a-binding, seven checks were written, six o'clock newscast, five golden rings, four people murdered, three years ago, two sets of books, and the reason your husband had to die."

A nine-year-old girl. Goosebumps slid up Anna's arms and down her legs. She knew all of this had to do with that little girl! She should never have let her out of her sight. Wait. Could she be nine? That seemed way too old. But maybe. It had to be her, didn't it? Nine years old was what? Third, maybe fourth grade? Too old for teddy bears and tea parties. But...

Kathy stopped singing, and Anna figured she should probably say something so Kathy wasn't totally flipped out. "Don't worry." It was the best Anna could come up with.

"Don't you tell me not to worry. You're fainting. Probably pregnant. You've got some strange live-in, and now, you're getting bizarre faxes from people talking about murders and your dead husband!"

Well, when she puts it that way. "I'm not pregnant. We're not sleeping togeth—"

"Who is he?" Kathy spat the words out.

"It's okay. I'm okay." Anna squeezed her eyes shut, trying to force a quick, non-question-provoking explanation. "Do you remember Jake's friend, Ryan?"

"Kind of. Tall. Always wore obnoxious neckties. Been lurking around you ever since Jake died."

Lurking? Anna's ire rose, but she refused to get into it. "Yep. Ryan's staying with me *temporarily* because he broke his ankle, and he has no one else. So, I—"

"Anna. Stop. Just stop."

"What?" Anna wasn't sure what Kathy would say but didn't need a lecture.

"There's a gigantic difference between having no one else and being unwilling to find anyone else."

Anna wasn't sure how to respond.

"When did you start getting these notes?" Kathy continued before Anna could get a word in.

"Nine days ago." Strange to be talking so freely about something Anna had kept secret. "Basically, I've gotten one note per day since Christmas. Some mailed to me, others shoved against my front door, another left under my windshield wiper."

"And when did this guy...What's his face?"

"Ryan."

"Yeah. When did Ryan move in with you?"

"About a week ago—give or take." Anna knew where Kathy was going with this. "But he's not the one sending me these notes. He was just as surprised as I was when I told him about them."

"Was he now?" Kathy blew into the phone, clearly frustrated. Kathy didn't believe it, but Ryan couldn't be involved. "Have you called the police?"

"Yes." Anna lied. She shouldn't have, but otherwise, Kathy would never stop, and Anna didn't want to go round and round about this. A phone tolled in the background.

"Crap. I've gotta answer this," Kathy said.

Saved by the bell. The advertising agency had to be crazy today.

"At least law enforcement is involved. Listen, I've got to go. I just missed that call, and Larry walked by for the third time in three minutes."

Larry, the boss.

"Is he grabbing himself again?"

Kathy laughed. "Call me later. I'm worried about you. And I need to talk to you about this. I don't like these creepy notes or this guy living in your house. It's just too much of a coincidence for me, and you know I don't believe in coincidences."

"Kathy, wait." Anna didn't want her to hang up.

"What?" She sounded aggravated, but Anna knew Kathy loved her.

"What's the fax number?" Papers shuffled. Kathy read her the number, and Anna jotted it down with her makeshift pencil. At this rate, she'd be out of eyeliner by day's end. "Thanks for the call. I'll see you tomorrow."

"Sure. I'm not done talking to you about this."

"I figured."

"What? Of course, I'll let Larry know you're missing him." Kathy spoke loud enough for everyone, especially Larry, to overhear. Kathy snickered in Anna's ear, and, despite her tense mood, Anna couldn't hold back the giggle.

Larry was already convinced Anna was into him. Wishful thinking.

Anna ended the call and tossed her cell on the passenger seat. The windows started to fog. She wiped the condensation with her fuzzy coat sleeve, leaving behind a slew of tiny, maggot-shaped lines.

Could Kathy be right? Could Ryan be the one writing these notes? No, he wasn't even around when she got all of them. But why did that matter? He certainly had access, especially in the last week.

One note was shoved against her front door. Another mailed. Stuffed under her windshield wiper. In her purse. The church hymnal—he knew where she sat. The flower delivery.

Email. Ryan volunteered to help her trace it and was the one who said it was a secured sender.

It was Ryan's accountant going through Jake's books.

Her purse was left in Ryan's store…

Could it be? No. She would know. Wouldn't she? *Like I knew my husband went to find Tommy Peters?* Anna exhaled a shaky breath. Despite the cold, a bead of sweat trickled down her ribcage.

Chapter Thirty-One

Children played in the park. Snowballs sailed across the field. Random snowmen provided cover and then disintegrated under attack.

That little girl. Is she out there playing too? At least Anna knew the child lived close by or was in the area temporarily. Anna could post a sign on the message board at Ryan's General Store with her phone number and ask anyone with any information on the child to call. How many girls in Potrage wore a pink boa as a scarf?

No. That was silly. And creepy. She wasn't thinking clearly. The stress must be getting to her.

Anna had been positive these notes had to do with that little girl and now... Nine years old. The little girl she saw couldn't have been older than six or seven. Regardless, she had to help her. She had to stop this.

The news spoke of a different child kidnapped from a Rochester mall. Anna couldn't recall the details.

Oh my. A thought cut through her. What if the person penning these notes is the kidnapper?

The notes mentioned a six o'clock newscast. And then a nine-year-old girl and eight ties a-binding. If the notes were actually about the little girl Anna had seen, then the author would have to know about the crime beforehand. No. Why send notes and telegraph actions? And why to Anna? It made no sense. *God, no. Please, no.*

Maybe she was wrong. Maybe she should go to the police.

Two sets of books. Three years ago. Tommy, Hartman, Daisy, Jake. What did they know, and how did this all tie together? Five golden rings. The only verse the same as the song. Significant, but Anna still didn't know what it meant. The way they interlocked, like the Olympic rings? Tommy, Hartman, Daisy, Jake. Who was number five? Anna?

Leo?

If Leo was involved, then his brother—Vince, the town's only full-time police officer—would never help her. And Leo had information. He killed Tommy in a hit-and-run, and Leo knew about a body. *Her body's not even cold yet.*

The Adams could reel a punch from anywhere. They could destroy her, or Ryan and his business, with the wave of a hand.

Surely, the state police or FBI or somebody worked on missing person's cases. What if the child wasn't missing yet? What could she report? She was being haunted? There was that little missing girl in Rochester, but Anna had no proof she tied into this. Six o'clock newscast could have referred to anything.

Anna needed to talk to Ryan. She had to get his take on this. *Ryan would never allow someone to harm a child.*

Ryan...oh... Anna took a deep breath and let the air flood through her. *He can't be involved in this. No.* She couldn't allow herself to believe that. She, too, didn't believe in coincidences, but she did believe in fate. Fate brought them together. Ryan needed help with his broken ankle, and she... she needed Ryan and the safety and comfort found in a familiar face.

Anna raced out of the house today and didn't even leave a message about where she was going or who she was with. If Ryan had done that to her, she'd be hurt. Angry.

She couldn't define her feelings for Ryan. He made her smile. He made her feel safe. He made her feel at home. Maybe some relationships didn't need a definition. Maybe they could just be.

When she was with Ryan, she didn't want to be anywhere else. While Jake and Ryan had been the best of friends, Ryan wasn't like Jake. Jake had a way of doing things and keeping things. Everything had to be perfect. Ryan... way more spur of the moment...relaxed. *A lot more like me.*

What harm would there be taking their friendship to the next level? What would Jake tell her to do? Would he understand? Surely, he wouldn't want her to go on the way she had been. Just going through the motions. Life going on all around her but she wasn't a part of it. She was an accessory to the main event. *An accessory in my own life.*

So many nights she cried herself to sleep and wondered if she died, how long would it take to find her? Who would notice? Who would care? And the answer was always the same. Ryan would notice. Ryan would care, and not out of obligation, not anymore.

For a while she thought the attraction was in her head, but now...

The way he looked at her...that smile...And he'd done what a gentleman would do. He threw the ball in her court and waited—longer than he should have, longer than she would have. *And what did I do? First, I pretended it didn't exist, and when that no longer worked, I got in my car and drove off like a fool.*

Anna picked up the cell phone and dialed Ryan's cell. No answer.

It took a second to remember her home phone number. *Man, I'm getting old.* She called the home phone. No answer. The home voice mail clicked on. *Caller ID. I wouldn't have picked up either.* Anna hung up before the beep.

As long as she had her phone, she checked her messages. She had two, both from Ryan.

"Hey, Anna. It's me. Where are you? Call me. I'm worried." Then, with more force, "And you just fainted. You shouldn't be driving."

An automated voice said, "Press seven to delete this message and hear the next. Press five to save this message and hear the next. Press three to play this message again."

She deleted it and listened to Ryan's second message. "Anna, call me. I've got something."

She dialed her house and Ryan's cell again. No answer.

Now, it was her turn to worry.

Chapter Thirty-Two

Anna was on to him. The man sensed it. The questions. Her impromptu visit to the storage garage. She was going to find out.

Her brick two-story house stood before him, camouflaged against the surrounding trees. *Why am I here?* She was on to him. He nodded and continued walking up her gravel driveway. Was she back home yet? He couldn't be sure. She could've parked inside her garage.

The scent of burning logs from distant fireplaces drifted along the crisp winter air. A snow removal service had plowed out Anna's driveway. The perfect pitches of the snowdrifts gave it away. The ridges of snow on either side were waist-high, providing cover to duck behind should anyone peer out.

The blood throbbed in his hands, and he opened and closed his fists so they didn't swell from the excitement. What would he say when he got to the door? Didn't matter. There was only one way to stop a leak. Plug it shut. He touched the gun holstered on his hip concealed beneath his jacket. Yes, he needed to plug this leak shut.

Something moved upstairs. The beige drape wafted close. *She's home. No, not yet.* Then, he thought a moment. *Ryan.* A smile crawled through him. It started somewhere deep inside and snaked through his system. Yes, Ryan. It was amazing how fate had a way of filling in the blanks. He wasn't sure why he'd come, but now he knew.

Anna had a new kinship with Mr. Ryan Martin. Someone to fill all those lonely, empty nights, no doubt. Did she think of her husband when she and

Ryan made love? Did she feel his dead eyes? Did her husband watch from the world beyond? Could Jake, in death, still feel the blade of betrayal in his back every time his best friend slid into his bed?

Just keepin' it warm for ya, buddy.

Ryan had bitten the forbidden fruit. What guy didn't want to just once tag his best friend's wife? Just once. Just to see. A sample. Seeing if the grass was greener, having cake and eating it too, and all that other sweet stuff.

Well, Ryan was off the hook. Till death do us part, and Ryan sure made certain he made a mental note of that part of their wedding vows. Oh, it wouldn't last. Something based on curiosity rarely did.

Kinships were a weakness, and weaknesses could be exploited. Everyone had that someone. That one person they couldn't live without. For many, it was their babies, but Anna was barren. She and her husband never did make that family Jake had talked about starting. Lucky for Jake, they waited. Wouldn't it be like glass in your veins to have your child call your best friend daddy?

A black bird chirped and then swooshed down between the leafless trees before soaring back toward the sky. Birds in winter went against the natural order of things. If he were a bird, he wouldn't fly south either, nature or not.

Nature. What was his nature? Surely, he wasn't a monster, although he'd been called one. No. He had a need. A burning desire he couldn't suppress, a desire afforded unto him to carry and act on. There were signs all around him, telling him he was doing the right thing.

That little girl at the park, she was a sign. Her heart beat in sync with his, and he knew it from the moment he laid eyes on her. She had called to him in a silent tongue only his ears could hear. He alone would touch her and teach her. He would give himself up to her, and she would take him. She was proof. Proof what he'd done wasn't so bad. He would be forgiven and anchored at her port.

Finally, anchored.

Only one person stood in his way. She stopped him at the park. Somehow, she was there, getting closer. He stopped asking why now. It didn't matter. All that mattered was that child, and their life together, and he would do whatever it took to have that. It was, after all, his destiny. Nothing, and no one, would stop him now.

Branches cracked beneath his boots as he made his way toward the concrete porch. In an upstairs window, he saw something and stopped. The element of surprise was no longer his ally. He forced a smile and turned his gaze upward, already raising a hand to wave. Did they suspect him yet?

A cat. His smile widened. His ally remained intact.

The cat looked at him and arched his back. He knew, even at this distance, that its orange hair stood on end. Animals knew; they sensed things. With just one look, they could break a person's spirit open like a coconut. They saw the true soul, not the person one pretended to be.

Animals listened to that tiny voice in their head. The voice most humans ignored. People were far more worried about how they were perceived than their own personal safety.

"Well, I didn't want to be rude and just ignore the guy," an old biddy would say while her white-haired friend nodded like the insanity somehow made sense.

No, don't be rude. When the guy grabbed your purse, he was thinking, boy, what a sweet lady.

That would never happen to a wolf. A wolf would take one look at the guy and tear his arm off. The wolf was a step ahead. Today, he was The Wolf. A wolf in lamb's clothing.

He knocked on the door.

Chapter Thirty-Three

Anna drove home. What could Ryan have found? It could have been a ploy to get her to call, but that didn't fit. Ryan knew she'd turn up sooner or later. *Why isn't he answering?* She pressed redial and when he didn't pick up, she pressed a little harder on the accelerator.

The park was fifteen minutes from her house—fifteen long minutes. The leafless branches that arched above the road looked like interlocked fingers, trees forever praying.

Please let him be all right.

Anna passed a dark blue state police car and tapped her brakes. The last thing she needed today was a speeding ticket. She had enough to think about. Speed limits weren't even on the radar, although she doubted that excuse would hold up in court. Anna checked her rearview mirror. Thankfully, the cruiser didn't follow.

Was the author of the notes also a kidnapper? Anna just never felt that. She tried to trust her instincts, but... The song had twelve days, which meant on the first day of Christmas, the author already knew there would be twelve notes. The writer plotted and planned days beforehand. Nine-year-old girl, eight ties a-binding. How could he or she not be involved?

What if they knew the person committing the crimes? A relative? A spouse? They wanted to implicate them but not do so directly? Then, why send her the notes, especially over multiple days? Nothing made sense.

Something guided her. Something, or someone, she didn't understand. She didn't know why she had the horrific glimpses of that child, but now that she had, to deny them would be to deny the existence of everything she held true. Anna didn't believe in a lot, but she did believe in God, in fate, in a plan. Had her life unfolded differently, maybe she wouldn't be so sure, but in the days, and weeks, after Jake's death, her faith was all she had. There had to be something beyond this world.

Why the notes? There had to be a reason. If someone knew something, why not just tell her? Anna felt like she was on a scavenger hunt but had lost the master list.

She'd go insane if she turned it over too much. Trying to figure out the plan for the universe was like trying to figure out an affair of the heart. Some things that were totally illogical turned out right, even if you didn't understand why at the time.

Nana was infinitely wise, and it was times like this Anna missed her the most. Anna knew what Nana would say. "This too shall pass."

Anna knew her grandma was right. *What will it leave in its wake?*

Chapter Thirty-Four

Slowly, he twisted open Anna's front door. Unlocked, like the rest of the village. Potrage was a great place to live, and die, and hunt.

He stepped inside, carefully guided the door shut, and listened. From the den, he heard the hum of a computer and saw the blue screensaver's reflection in the glass panels of the French doors. The computer was on, but no one sat in front of it.

Where was Ryan?

The house smelled like cinnamon, and he could almost feel Anna's touch in every furnishing. Soft lines, romantic colors. Yes, definitely a woman's home. Ryan must feel like the guy from *Three's Company* living here, smothered in femininity.

Three's Company. He cracked himself up. *Just keepin' it warm for ya, buddy.*

The cat sauntered in from the kitchen and peered at him. It meowed, and he put a forefinger to his lips. He imagined it skinned and bloody, hanging from one of the trees outside, while the birds that didn't migrate plucked at it. Little bloody cat chunks would dangle from its beak, and the bird would look at him with reverence and appreciation. Although, he was here to hunt much bigger prey. A dead cat wouldn't help him. The cat would scare, not silence.

He'd scared Anna already, and scaring her hadn't worked. This time would be different. He understood now. The answer revealed itself to him like an angel to the shepherds.

Ryan's death would provide a glorious distraction. The shock would derail Anna until he had the child from the park safe and sound. Then he could leave. What did it matter if the truth came out after he was gone? In a way, it would be a relief, especially now that Valerie was dead.

In fact, he could kill Ryan but make sure the body wasn't found right away. Yes. The angel of fate had come to him. He followed the path she lit like the kings followed the star of Bethlehem. Their feast was coming, and so was his.

He moved through the house, The Wolf on the prowl.

Chapter Thirty-Five

Anna pulled into her driveway. Her chest tightened. Fear flooded through her. *My home.* It was her sanctuary, but it felt different, like it had changed. Something about it seemed foreign, although Anna couldn't articulate what. It was the same way the night Jake died. Everything looked the same, but somehow, she had sensed something was horribly off.

Don't go there. Anna turned off the truck. Her pulse pounded in her neck. *I'm nervous. Nothing more.*

Anna sat a minute and tried to think of what she would say to Ryan. She needed to articulate why she ran off this morning in a way he would understand. She had to tell him how she felt. She came close the other night when they played Scrabble and drank wine, but she wasn't ready to have that conversation yet.

Was she ready now? Would she ever be?

Anna picked up her cell phone, opened her truck's door, and stepped out. A bird chirped from a branch above, welcoming her home, or warning her off?

Little Red Riding Hood. I'll huff, and I'll puff, and I'll blow your house down. What a random thing to pop into her head. A child's tale. She hip-butted the truck door closed.

Any time a bizarre thought occurred to her, she wondered if it was Nana speaking to her soul in whispers from heaven, with no living proof.

Funny, she never thought about Jake that way. Maybe the loss was too painful, or maybe it was too soon. Or maybe that would mean accepting

Jake would never return, and, even though she knew it, a part of her didn't want to believe it. Although, that part grew smaller each day, and somehow that realization made her heart sting anew.

Something moved upstairs in her bedroom window. Ryan? Not upstairs. His leg was getting better, but he wouldn't go upstairs.

Probably the cat.

Kathy, at work, had cats. She should've asked her why a cat would meow all the time. What could it possibly be trying to say? Feed me. Pet me. Change my litter.

Anna stepped onto the porch and pushed open the front door. "Ryan, I'm home."

A puddle glistened on the hardwood floor. The pulse in her neck pounded faster.

"Ryan?"

Chapter Thirty-Six

Avoice woke him. A woman's voice.

What was he doing? The Messenger looked around, and it took a second to remember where he was or how he had gotten there. That always happened when he fell asleep anywhere other than his own bed.

He sat up and shook off sleep's blanket. His cheeks felt damp. He must have been crying.

Some pain flooded every consciousness.

He dreamt of her again—Valerie. She played in a beautiful field full of flowers and soft, green grass. A mote surrounded the field, and she helped him across a wooden bridge. He hadn't seen the bridge until he was on it. The wooden planks vanished when he crossed, as if they never existed at all.

Peace, unlike any he'd ever known, filled him; a silent tranquility that, until this point, he would have been incapable of knowing. The gentle grass folded under his feet, although, at the same time, he also understood he was weightless.

Valerie led him to a scrolled concrete table and chairs, but when he sat, he found it wasn't concrete at all. It looked like concrete but mushed like puffs of down.

It smelled of lilacs here, his favorite scent, but he couldn't see the blooms. It was like a warm summer day. Not too hot, nor too cold. A soft breeze fluttered the tree branches, sending the lilac scent through him.

"Hi, Uncle," Valerie said and she smiled.

He was positive she had never looked more beautiful. This was how she would have looked on her wedding day. Her blonde hair flowed around her, and she wore a white dress, not quite satin, not silk. A material so soft it almost seemed liquid. Like him, she was barefoot. She glowed, and he looked for the scars on her wrists and ankles, but they were gone.

Emotion flooded him, and the words poured out. "Did you know I loved you?"

"Yes." Valerie seemed to have a wisdom about her. Something far more detailed than her twelve years on earth could have provided.

She reached out and wiped the tears from his cheek, and he kissed her palm, wanting to stay there.

More than anything, he wanted to stay in the garden that smelled like lilacs, that was not too hot and not too cold. *Let me stay. Please, don't make me go.* "I love you," he whispered, and the words caught in his throat.

How he had prayed for this. To hold her just one more time. To tell her how sorry he was that he didn't do more. That he didn't save her. If he'd known. If he could have, he would have stopped it. He would give anything, anything to have stopped it.

"It's okay." Valerie laid her warm hand on his. "I'm okay."

"I loved you so much." His heart ripped open again. Why didn't he help her? How could anyone hurt her?

Valerie slid closer and hugged him, and he knew he'd never let go.

"You have to go now," she said as if she could read his thoughts.

"No." He could barely squeak out the word. His heart swelled and sucked the air from his lungs. Tears streamed down his face. *Thank you, God. Thank you for this time.* He would never let go.

"You have to finish," Valerie whispered in his ear. "It's not over."

"I can't." He held her, and she him, and he wept like a child. "I can't leave you." *I love you so much.*

The Messenger didn't know how long he stayed there, and it didn't matter, for he was past the point where time tolled.

"Valerie?"

She didn't answer.

"Valerie!"

Then, there was water. It was in his ears, in his nose, in his mouth. He tried to breathe, but his lungs filled. "Valer—" His voice was smothered in the buttery liquid.

All of a sudden, he clutched something hard, something very different from Valerie. How? He hadn't let go. "Valerie," he tried to scream but couldn't. He had to breathe. Breathe. He lifted his head out of the liquid, out of the water.

No. No. Please, no.

A horrible realization crashed through him; it was too late. He gripped the edges of a casket full of water. He was drowning in it.

"Valerie!" he screamed again and then he woke up.

It was a dream. Just a dream. Although, he couldn't help but feel like he'd gone somewhere.

Please let her be okay, he prayed, and then wished he could take it back. God let this happen. Prayer was like fool's gold, only valuable until you were shown the truth. And he had been shown. He'd seen what the power of prayer could do. He watched as they buried her in the dirt where maggots would eat her flesh.

Where was the power then?

Rage flooded The Messenger's spirit as the comfortable hatred that filled so many of his days returned. He could taste it, and it ate at him like those maggots in the ground. He ran a hand over his wet cheek and prayed again. *Where were You when she cried out for You?*

Where was I? Tears filled his eyes. "Where was I?"

Chapter Thirty-Seven

Anna slid her purse off her shoulder and tossed the purse and her keys on the writing desk. Nothing appeared out of place. The house smelled of cinnamon from the decorative pinecones. The Christmas tree's white lights glistened in the corner. "Anybody home?"

"Yeah." Ryan croaked. "I'm awake. I'm awake."

Anna sifted through the stack of mail on the desktop. *So, this is where the water came from. Ryan must have gotten the mail.* Cable bill, furniture sale flyer, direct TV mailer, credit card offer. The usual junk. Ryan appeared in the doorway of the den, clutching his neck.

"You okay?" Anna expected a wave of relief when she saw him and knew he was okay, but it didn't happen. She was still tense.

His eyes were puffy and pink. "Fine." He cracked his neck. "A little sore, but—"

"Were you asleep?"

"Yep." He gestured toward the den. "Passed out on your leather sofa in there. I heard you come in a few minutes ago, but I must've dozed back off."

"Nope, I just walked in." Anna slipped off her coat and looked back at the foyer's floor. "Thanks for grabbing the mail."

"That's not today's mail. I didn't go out and check it yet today."

The puddle. Her heart beat faster. "You didn't go outside at all?"

"No." He nodded at his cast. "Can't exactly drive. And the doctor said you're not supposed to be driving either."

Something was off. "Where'd this water come from?" Anna pointed toward the floor.

Ryan shrugged. "You?"

"No. It was here when I got home. You're sure you didn't go out?"

Thud.

The sound came from upstairs. Ryan's eyes widened.

Her pulse spiked. "Someone's here. Someone's in the house."

"Are you sure?" Ryan moved around her. He picked up the poker from the fireplace and hobbled through the living room.

Anna followed. Her right eye started to twitch, and a knot formed at the base of her shoulder blades. The house hummed. The low methodical buzz of the refrigerator. The steady gush of air from the heating ducts. The sounds of the house that so often went unnoticed, but not now. The clock ticked, and Anna mentally counted with it. *One. Two. Three.*

Anna reached out and touched Ryan's back. Tension radiated off of him. He turned, put a forefinger to his lips, and pointed the poker upward. They stopped, and she strained to hear. Ryan was right. Faint footsteps that moved in tandem with the numbers in her head. One. Two. Three. Methodical. Like a caged lion moving back and forth. Back and forth. Then, it stopped.

The cordless phone lay on the desk next to her; the desk her Nana left her. One more of her gifts? The receiver nearly slipped from her sweaty palm. Anna pressed talk and dialed.

"Nine-one-one," an operator said. The sound ripped through the house like a gunshot. "What is your emergency?"

"This is Anna Greenan at one oh one Whispering Pines, and I think someone's in my house." Anna spoke as quickly and quietly as she could.

Computer keys clicked on the other end of the line. "Are you inside the home right now?"

"Yes, and I think someone's upstairs. There was a puddle by the door."

"Whatever you do, I want you to stay on the line with me. Okay?" More clicking. "If someone is close to you, you don't have to talk, but don't hang up the phone."

Ryan snatched the scissors out of the pencil can and slid them into his back pocket. He waited at the base of the steps, ready to strike. He held the fireplace poker so tight veins popped in his hand.

"Okay." Anna touched Ryan's back.

The operator spoke in a soothing voice. "The police are on their way. Can you hear the intruder inside the home now?"

"Yes...I...I think so." Nothing appeared broken or disheveled. *Am I mistaken? No. I know what I heard.*

"And where are you inside the house?"

"Living room. I just got home." A drop of sweat trickled down her ribcage. "We're downstairs. I mean the main level."

"Is anyone else with you?"

"Yes. Ryan's here."

"Is Ryan male or female?"

"Male."

"Is it just the two of you that are supposed to be there?"

"Yes."

"Are you and Ryan able to get to a bathroom or closet? Someplace where you can lock the door and hide until police arrive?" the operator asked. "They're almost there."

Ryan pointed toward the front door. He mouthed, *go.*

Anna moved toward the door and motioned for him to come too. He walked backward never taking his eyes off the stairs. "We can get outside." Anna pinned the phone with her shoulder, snatched her car keys off the desk, and yanked open the door.

"No, you and Ryan want to stay—"

Anna stepped outside. A scream tore from her throat. The phone fell and smashed. Its battery skidded into the snow.

Chapter Thirty-Eight

Anna's scream echoed in the thin winter wind. Father Matthew jumped back. His jaw dropped. Snow streaked the bottoms of his black pants and long coat. His round glasses were fogged.

"Someone's in the house." Anna squeezed out the words.

"Keep moving." Ryan put a hand on her shoulder and ushered her past.

Father Matthew caught up. "What happened? Did you call the police?"

"They're on their way." Ryan hobbled down the drive, urging Anna forward.

Father Matthew stepped beside Anna, shielding her from the house. "Are you okay? This is awful."

Anna nodded. Her throat too dry to speak.

Ryan rested a crutch against Anna's SUV and pulled her close. She buried her face in his chest. The uneven pattern of his cable knit sweater pressed against her cheek. The familiar aroma of his cologne enveloped her as his body blocked the bitter wind and the driveway.

Vince pulled in. Sirens silent. "You guys okay?" He stepped out of the police cruiser.

Anna nodded.

"Yeah. They're upstairs." Ryan pointed toward the house.

Vince spoke into the walkie clipped to his shoulder, likely letting everyone know he had made it to the scene and found everyone unharmed.

Father Matthew moved around them as a sheriff's car careened into her drive. Vince stood on Anna's porch, his hand on his holster. The sheriff exited his vehicle and bolted toward her open doorway. The two vanished inside.

Neighbors started to peek out their windows. High school kids filtered into the street, suddenly inspired to ride bikes in January.

This isn't happening. Not in Potrage.

"Let's wait inside the truck." Ryan opened the driver's side door, and Anna slid into the seat. He hobbled around to the passenger side as Father Matthew climbed into her back seat.

Ryan filled Father Matthew in on what happened. Father Matthew pulled out a white handkerchief and wiped the fog off his glasses.

Lights went on and off inside her home, and Anna could almost see the shower curtains being yanked back and closets being opened and shut.

Sometime later, the sheriff appeared on the front porch, followed by Vince. Anna opened her door and stood.

The sheriff took the lead. "Miss Greenan?"

"Yes." Her voice shook.

"Just want to verify—you don't have any kind of attic or crawl space or anything. Is that correct?"

"Yes. Correct. We had to have a firewall built in the garage when we moved in. Something about it not meeting code. There's no way to access that space from inside."

"Okay. Thank you."

Vince gave her a reassuring nod.

The sheriff and Vince chatted on the porch. Anna walked toward them, stepping closer to hear.

"Up to you." The sheriff shrugged.

"Your call, Randy." Vince patted his shoulder. "But if you're asking if I'll take it," Vince held his arms out, "what else have I got to do?"

The sheriff glanced at his wristwatch. "You sure you don't mind? Nancy does aerobics tonight, so it's my night with the kids."

Vince nodded toward the sheriff's car. "Go ahead. Get outta here."

The sheriff walked by the group with a little more spring in his step. He wasn't much older than Vince. Kids, already? They started younger in the country, or maybe Anna was just getting older so everyone seemed young to her.

The sheriff smiled as he passed. "You're all set. Must've been the wind."

"Thank you." Anna climbed her porch steps. No way what she heard was wind.

Vince's normally present air of entitlement vanished and was replaced with genuine concern. "You okay?" He stepped aside and, before she could answer, added, "Come on out of that cold."

She never liked Vince, but, in truth, had no reason not to. He seemed like a good man and a good cop. Yes, he was kind of a prick when Daisy died, but he was doing his job. She probably would've done the exact same thing. He had to solve a murder, and, at the time, she was a potential suspect.

"You know, I think I'll take off." Father Matthew gestured toward the street.

"In a minute, Father." Vince nodded toward the living room. "This'll just take a second."

Father Matthew, Ryan, and Anna stepped inside, and Vince closed the door after them. He slid off his coat and hung it with his hat by the door.

"This is so surreal. I know we heard somebody upstairs." Ryan hobbled into the living room.

Vince didn't seem to be listening. He pulled out a pen and small green notebook as he took a seat in the club chair across from the sofa.

Anna sat on her couch. She picked up one of the pillows and snuggled it on her lap. She ran her fingers through its fringe, letting the wound strings slip through over and over. She just wanted to go to bed, but she'd never be able to sleep. Not here. Not now.

"We didn't find anyone in the house. No evidence of a break-in and nothing looks out of place." Vince regarded Anna. "But I still wanna take some notes. Just to have something on file." Vince smiled, and she could tell he was assessing her. "Can you please start at the beginning and tell me what happened? And why you thought someone was upstairs."

Ryan rested his hip on the sofa's arm. "I was just telling Father Matthew outside. Anna came home, and I was asleep."

Vince shifted his attention to Ryan. "You were in Anna's house?"

"Yeah." Ryan nodded.

"Sleeping?" Vince's single word full of unspoken accusation.

Ryan gestured toward the French doors. "Yeah. I passed out on the couch in the office."

"You live here now?" Vince's eyebrows rose.

Father Matthew walked over and took a seat beside her.

Oh gosh. What is my priest going to think of Ryan living here? Heat burned Anna's cheeks, even though she had nothing to feel ashamed of. "I'm helping Ryan out. Nothing's going on between us."

Ryan must have sensed Anna's discomfort and filled Vince in on his broken ankle, not being able to climb steps, staying with Anna only until his leg was better. He brought Vince up-to-date on the story about the puddle and Ryan hearing Anna come in minutes earlier, but she said she had only just arrived. Then, they both thought they heard footsteps upstairs.

How could this have happened? How could I and Ryan both be wrong? And if we were, why is Vince taking notes? Do police always have to explain when they answer a call?

Vince said something Anna didn't catch. He looked at her expectantly as if waiting for an answer.

"What's that?" Anna stammered. "Sorry, I..."

"Oh, no problem." Vince smiled a warm, gentle grin. Laugh lines etched his eyes. "I asked if you have pets."

"Ryan's cat is staying here until Ryan's able to go home. I didn't want to leave it in his apartment." Anna didn't see the cat anywhere. Or hear it, for that matter.

"Where's the kitty now?" Vince seemed to read her mind and then looked at his notes for an answer. He must have found one. "Hiding, no doubt."

"Haven't seen him," Ryan glanced around. "But it likes to hide under the beds."

"Okay. You're sure the sound you heard couldn't have been the cat?" Vince lowered his chin and peered at her. "I mean, is it possible it was the cat?"

"Anything's possible," Ryan adjusted his weight.

Vince jotted something down.

"That doesn't explain the puddle on the floor." Anna pointed toward the entryway.

Vince shook his head, as if shaking off an idea. "Other than water pooling by the front door, and some noise upstairs, is there anything you can give me to substantiate the idea someone was here who shouldn't be?"

"No. I...I thought I was sure of what I heard." Anna felt silly having called the police. What a waste of everyone's time.

Ryan touched her shoulder. "I heard something too."

"Was anything taken? Is there anything missing or out of place?"

"Not that I know of." Anna shook her head. "I can take a walk upstairs and look, but everything seems the way it should be down here. Honestly, I probably overreacted. It's been rough since Christmas."

"What do you mean since Christmas?" Vince leaned forward. "Are you in some kind of trouble?"

"No." Anna leaned back. Vince's sudden attention made her uneasy. "Not trouble but—"

"The holidays are always hard when you've lost someone." Ryan placed a hand on Anna's and squeezed. "I'm sure you understand."

What is Ryan doing? She needed to tell Vince about the notes. Not for her sake, but for the little girl. If things could be prevented...

"Did either of you notice anything else besides the puddle? The door ajar, a window askew, lights on that shouldn't be, anything?"

"No." They answered in unison.

"What about footprints in the snow?" Vince rose and walked to the back window. "I didn't notice any, but the wind is really whipping out there."

"Nothing." Anna clutched the pillow. "Just the puddle."

"And how long after you got home did you hear the footsteps?"

"Right away," Anna said, "and then I picked up the phone and dialed nine-one-one."

"I see." Vince returned to the chair. He glanced at his notebook and then at Father Matthew. "What time did you get here, Father?"

Father Matthew shifted on the sofa beside her. "Right when Anna—"

"He was standing on the porch when I opened the door to go out." Anna smiled at Father Matthew.

"That must have scared the hell out of you." Vince chuckled.

Anna nodded. "You have no idea."

"She screamed so loud my ears still hurt." Father Matthew cupped his ears as he smiled.

"Father, you see anything when you pulled up?" Vince returned the smile. "Anything out of the ordinary, I mean."

"No." Father Matthew shook his head.

"There's something that's bothering me." Vince flipped through his notes.

"What's that?" Father Matthew asked.

"Don't know." Vince looked at their priest. "Can't quite put my finger on it. At any rate, I just need some basic information, and then I can be on my way. Anna, your full name, address, date of birth, and number where you can be reached."

She gave it to him, so did Ryan, and Father Matthew.

"Anna, before I head out, why don't you take a walk upstairs and make sure nothing looks out of place. I can go with you if you want or wait here. Up to you."

"No, I'll be okay. As long as you promise no one's up there." Anna got up.

"I promise." Vince winked.

Chapter Thirty-Nine

Anna headed up the staircase. Her palms were clammy as sweat leaked from under her arms. Regardless of Vince's reassurance, she couldn't help the unease trolling through her.

She strained to hear anything, but the murmur of voices in the living room blurred everything else. *What a day.*

Ryan clearly didn't think she should mention the notes to Vince. *Why? What changed?* But Ryan had mentioned he found something in his voice mail. *What? And could it have had to do with Vince? Or even Vince's family?*

Everything looked the same in Anna's bedroom. She tugged open the top drawer of her nightstand. Her only valuable—a gold necklace with diamonds—glistened in its case. Her room, and all the others, appeared undisturbed.

When she returned downstairs, Vince was waiting by the door. "Anything missing?"

She shook her head. "Nope."

"Didn't think so. I think that's it then. There's not really much else I can do. Make sure you lock your doors. I'll keep a close eye on the property. If you need anything else, just call." Vince handed Anna a business card with his name, office number, and cell phone number.

"I will." Anna read the back. On it, Vince had written, *Call me if you're in trouble or need help.* She tucked the card in the back pocket of her jeans. "I'm really sorry I wasted your time."

"With Daisy being killed, the entire town is on edge. I get it. Making people feel safe is time well spent." Vince turned toward Ryan. "Oh, Ryan. I had a little talk with Jason Barnes the other night about stealing the beer."

"What'd he say?" Ryan leaned on his crutch.

"I bowl with his old man Friday nights, so, needless to say, the kid was petrified I'd tell his pops. Let's just say I don't think you're gonna have any problems with little Barnes from now on."

Ryan laughed. "It takes a village."

The radio on Vince's belt chirped. "I've gotta run."

"See you later." Ryan lifted a hand.

"We'll see ya." Vince put on his police issued cap and opened the door. "Oh, I just thought of it."

"Thought of what?" Anna placed a hand on the stair rail.

"Something I forgot to ask." Vince stepped back inside, closing the door. "I was just wondering something, Father." He smiled at Father Matthew.

"What's that?" Father Matthew's brow wrinkled.

"Why did you stop by?" Vince asked without a trace of accusation.

"Oh...ah..." Father Matthew looked at his feet and then back at Vince. "The Western Greyson Planning Board meets once a month. Anna's been on the board for about a year. This is the first meeting she's ever missed. I came over to make sure she was okay."

The meeting. I totally forgot. She had so much going on. *Is it the first week of the month already? Wait. I thought it was canceled with the holiday.*

"I see." Vince looked to Anna as if for confirmation.

"It completely slipped my mind. I'm so sorry, Father."

"Oh, it's okay. It seems you've had a lot going on with a houseguest and all." Father Matthew gestured toward Ryan. "I'm just glad to see you're okay. Am I good to go now? I told Mrs. Forrester I would stop in and check on her. She's on bed rest with a fractured foot."

"Of course." Vince pulled back open the door and moved aside.

"Good night." Father Matthew stepped out onto the porch.

"Good night." Ryan and Anna watched as he walked down the drive.

Vince waited until Father Matthew was out of earshot before he spoke again. "Anna." Vince stood in the open doorway. The cold seeped in around him. "One more thing."

"What's that?" Anna fought the shiver.

"The marks on your neck." Vince touched his own throat.

Ryan whirled around, his eyes wide in a stunned silence.

"What're they from?"

So Vince hadn't heard about the run-in with his brother. She wasn't about to explain. "Nothing. I scratched my neck with my zipper."

"I see." Vince sighed. "I gave you my card, right?"

"Yes." She nodded. "I saw. Thank you."

They said their goodbyes, and Ryan locked up after Vince left. "What happened to your neck?" He followed her into the living room. "There's no way you got that from a zipper. Where were you today? I can't believe I missed that." Ryan leaned closer, and his fingers grazed her neck. The raw skin sent a chill through her as goose pimples slid up her arms.

"Stop." Anna held up a hand and backed away toward the sofa.

Ryan stood with his hands on his hips. He was going to blow a gasket. No sense putting off the inevitable.

"I went to see Leo."

"What?" Ryan balked. "You did what? Have you lost your mind?"

"Calm down." Anna flopped onto her couch.

"Do *not* tell me to calm down. You race out of here. Don't tell me where you were going. What the hell were you thinking?" He wouldn't meet her gaze. "You know Daisy was murdered."

In all the years they'd been friends, this was the first time she'd ever seen Ryan really mad. "I needed some time to sort things through." Her eyes burned.

"Sort through what?" Ryan paced. "How to rile up the entire community in twenty-four hours?"

"No." Her voice cracked. She held her face in her hands. *What was I thinking? This entire day has been a disaster.*

"I'm sorry," Ryan said suddenly, and she looked at him.

What? His anger seemed to dissipate.

Anna's chest ached, like her heart was bruised and Ryan was standing on it. "I needed to—"

"No, you don't." Ryan didn't meet her gaze and stepped away. "You don't owe me an explanation. I'm *just* your guest. You've been kind enough to put me up. You don't answer to me."

The floor blurred. "You're more than my guest." Anna looked at him, but his back was to her. He had a hand on the oak fireplace mantel and the other on the small of his back.

"I was just worried." Ryan exhaled. "The thought of you in danger. I mean...ah...What if..." He sighed. "I was worried, but I shouldn't have blown up like that. You don't deserve that. I'm sorry."

There were so many things her heart wanted to say, but her head couldn't find the words. "It's okay. I'm sorry too. I should've left a note."

Ryan hung his head. The distance between them seemed to multiply with every second of silence, and Anna had no idea how to stop it.

She couldn't take it anymore. "I saw her."

"Saw who?"

"The little girl. The one I dreamt about."

"Saw her?" Ryan turned. "What do you mean you saw her?"

"At the park." Anna filled him in on everything that happened that day. Everything but the one thing he needed to hear. The one thing she still couldn't bring herself to say.

Chapter Forty

The scratch that ran down his calf burned, and dark pants stuck to the warm blood. A stray tree branch caught his leg when he leapt off Anna's garage. The snow behind the house provided ample cushion, and he made damn sure all his tracks were covered. By now, they were trampled over.

He sat in his car and licked his wounds, The Wolf still hungry after a fruitless hunt. With each gust of wind, snow splattered his windshield. Like bird crap, it plopped from the branches.

The wind howled.

Something stirred deep within his bones. Yes, something good would come of this.

Two doors down, he spotted a newly sided one-story house with its lights still on. The only house on the street without Christmas lights. Jews, maybe. Or atheists. He nosed his car forward.

A white Big Men moving van sat parked in the drive, along with a little dark blue or black Chevy sedan. He peeped through their picture window. A woman chatted with someone he couldn't see.

The woman looked like a countrywoman—stocky, with dark, curly hair and glasses. A woman who could pull her own weight. Out here, in rural America, she'd have to. She lifted an oversized cardboard box and walked it around the corner. A rectangular cutout divided the living room and the kitchen and framed her like a movie screen. The woman unloaded plates and bent and straightened, bent and straightened. Either she was sticking them into a dishwasher or doing slow motion calisthenics.

A man appeared suddenly in the front window and blocked The Wolf's view. The man, skinny with red hair and a trimmed beard, stared out, almost as if he could sense The Wolf watching and wanted to protect his keep. Then, the man vanished.

A few moments later, the red-haired man reappeared behind his wife. The Wolf watched as he put his hands on her shoulders. She leaned into him. The man kissed her cheek, her neck. His hands slipped below the screen, and the woman turned to face him. She forgot about the dishes and kissed him hungrily on the mouth, her hands groping his shoulders and back.

They stopped suddenly and let go of each other, as if they were teenagers caught by an angry parent. They both looked downward, and the woman smiled and spoke to someone. The man did something that made the woman jump, and she swatted at him, smiling, and then refocused on whoever she was talking to.

The woman turned and lifted a glass from the cupboard behind her. She filled it at the sink.

A moment or two later, a light went on in the front bedroom. The entire room looked pink.

There she stood!

He couldn't believe it. His pulse spiked, and his tiny car seemed to spin. He stared, unable to pry his gaze off her. *What luck! No, not luck.* Luck was for losers, something intangible for them to blame, a pathetic excuse. This, this was something that went far beyond good luck.

Instead of her pink boa, she wore a white nightgown and carried the glass from the kitchen. The little girl moved slowly as if careful not to spill. Her brown hair grazed her shoulders, and she set the glass down on a cherry dresser, crossed the room, and climbed into her canopy bed.

The red-haired man, probably her father, appeared in the doorway and looked out toward the street. He walked to her window and closed the blinds. The Wolf could still see his silhouette as he waited beside her bed, presumably to tuck her in.

The Wolf tried to control his breathing. He listened to the howl of the wind and wanted to stand outside and howl with it, but now wasn't the time.

He had to wait. There was work to be done.

Thank you. He sat in his car and waited. He no longer felt the gash down his leg, or the blood that stuck to his clothes. All he felt was a renewed sense of purpose.

Time passed, and he watched as the husband and wife went back to necking in the kitchen, and then he imagined them moving into the living room, the bedroom, the hallway, christening the house. They would need all the blessings they could get, but it wouldn't help. For he had seen what they hid in the room painted pink. He knew now where the treasure lay, and he no longer needed a map.

Destiny worked in strange ways. The fiasco at Anna's had helped him reach his final destination. He watched and waited until the shadows on the moving van played tricks with his eyes, and his breath fogged the windows. He wiped away the haze and took a deep breath.

The white snow beneath her window glittered in the moonlight like angel dust.

Once again, he'd been blessed.

Chapter Forty-One

In honor of her first day back to work, Anna chose her favorite outfit, a royal blue suit that flattered her figure and brightened her eyes. A quick cup of coffee and she'd be ready to roll. Anna headed downstairs but stopped at the writing desk adjacent to the front door. She picked up the latest note.

"On the tenth day of Christmas, my true love gave to me Ten Commandments broken. nine-year-old girl, eight ties a-binding, seven checks were written, six o'clock newscast, five golden rings, four people murdered, three years ago, two sets of books, and the reason your husband had to die."

Anna flung the note on the desk, where she'd found it. *Ryan must have brought it in. Not only do I have to go to work, but I start my day with this.*

Anna glanced at the stove's clock—8:15. She'd be late for work if she didn't take off in the next few minutes. *Ten Commandments broken.* Anna inhaled. Two more days. Two more notes. Then she'd take the stack to the police and be done with this. She and Ryan agreed last night if she went to the police too soon, the notes might stop coming and any clues would go away along with them. Ryan was right. Confidentiality couldn't exist in a small town. She was glad Ryan stopped her from telling Vince, especially when Vince's brother, Leo, knew more than he said. *Her body's not even cold yet.*

Since nothing had happened to Anna in the first nine days, there was no reason to think anything would happen in the last two or three. The notes weren't about her. They were about a nine-year-old girl, and Anna had every intention of protecting that child.

The downstairs shower water turned off. Anna wasn't sure if she wanted to see Ryan this morning. Even though they talked for over two hours about Leo and the little girl and debated whether or not to go to the police, a lot of things were unresolved. All of them personal.

Anna pulled another coffee cup out of the cupboard, filled it, and took it to Ryan. She knocked on the bedroom door. "Ryan?"

"Come in."

She opened the door and gasped. Ryan stood still, a white towel wrapped around his waist. His skin glistened and his shoulders seemed broader than usual. Anna couldn't help but notice his toned stomach and the bulges in his arms. He ran a hand through his wet hair.

Wow. She realized she was staring and looked away. *Oh, man.* "I…ah…I…um…I brought you coffee." She lifted the cup and hot liquid doused her hand, slid down her wrist, and up her arm. "Ow. Son-of-a." Her whole arm stung.

Ryan hobbled over and grabbed the cup.

Her entire right sleeve was soaked, and she somehow managed to splash her left pant leg. "Shoot." She looked up, and Ryan smirked. "I have to go change my suit."

"I wouldn't change a thing." Ryan raised his brows as he took a sip of the coffee.

Anna ran back upstairs and peeled another suit out of another plastic dry-cleaning bag. *The cleaners should give me a discount. I shouldn't have to pay full price if I never wear the outfit in public. If only this morning were atypical, but it wasn't. Just a day in the life.*

Black. I'll wear black and mourn the loss of six more dollars to Sandy's Dry Cleaning.

God, Ryan looked good. I wouldn't change a thing. With that smug, I'm so sexy smile. Anna pushed the image out of her head, but she'd be a liar if she claimed she forgot it entirely.

The forty-minute ride to work, Anna spent trying to think of all Ten Commandments. One must head straight to hell if you couldn't name all ten. *And I call myself a Catholic.*

Anna counted on her fingers and tried to steer the truck at the same time. Thou shall not steal, kill, bear false witness, use the Lord's name in vain, honor any other God, commit adultery, covet thy neighbor's wife and possessions. Thou shall honor thy mother and father, keep the Sabbath holy. *One more. Holy hell. I don't know the Ten Commandments.*

Oh, Lord, forgive me.

This must be one of those things that you know so well that you forget from time to time, like your age after you hit thirty.

Larry was playing with his balls again when Anna walked into work. Nana would say the man would go blind, but apparently, Larry was immune.

"Hi, Anna." Larry pulled his hand out long enough to give her a wave. "Welcome back."

"Good morning." She scurried past, afraid he'd try to tap her back or worse, shake her hand.

Anna entered the lair of the creative department. Somebody had told Happy Hands that primary colors stimulated the brain, so the office could have doubled for a preschool room. Who would have thought bright red, yellow, and blue could be so annoying? *No wonder my second-grade teacher was so nasty.*

"Welcome back, Annie." Kathy was the only person on the planet who could call her Annie and live. Kathy looked stunning in her trendy clothes and short, dark hair. The black glasses she wore would have looked awful on anyone else but looked great on Kathy.

Kathy's all stylish and sophisticated while I'm chaos in a suit.

"Good morning, sunshine." Anna breezed over to her desk. *Good to be back.*

"We've got a ten o'clock with North Carolina Coffee, and Dave called and wanted to know if you got a copy of the voiceover yet."

"Anything else?"

"Nope. How's the live-in?"

"Fine." Anna unpacked her overstuffed briefcase and didn't dare look at Kathy. A storm of Post-its and crinkled papers rained onto the floor.

"Really?" Kathy bent down to help pick up Anna's mess. Kathy had a smile that stretched across her face and wrapped around her head. Anna needed an officemate who didn't know her so well. "Gosh, I missed you."

Anna smiled and got right to work, letting Dave know she already received, and approved, the voiceover and then focused on the North Carolina Coffee campaign.

Later that afternoon, Anna did what any sane person who missed the last eleven days of work would do; she surfed the net for the Ten Commandments and found she indeed did know them all. *Phew.* Thou shall not covet thy neighbor's possessions and thou shall not covet thy neighbor's wife, separate but equal.

She went to Google and typed The Twelve Days of Christmas in the search bar. Maybe notes were being sent all over the world, and people were blogging, Facebooking, tweeting, and boasting about it. Ridiculous, but... Anna scrolled down the list of links that were of no help and even less interesting until she hit one, The Urban Legend of The Twelve Days of Christmas. *Bingo.*

Everyone has heard of the song "The Twelve Days of Christmas." A happy song sung during a joyous season, but the origin of the song reflects a much darker time for the Catholic Church. From the mid-fifteen hundreds to the early eighteen hundreds, when Parliament finally emancipated Catholics in England, Catholics were prohibited, under penalty of death, to practice their faith. Several historians believe that the song "The Twelve Days of Christmas" was developed as a coded message. A way for young Catholics to learn the tenants of their faith. This is known as a "catechism song."

A coded message? Anna couldn't believe this. She had never heard of this.

The partridge in a pear tree = Jesus Christ.
Two turtle doves = The two books of the Bible: the Old and New Testament.

Three French hens = The three theological virtues: faith, hope, and charity.

Four calling birds = The four gospels.

Five golden rings = The five books of the Old Testament.

Six geese a-laying = The six days of creation.

Seven swans a-swimming = The seven gifts of the Holy Spirit.

Eight maids a-milking = The eight Beatitudes.

Nine ladies dancing = The nine fruits of the Holy Spirit.

Ten lords a-leaping = The Ten Commandments.

Eleven pipers piping = The eleven faithful apostles.

Twelve drummers drumming = The twelve points of the Apostle's Creed.

Anna had never really thought about why the author chose the song. The person had a purpose, and perhaps, that purpose could also explain why he sent notes rather than told her directly. Ten lords a-leaping, Ten Commandments...broken? Could this really be? *Fear of persecution? Coded messages?*

The rest of the day, Anna did complete some actual advertising work and was in the middle of brainstorming with Kathy about Big Ted's Used Cars upcoming ad campaign when the phone rang.

"Crap," Anna blurted. "We almost had it."

"You answer it." Kathy got up. "I'll start jotting down what we've got so far."

"Hello. This is Anna Greenan."

"Hi, it's Ryan."

"Why hello there." Anna smiled.

"How's your arm?" Ryan asked.

"What do you mean?"

"The coffee spill."

"Oh, I'm fine." Anna pictured him standing in the bedroom in the towel and grinned. *I need to buy smaller towels. Oh my gosh! I'm such a pig. Personal commandment eleven, Thou shall not be a swine.* "My favorite suit may not be happy, but the arm's okay."

"Coffee'll come out. How's your first day back?"

"Good." *All right. Odd. There's no way he's calling me at work to chitchat. Ryan took work way too seriously for anything that frivolous. I, on the other hand...*

"Busy?" Ryan asked.

"Not too bad. What's up?"

"I forgot to tell you something yesterday."

Anna remembered the message he left on her cell phone. *Call me. I've got something.* There was so much going on yesterday she had forgotten about it. "What's up?"

"The King found something in the boxes we gave him."

"You're kidding." Anna sat forward and sent an avalanche of papers cascading to the floor. She picked them up. "What?"

"Don't really know."

Anna restacked the mountain. *You called to tell me this?*

"He called, said he was on to something and he was goin' to Tennessee to check it out."

"Does he need money for gas and a hotel?" Anna hoped not. With the expense of the holidays, and higher than normal gas bills from the colder than normal winter, her bank account was almost depleted.

"No. I asked him that. Guess he's got relatives there. Said he'll call as soon as he knows more."

"Tennessee?" Anna asked a little too loud, and Kathy whirled around and looked at her.

Kathy wrote something on a yellow legal pad and held it up. *Is it your live-in?* Anna nodded. Kathy jotted down something else, and Anna swiveled back around in her desk chair, because she knew she didn't want to know whatever it was Kathy wrote.

"Why Tennessee?" Anna asked. "Oh my gosh. Holy cow. Jake went to Tennessee a week or so before he died. Said he had a conference there. I never gave it a second thought. Did The King say where in Tennessee he was headed?"

"Don't know. Didn't say."

"Tennessee." Anna stared at the picture of Jake on her desk. How many secrets had he kept, and how many times had he lied? She hadn't wanted to believe he could have been caught up in this, but he had been and, because of him, she was too.

"You still there?" Ryan asked.

"Yeah. Just daydreaming. So, The King's got family there?"

"That's what he said."

"Wait a minute. Ryan, isn't Graceland in Tennessee?" Anna shook her head. "You know what? Don't answer that. I don't wanna know."

"I'm not sayin' a word." Ryan laughed. "Oh, I also called to let you know I had them hang the sign for the little girl with the boa on the bulletin board at my store like we talked about. I made a few calls, but nobody seems to know who she is. I'll keep trying, though."

"Thanks," Anna said. "I hope we're doing the right thing with that." Anna still wasn't sure whether or not hanging a sign asking about a child was the best option, but she and Ryan both didn't see any other choice. "Did The King ever pick up the books from the house? My personal tax returns?"

"No. They're still here. He wanted to get through what we gave him first. Why?"

"As I mentioned before, there must be some record of Jake's trip when he went to see Daisy's son, Tommy. Plus, I'd like to look and see exactly where in Tennessee Jake stayed and whether or not there actually was a conference there then. We can talk about it when I get home. Oh, and I learned there's an urban legend involving 'The Twelve Days of Christmas' song. I don't have time to get into it now."

"Oh, I got the note you left me. It gets stranger by the day."

"What note?" A yellow sheet drifted over Anna's shoulder and floated into her lap.

"Ten Commandments broken."

"I didn't leave it for you. I thought you left it for me. I found it on the desk when I got up this morning." Anna unfolded the yellow piece of paper.

"How'd it get there?" Ryan asked, and she could tell he wasn't kidding.

Anna read the note Kathy wrote, *Is your pulse racing?*

It was, but not for the reason Kathy suspected.

Chapter Forty-Two

When Anna arrived home, Ryan sat at the kitchen table. He wore a pair of black shorts and a white T-shirt. Not normal January clothing, but she wasn't the one in a cast. Rich, Italian spices wafted from her stainless-steel oven.

"Hi." Anna heaved her briefcase onto the counter. "Something smells fantastic."

"I made dinner." Ryan pointed toward the stove.

"Delish." Anna flopped onto a kitchen chair.

"Be ready in ten minutes. How was work?"

"Works work. How did someone get in this house to leave a note on my desk?" Just the idea made her skin crawl. Someone creeping into her house while she slept upstairs…

"I must have accidentally left the front door open this morning. I couldn't find my cell so I called it. When it didn't ring I thought maybe I left it in your truck. I didn't, but…I'm so sorry. I'll be more careful."

Anna sighed. What more could she say? "Tell me more about what your accountant had to say."

Ryan opened the side-by-side refrigerator. "He didn't say any more than what I already told you. Said he found something, and was going to check it out. Said he'd call us when he had more. What do you want to drink?"

"Diet pop's fine."

Ryan passed her a chilled can from the fridge. "Do you want a glass?"

"Yes, please." Anna popped the top and took a quick swig. The fizz tickled her nose. "Let's call The King's cell. I wanna talk to him."

"He doesn't have a cell phone."

"What? That's crazy."

"He says cell phones are a fad and when this craze ends, he'll be ahead of the curve."

"That is beyond insane."

"The man is an Elvis impersonator *and* an accountant. How *normal* did you think he was?" Ryan pulled a Mickey Mouse glass out of the cupboard and inserted it under the icemaker. The icemaker grinded but didn't cough out any ice.

"You know the icemaker's broken." Anna grabbed a napkin from the holder and wiped condensation from the aluminum can.

"I keep forgetting. When did this break?"

Anna had to smile. "Almost two years ago. But if you open the door, there's always ice in the holder."

Ryan opened the freezer and reached inside. "You know this would've made Jake crazy."

"I know." *Payback for him keeping so much from me.*

Ice rattled in the cup as Ryan passed it across the table to her.

"Thanks." She took it and poured in the remaining pop as bubbles fizzled across the top. "If The King checks in, have him call me on my cell."

"Okay. Why?"

"I wanna know what he found and where in Tennessee he is because, like I said before, Jake went there shortly before he died, and that's a hell of a coincidence."

"And you don't believe in coincidences." Ryan smiled.

"Exactly." Anna got up. "I'm going into the office to go through my old tax returns. Call me when dinner's ready."

"Will do." Ryan pushed himself up. "This house felt so empty without you here all day. It was weird."

"Yeah...well..." She shrugged. *Will it be the same for me when Ryan leaves?*

After dinner, Anna sat on the office floor, surrounded by a sea of paperwork. Ryan knocked on the door.

"Want help?" Ryan hunched on his crutches.

"Sure." The knot at the base of Anna's shoulder blades ached from sitting on the floor for too long. "What time is it?"

"Almost ten. You've been in here all night."

"I guess so." *No wonders my bones ache.*

"Find anything?" Ryan nestled into the brown leather desk chair and wheeled it behind her with his good leg.

"Maybe." Anna sifted through the paper storm and pulled out Jake's client notes from spring. Tax time. She was still amazed Jake had kept such intricate files. Anna held up the top page so Ryan could see it and pointed to the writing in the margin. *Client: American Salt Company Independent Contractor? Schaeffer. Relocate 12/7???*

Ryan leaned in over her shoulder. "What's it mean?"

His breath warmed her neck. His cologne was intoxicating.

Anna scooted forward. "Don't know, but that's the only thing in all the client notes that seems out of place. It could be nothing. It could be something." She pointed toward the stack of folders. "I still haven't gone through all of that. I figured I'd start here and see if anything seemed odd, whether there was any reference to Tennessee, Tommy, or anything. I didn't know it would take me so long." She scooted around and leaned her back against the desk leg. "Dinner was great, by the way."

"Must have been." Ryan pointed at her shirt. "You saved some."

"I wanted to share. My shirt was hungry too."

Ryan smiled. Handsome laugh lines etched his blue eyes.

Anna shuffled paperwork, trying to distract herself. *What is wrong with me? Focus.* "Hey, when we pulled those boxes from the storage garage, it was the Potrage files A-D that were missing, right?"

"Yep. American Salt Company. Is that what you're thinking?" Ryan asked.

"I don't know." Anna pursed her lips.

"If you're going to take on the Adams family, you better be darn sure you're right."

"I know, and I know I shouldn't say this. I shouldn't even put it in the ethers..." Anna pulled the pen from her pigtail.

"What? What are you thinking?"

"Jake did some accounting for Saint Andrew's too. Helped out a bit. Pro bono."

"Okay? Wouldn't that be filed under the letter S, not the letter A?"

"That's not how Jake filed it. Have The King look there too. I mean, it's probably nothing, but Old Man Baker said the church gave him money… and well…just have him look."

"All right. I'll tell him. Listen, I wanted to talk to you about something else." Ryan leaned forward and rested his elbows on his knees. His well-defined chest shown through the thin white T-shirt. "But, if now's not a good time then…"

Uh, oh. "What's up?"

"The thing is, my leg's a ton better, and I've got to go back to work."

It figured. "Well, I think you should take it easy for a while, but if there's no talking you out of it, I am happy to drive you."

"No." Ryan sat back and looked away. "I can't ask you to do that. You've done so much already."

"I haven't done a thing." Anna closed Jake's notebook. "I let you camp out. So what? You cook. If you did laundry, I might bolt you to that chair and hold you hostage." An ache echoed through Anna's bones that no longer had a thing to do with where she sat.

Ryan laughed. "Nah. I've gotta get out of your hair. I wanna wait, if it's okay with you, until the twelve days of Christmas are over and everything is sorted out with that."

She couldn't think. *Where did this come from?*

Ryan stared at her as if waiting for something.

"What?" Anna choked out.

"Do you care if I hang out until the notes stop?"

"Oh, yeah, that's fine. Whatever." Anna couldn't meet his gaze.

"I think I can manage the stairs now, and one of the stock boys lives in an apartment three doors down from mine. I called him today, and he said he'd be happy to cart me around."

"I see." She couldn't believe this. *He's leaving? What brought this on?* She tugged at a string on her white sock, and the entire top started to unravel.

"What are you thinking?" Ryan asked.

She looked up. *Is he kidding?* "What am I thinking? This morning, I woke up to a note on my desk with no explanation of how it got there. Leo held me by my neck, and last night, I thought someone broke into the house." She gestured toward his leg. "Daisy and her son are dead. You got assaulted at your store. So, I guess what I'm thinking is your timing is pretty crappy, but I guess when the notes stop, it'll all be over, right? Everything will be a–okay."

"Wait a minute." Ryan slid off the chair next to her. "I'm giving you what you want and I'm in trouble for this?"

"How is this what I want?" She stared at him. "You a mind reader now?"

"No. Wait. Stop. Listen, you left here and needed time and space, and I understood that. I don't want to be a burden to you, and I definitely don't want to overstay my welcome."

Anna got up and felt like crawling out of her skin. Every part of her was uncomfortable. "I'll let you know when you're a burden. I leave for work at eight-fifteen. If you want a ride, I drive by the store anyway." She headed toward the living room. "Be ready to go in the morning. I don't want to be late for work."

"Anna."

"What?" she snapped.

"Where are you going?" Ryan fumbled for his crutches.

"To bed." She didn't turn around.

"Wait a minute." Ryan rose and hobbled toward her. He grabbed her hand and whirled her around. "I'm not going to let you do this."

"Do what?"

"Walk away again."

He stood so close the heat of his body raced through her.

"What is it you want from me?" Her voice caught, and her cheeks burned.

Ryan let go and sighed. "I know you must be scared, and I would never leave as long as I thought you may be in any danger. You should know that." He hung his head. "I don't know what you want or where you stand. I feel like…" He blew his bangs out of his face. "I mean…" His gaze met hers, and his blue eyes seemed to probe for answers to questions he wasn't asking.

"Here's where I stand. I like having you here. That's it. You're not in my way, and you're not a burden. If you've got to go back to work, I can drop you off on my way. No big deal."

He'd put her on the spot, and she didn't like it. His attempt to leave was starting to feel more like a threat than something he actually intended to do, and Anna wasn't into games. She was playing all she could handle.

"I'm beat. I'm turning in. Tomorrow, I'll go through the rest of those papers. Leave everything where it is for now."

Ryan nodded. "Anna?"

She paused, her hand already on the staircase banister.

Ryan looked down and then at her. She thought he might cry and then scream. Instead, he whispered, "Good night," turned, limped to his bedroom, and closed the door.

Anna stood at the base of the steps and couldn't help but feel like she had just ruined something, although she wasn't sure what that something was.

She double-checked the doors and windows. All locked. When she returned to the base of the stairs, she looked back toward Ryan's room. Even though he was in the house, she had never felt more alone. She wanted to talk to him, to tell him she needed him and that she didn't know if she'd ever want him to leave, but she couldn't. She was too angry, and it would come out wrong.

Anna went upstairs, flopped into bed, and stared at the ceiling. She had too much to worry about to focus on whatever it was that Ryan was searching for. And maybe that was cold, and maybe that was unfair, but that was the truth. All she could think of was that little girl from the park.

How that child wove into all this, Anna wasn't sure, but she also knew with every fiber of her being, she did. *Jake. His trip to Tennessee. So many lies told and secrets kept. Then there's poor Daisy and her son. And Ryan.* Anna sighed. Things couldn't stay the way they were between her and Ryan. She knew that. It hurt too much. *Love? Lust?* She didn't want him to leave, but what did that mean?

The twelve days of Christmas were starting to feel like a countdown, to what, Anna had no clue. She was on her own and could almost envision the ticking clock.

Two days left.

Chapter Forty-Three

Anna couldn't sleep. She kept thinking about American Salt Company. Leo was involved. He worked there. Yet, there was something that didn't mesh, some part that didn't fit.

Old Man Baker. "I not crazy. The church. The church gives me money." That was the piece that didn't fit. Somehow this had to do with her church.

The hardest part was she knew she had all the parts of the puzzle, but, no matter what she did, she couldn't jimmy them together to form a complete picture. *Ten Commandments broken has to be literal. Whatever it is will break all ten. Nine-year-old girl. The missing child. The girl on the news, the girl at the park? Why those visions?*

Holy cow.

The ninth day was a fax. She had a fax number. She had written it down. Anna grabbed her purse, dumped it, and sifted through the crap until she found the smudged receipt. Anna picked up her phone and dialed zero.

"Operator. How can I help?" a woman asked.

"Yes, I just received a fax and was wondering if you can tell me who sent it."

"Well, I can cross-reference the directory, but if it's not listed, it's not going to show up."

"Can you check the directory, please?" Anna pinned the phone to her shoulder while she picked up the loose change off her bedspread. Amazing how many pennies could accumulate in the bottom of a handbag.

"Sure."

Anna read the operator the fax number.

Anna had to find that little girl from the park. So far, they hadn't received any calls to the sign Ryan posted. He had written just what she told him to.

Desperately searching for little girl with pink boa seen at Highlander Park on Thursday afternoon. Please call if you know who she is. Reward. Must speak with her parents immediately.

Ryan left her home phone and cell numbers.

The wind rattled the windows. The morning sky looked gray and bloated, and Anna could barely make out the house across the street with the blowing snow. She flipped on the bedroom television and channel surfed until she found the local weather. With those snow clouds, she'd need to give herself extra time to drive to work. Anna wore a beige sweater and a pair of khaki slacks. No meetings meant no business suit needed.

The operator came back on the line. "Ma'am, the number you gave me is for Ryan's General Store, Potrage, New York."

"What?" Anna's voice cracked, and her mouth felt chalky.

The operator repeated the number and the address. *Ryan's store?* Anna hung up. *No. Ryan's store? There must be a mistake.*

The bedroom television beeped as a message scrolled along the bottom.

The National Weather Service has issued a Winter Weather Warning until ten p.m. tomorrow for Monroe, Livingston, Wyoming, Erie, Greyson, and Allegany counties. High winds, reduced visibility, and several feet of snow are expected. Monroe County has declared a state of emergency—no unnecessary travel. Stay tuned to News Channel Two for the latest.

The television beeped again, and the scroll repeated. Anna's heart thudded. Ryan was in the house, so were some of the notes. It was *his* accountant that was going through the books. Certainly, he knew he would have access to her for the twelve days of Christmas, especially after he broke his ankle. He—

179

"So you heard?" Ryan asked, and she jumped.

"What?" *Oh, God, help. Please.*

"About the snow day."

How long has he been standing there? "Yeah." Anna busied herself with the catastrophe of hairclips and makeup strewn on the bed, sweeping them back into her purse. *No, he can't be. No, please.* "How'd you get up here?"

"Magic." Ryan smiled as he leaned on her doorframe. "Listen…um… I haven't been myself the last few days. So, if I've done anything, or said anything that's been off, or upset you, I'm sorry. This ankle's making me miserable."

"No, you're fine." *I would've suspected. Wouldn't I?* "I think it's just been a really intense few days."

"Yeah." Ryan straightened. "At any rate, I came up to tell you there's a driving ban in Monroe County, so you can't go to work. We're still okay, but we should go grab some staples because the bulk of the snow's supposed to hit here later tonight. We're out of milk and almost out of coffee."

Anna peered out her bedroom window. "Looks like the storm's already here."

"They say it's gonna get worse. Hey…what's this?" He balanced on his crutches, bent, and picked up the crinkled paper. "This is the store's fax number."

"Yeah."

He held it out. "What're you doin' with this?"

"I…um…" Anna studied her bedroom carpet. *What do I say? What if he's sending the notes?* "I don't remember. I think I wrote it down just in case I needed to have anything faxed while I was out on vacation."

Ryan studied her. "What's wrong with the fax machine in the den?"

"Nothing." Anna rose and flicked off the television. "It's fine now. It was eating paper for a while."

That seemed to do it. Ryan propped himself on his crutches. "Let's head out and grab groceries. I'll even treat you to breakfast to celebrate your snow day."

"Sounds good." *Jake lied to me. Could Ryan be lying too? Were they both involved in this?*

"But we should get going before the weather gets worse. When we get back, if you want, I can help you go through Jake's books and see what else we can come up with."

"I think I can handle it myself."

Ryan's eyes narrowed. "You sure you don't want help?"

"Yep." Anna clung to her purse strap as if it could anchor her from the tornado of doubts tumbling through her.

Ryan glanced at his watch. "How much longer do you need to be ready to go?"

"Three minutes."

Ryan smiled and hobbled back down the hall. The clank of the crutches on the hardwood paused. "I know that means ten."

Should I say something about the fax number on the Christmas note? Maybe it wasn't Ryan. It could be anyone who had access to the fax. He's been with me. When would he have had time?

"Ryan, wait." Anna met him in the hall. "If I needed to send a fax, not receive one, could I pay and do it from your store?"

"Always." Ryan paused and turned to face her. "Why?"

"Could anyone?"

"Of course." He nodded. "We're a one-stop-shop. We do copies. Sell stamps, too. Wait a second. Did someone fax you from my store?"

"Never mind." Anna held up a hand. "I'll be ready to go in a minute."

Snow and ice crunched under the tires, jostling the SUV right and left. Streams of powdery wisps blew off the top of the snow mounds that lined the roadside. The plows had been out but still hadn't finished the main thoroughfares, let alone the side streets. They simply needed more time to clear the roadways. Thank goodness for four-wheel drive.

Anna pulled into Will's Restaurant and parked. "Let's eat breakfast first and allow some time for these roads to get cleared."

"Good idea." Ryan unclasped his seat belt. "I was just about to tell you to turn back."

"I wanna pick up what we need before the next wave of snow hits." There was no way she would be snowed in for days without coffee. She would kill someone.

Anna grabbed her handbag and followed Ryan inside. The blowing snow stuck to her hair and eyelashes.

The restaurant had six cars in the lot and even fewer people inside. A converted barn, the eatery held true to its origin with farm animal wallpaper and barn stall doors to enter. The table's pedestals were donned in jeans and cowboy boots as if half of a man stood under every table.

"Always wanted to know where the upper half of each cowboy's at." Ryan gestured toward the table legs with his crutch.

"Will's secret stew," Anna chided as the waitress met them at the hostess stand, all the while waiting for the underside of each table to twitch or break into a cancan.

"Hi, Ryan." The waitress's dark hair was scrunched into a hairnet, and she wore a black apron over jeans and a navy top. "How the foot feeling? Wait. Was it your foot or your ankle?"

"Hi, Nancy. Ankle. It's doin' okay. Good days and bad ones, ya know?" Ryan stepped forward.

"I do." The waitress picked up menus and walked through the dining room. Anna and Ryan followed. "I heard someone tried to break into your store, but you stopped them."

"Something like that." Ryan slid out Anna's chair. "Hi, Father."

"Hello, Ryan. Anna." Father Matthew sat at the table to their left.

"Hi, Father." Anna scooted her seat closer to the table. "How are you?"

"Thought he could come in here and pick up a gift certificate for the Sunday school's Chinese raffle and not have breakfast." Will Masters stepped out of the kitchen, a giant, obese man with a head full of wild, gray hair. "You believe that? Hi ya, Ryan." Will extended his hand.

Ryan shook it. "Hey, buddy. Good to see you."

"If I can't make a free meal for my priest, then what am I doin' here? There are some people ya take care of, ya know what I'm sayin'?" Will looked at Anna. "Hi, hon. Nice to see ya."

CHAPTER FORTY-THREE

Hon. If someone calls you hon in Potrage, they have no idea what your name is.

Will grabbed Ryan's shoulder, nearly knocking him off balance. "How's the leg, Rye?"

"Looks worse than it feels."

"Thank you for breakfast." Father Matthew stood and set his napkin on the table. "You didn't have to do that. And thanks for donating the gift certificate. If I'd have known you were going to feel obligated to feed me, I'd have sent someone else to pick it up."

"It's not obligation; I wanted to. It's the least I can do. I've got five kids and a great wife, all the blessings a man can ask for." Will began clearing dishes.

"Well, if you feel that blessed…" Ryan wiggled his eyebrows up and down.

"Not you. You're payin' double."

"Anytime I don't have to do the cookin' in this town, I'm happy to pay whatever." Ryan sat in the chair across from Anna and picked up the menu.

"Ain't that the truth." Will chuckled as he headed toward the kitchen, pausing to check on the other diners on his way.

Father Matthew reached in his pants pocket and pulled out a small wad of cash. He tossed a few dollar bills on the table.

The church. The church gives me money. Hush money?

"You okay, Anna?" Father Matthew slid on his black coat.

"Fine." She tried to shake off the unease.

"I need to head back to the rectory before those skies open up." Father Matthew pulled gloves out of his coat pocket. "Stay safe. I heard more snow is headed this way."

"Will do. You too." She smiled.

"See you Sunday." Ryan leaned his crutches against the wall.

Father Matthew paused, chatting with an elderly couple. Anna recognized the two from church but couldn't remember their names. Pretty bad since the man was an usher and greeted her every week.

The cold weather seemed to settle in her bones and chilled her from the inside out. Anna rubbed her arms.

Ryan set down his menu. "You cold?"

"Freezing."

"Here, order me the breakfast sausage and gravy." He eased back his chair and reached for his crutches.

"Where are you going?"

"I tossed an extra sweater in your back seat." Ryan tucked his chair in. "I'll be right back."

"I'll go get it." Anna stood and slipped on her coat.

"Nonsense. You're already frozen."

"Sit down. Besides," Anna held up her key ring. "I drove."

Anna hustled to her SUV and grabbed Ryan's sweater off her back seat. The cold singed her nose and ears. Her breath fogged as she powerwalked back into the restaurant. A gush of warmth hit her as she opened the door. She went in as Father Matthew walked out. She held open the door. "Try to stay warm out there."

"Doubtful, but what can you do? Wintertime in New York State, right? If you don't like the cold and snow, you're living in the wrong area." Father Matthew shrugged and walked past. "Have a good day."

"Find it?" Ryan called out when she entered the dining room.

Anna held the sweater high, smiling.

At the table, she removed her coat and added the extra layer. Perfect.

"I noticed you're always cold, and I figured you would need it sooner or later."

"Well, thank you." Anna ran her hand over the worn material. "Very comfy."

The waitress lifted the money off Father Matthew's table and stuck it in the front pocket of her black apron. The dishes rattled in the bus pan as she set it on the arm of the chair and wiped off the red-and-white checkered tablecloth. "Are you ready to order?" She replaced the salt and pepper shakers and the sugar caddy.

"Yep, ready when you are." Ryan folded his menu and placed it on the tabletop.

When the waitress came to the table, they ordered and passed the waitress the menus. Moments later, she returned with two glasses of ice water and a basket of toast. "The coffee's still brewing. It'll be just a minute. I made a fresh pot."

"Thank you." Anna sipped her water.

As she set the glass back on the table, Ryan reached for her hand. Her tummy flipped. *What if Ryan's sending me these notes?*

The door opened and a gush of cold air filled the drafty restaurant. Leo stood in the doorway. He regarded her and smirked. He winked and then joined his father and brother, who were already eating at the table nearest the counter. Anna hadn't even noticed Vince or John Adams until Leo reached their table.

Ryan gripped the chair arms. *Great.* The last thing Anna needed was a fight between Leo and Ryan, especially with Vince here to make a quick arrest.

Ryan pushed his chair back.

"Let it go." Anna reached across the table.

"He grabbed your throat." Ryan spoke through gritted teeth.

"You're gonna make it worse. Please. Let. It. Go."

Before Ryan had a chance to move, Leo lifted a white plastic to-go bag off of the counter and left.

The waitress brought out their food. An envelope was tucked under her arm. She set down the plates and then peeled out the envelope. "Ms. Greenan?"

"Yes." Anna already knew.

"I found this beside the cash register. Somebody left it for you."

Anna opened the note, read it, and then passed the paper across the table to Ryan.

"Nancy, we need to take the food to go." Ryan tossed his napkin on the table and pushed back his chair.

Anna was already sliding on her coat.

Chapter Forty-Four

The SUV was in four-wheel drive, but four-wheel drive didn't help on ice. The wind whipped even harder than it had before, as if trying to toss the vehicle off the road. Anna loved her SUV, but it wasn't very heavy. She gripped the wheel, trying to steady it.

"Do you know where you're going?" Ryan adjusted his seat belt.

"Left at the blinking light, right?"

"Left, yeah. I think it's the third street just past the dentist's office."

Anna pushed the button to turn on her hazards and glanced at the speedometer. Twenty miles an hour and, in this weather, it still felt too fast, but she had to get there. She had to know.

The food stunk up the car. Plus, Anna was starved, and the smell of sausage wasn't helping her forget she hadn't eaten.

Firehouse sirens tore through the air. Eleven fifty by the clock on the dash. There was no way that was the noon siren. Something happened somewhere.

Please let everyone be all right.

As they drove through the village, people poured out of house after house. Men and women, throwing on coats, half-dressed, getting in their cars—their faces frantic. What was going on? They couldn't all be volunteer firemen. Not this many. Anna's pulse whooshed in her ears.

When she reached the outskirts of the village, the wind gusted. White. Everywhere—a wall of white. Ann glided to a stop. She inched the SUV forward, knowing it wasn't safe to stand still, but she couldn't make out anything in front or around her. She crept forward, glancing in the rearview

186

mirror, hoping she wouldn't be rear-ended.

Red and blue lights pulsed through the whiteout ahead. Were they stopped? With the blowing and drifting snow, Anna couldn't be sure.

In the distance, more sirens howled.

The high school towered on her left and stifled the relentless snow and thunderous winds. Finally, she could see. A state police cruiser cut off the left lane. Traffic was down to single file. The building provided some protection for the row of cops and firemen standing in the street as they stopped each vehicle.

Anna unrolled the window when she reached the roadblock. "Everything okay?"

A volunteer fireman leaned in and checked her back seat and inside the back area with a flashlight. "Go ahead," he yelled and tapped the roof.

Streams of vehicles with flashing blue lights passed on the left.

"Holy cow." Ryan turned in his seat as her SUV crawled through the roadblock. "What's going on?"

"I don't know." Anna's stomach plummeted. More red-and-white lights filled her rearview mirror.

Anna navigated her truck onto where the shoulder of the road should be, but, with the snowdrifts, she couldn't be sure. They waited and were passed by another state police car and a county sheriff's vehicle. The officers stayed straight up Route 15. Anna was tempted to follow but also afraid of what she'd find if she did. Instead, she made the right onto Potrage-Bystander road.

The SUV's wheels skidded and churned up the winding, snow-covered road. Thick, unplowed snow blasted the windshield. Anna made her way up the hill, but if she had to go much farther, they wouldn't make it.

Out her window, Anna spotted a baby blue trailer. A gold number eleven dangled by its door.

On the eleventh day of Christmas, my true love gave to me 11 Potrage-Bystander Rd.

"This is it!" With the snow, she couldn't make out what was driveway and what was lawn, and she didn't want to steer into a ditch. She pulled as far off the road to the right as she could and shifted into park. It probably wasn't the safest place, but what choice did she have? She'd come too far to turn back now. Anna looked at Ryan's casted leg. "Why don't you wait here while I see if they're home?"

Ryan sighed and nodded, clearly reluctant but resigned. "Yeah. Okay."

The bitter wind burned her skin as she opened the door. Tucking her chin in her coat's collar, Anna trudged forward. She didn't know who lived here, or what to expect, but it didn't matter. She didn't even know what questions to ask when they opened the door, but she had to go. She had to try. Her hands and face stung, and her ears hurt. She made it as far as the wooden utility pole.

Oh. My. No. The sirens. The roadblock. It all made sense. Sick horrible sense. *No. Why? God, no.*

Ryan opened the vehicle's door and crutched to her side. "Anna! What? What is it?"

She looked into his eyes and then at the pole. His gaze followed hers. She watched his face contort in horror when he too saw the thrown-together, handwritten paper sign with the picture of the missing little girl. The paper had been stapled to the wooden utility pole. Its left corner flapped in tandem with the gusty wind, taunting her, waving away, as if to say you're too late. You've failed.

Anna pointed to the paper sign. "That's the little girl I told you about. The one from the park that day. The little girl I dreamt about."

Chapter Forty-Five

"Get in the vehicle." Ryan shouted to be heard over the wind. He pointed to the Equinox. "We have to help find her."

Anna couldn't move. Her arms and legs were numb. *There's no way. This can't be happening. This is wrong. Off. No.* "I was supposed to help her. She told me. What did she want me to do? What was I supposed to do? This wasn't supposed to happen. I was supposed to stop this."

"Let's go." Ryan tugged her toward the truck, muscled her into the driver's seat, and closed her door. He rounded the SUV and slid in beside her, already barking into his cell phone. Saying something about the sign, taking down and destroying the sign, searching for the girl in the park.

Secrets. More secrets. Or I will be a suspect.

Anna still didn't believe it. They were too late. Whoever had that little girl would kill her. *How did this happen? I saw her in the park. I shouldn't have let her out of my sight.*

Oh, God. The notes, the countdown. No.

"Anna." Ryan grabbed her shoulder and squeezed. "Listen to me. We have to help her."

Her legs shook. Then her hands. Her whole body trembled. "How? And what if we can't? What if we're too late?"

"I don't know." Ryan touched her cheek. "But we have to try. You need to get ahold of yourself. Count to ten. Pray. Do whatever you have to do, because there's a missing little girl out there, and we need to find her. Now."

Anna took a few deep breaths. He was right. She knew he was. She still couldn't believe this had happened. *I thought I had time. I thought I could protect her.*

"They must have search parties set up somewhere." Ryan clipped his seat belt. "Let's go. Are you okay to drive, or do I need to call someone?"

Anna exhaled. *I have to pull it together.*

"Answer me." Ryan touched her quaking thigh. "I need to know if you're okay to drive. If not, I'll get someone to come get us. Can you do this?"

"Yeah. I can do it." Anna turned the SUV around and headed back down the hill. Her cold hands were clammy against the wheel. Beads of sweat trickled down her sides. *I have to stay calm.* Panic would help no one. There wasn't much time.

Anna came back to the roadblock.

"Where do we go to help?" Ryan asked when the same firemen came to the window.

"Saint Andrew's. They're sending out volunteers to aid in the search." The fireman leaned against the SUV. His face was red, wind burnt, and his eyes had dark circles beneath them. "Do you know where it is?"

"Yeah." Ryan nodded. "It's our church."

"There are people there that'll tell you what to do." The man stepped away and motioned for them to roll by.

"Thanks." When they pulled through the roadblock, she glanced at Ryan. His casted leg jutted out with nothing but a sock on his open toes. "Should I drop you at home on the way? It'll only take a second. You can't go out and look anyway."

"Absolutely not. I may not be able to join the search, but I can stay, make hot chocolate, take calls, pass out blankets. They're gonna need the help. But you should go get gloves and a hat if you're planning on going out to look for her."

She was planning on it but didn't want to waste the time. *If I'm cold and scared, wherever this little girl is, she's just as cold and ten times as scared.*

A white van with red letters passed by. *Greyson County Sheriff's Forensic Unit.*

Oh, please let her be alive. Let them just be collecting evidence. No body, please, no body. They'd know soon enough.

Ryan touched her shoulder.

She made a right on Fair Street and then a left onto Church Road. Saint Andrew's Catholic Church was on the left. A handful of parishioners congregated in the parking lot, most looked puffy eyed, and a few carried wadded tissues.

Anna hoped the little girl's family wasn't here. She couldn't see that type of despair and not carry a part of it with her. Anna closed her eyes and tried to picture the child she dreamt of. The harder she tried, the less she could recall. *Help me. Please, God, help me.*

They made their way toward the church. The handwritten sign on the double door read, *volunteers to church basement.* She held the door open, and let Ryan pass by.

Underneath the sanctuary lay a gigantic fellowship hall with a gray linoleum floor, florescent lighting, and a bingo board. Scores of large folding table and chairs were set up. It smelled of stale smoke and even staler coffee.

Will, from the restaurant, stood at the podium in front of the unlit bingo board. He spoke into a bullhorn. "Team Yellow." His boisterous voice echoed through the basement. "Team leader, Sandy Goodstein."

Sandy of Sandy's Dry Cleaning stepped on the platform beside Will, and a bunch of people circled around them, holding yellow cards.

A system? How long has the child been missing? They just saw Will. In a town this small, he would have said something. Unless he hadn't heard yet.

Anna followed the steady stream of residents forward to the table marked registration. The waitress from the restaurant was seated beside two other young girls that Anna didn't know by name but had seen around town. One, she recognized, worked at Ryan's General Store.

"Hi, Ryan." Their waitress tapped her pencil on the folding table. "This is unbelievable, isn't it?"

"It is. How'd you beat us here?"

She jotted down his name, adding it to the volunteer list, and then looked expectedly toward Anna.

"Anna Greenan." Ryan stepped slightly forward.

The woman kept writing. "You weren't even out the door when Will got the call. He came right over. You guys were my last table, so I hopped in with him. You must've gone the long way."

"I guess," Ryan said.

She passed him a navy-blue card and glanced at his cast. "I'm assuming you aren't going out, but they need help in the kitchen." She looked to Anna. "When they call for the Blue Team, take the card I gave Ryan and report to the podium."

Anna nodded and stepped out of line so the person behind her could register.

Wow. This was amazing. Ryan handed her the card. Volunteer number one hundred thirty-two. There were only five hundred families in town.

"I'm going to go to the kitchen." Ryan made his way through the crowd. "Come see me before you go out."

"This is so..." Anna looked around. Everyone seemed to have a task. "Organized. I mean, I don't see any police, or anything. How fast everyone came together."

Ryan shrugged. "Practice."

"What?" She gawked at him. "What do you mean?"

"Ryan." The elderly man from Old Man Baker's trailer park tapped his shoulder. "They need you in the kitchen. Somebody started a small grease fire. It's out now, but they got a bunch of high school kids in there, and they need someone that knows what they're doin'."

"I'm on my way." Ryan followed behind him on his crutches.

"Wait a minute." Anna chased after him. "What did you mean practice?"

"This happened once before." Ryan paused and turned toward her. "A long time ago. Thank the Lord they found the girl, though."

A teenage boy came out of the swinging doors that separated the kitchen and the bingo room. "Kim just flooded the coffee pot. There are grounds everywhere. Can somebody come help us?" A group of students patted at something with towels. Smoke poured out of the gigantic double oven behind them.

Ryan shook his head. "I've got to go."

People moved around her. The air buzzed with the low hum of conversations. All these faces. Faces she'd seen a hundred times, but she didn't know anyone's name, just their face.

The little girl. She haunted her, and she would haunt her, regardless of the outcome.

Practice? This happened before? Anna couldn't believe it. Why hadn't she known about it?

Intrinsically, Anna knew every moment of these next few hours would forever be with her. A mental tape recorder switched on the moment she spotted the sign on that pole. The details might fuzz, and the faces would be forgotten, but she would remember this, like the way she remembered national tragedies or personal ones. Maybe it wasn't a tape recorder; maybe it was a mental camera. Will at the podium, Ryan in the kitchen, the young girls at the registration table. *Snapshots of hell. I should have gone to the police. Right away. This is my fault.*

An elderly woman handed her a tissue. "You okay, honey?"

She reminded Anna of Daisy. Petite with white hair in a winter-white wool suit dressed way too nice for Potrage. *Daisy. God, I miss her.* Another tragedy to add to the fast-forming list. *The reason Daisy died must be hidden in those notes. What other secrets do they hold? Four people murdered—how many more, and will their writer make an addendum if this child dies too?*

"Did you know the little girl?"

Anna shook her head. "No."

"My name is Elaine." The woman held out her hand, and Anna shook it. "You're Anna." She pointed toward the kitchen. "Ryan told me. He asked me to keep an eye on you. Nice boy. You lost your husband not too long ago."

"Feels like a lifetime ago." Anna's eyes stung.

"Gets easier." Elaine patted her shoulder. "Not better, just easier. Besides, Ryan's a keeper. He deserves a nice girl like yourself."

"Oh, we're not—"

Elaine raised her brows. Anna glanced at Ryan in the kitchen. He must have felt her gaze because he looked up, winked, and then went back to work.

"You're right," Anna said instead. "He's a great guy."

193

"Green Team, please report to the podium." Will's voice boomed.

Elaine glanced at the card. "You're Blue. You're next. It works like a rainbow. Red, then yellow, then green, see? They're sending them out ten minutes apart. Combing the town inch-by-inch." She glanced toward the exit. The glass doors at the top of the stairs looked like they had been spray-painted white. "I don't know how long you'll search for, but, with the snow, they won't let you be out too long."

"I was just saying to Ryan this seems so organized, and he said that this happened once before."

Elaine's eyes were wide with surprise. "Oh, it did dear. You didn't know?"

"No. How long ago?" Anna asked.

"Three years ago." Elaine shook her head. "I'm shocked you didn't hear about it? A nine-year-old girl went missing. It was all over the six o'clock news."

Chapter Forty-Six

"Here." Ryan handed her an orange, knit hat, and a pair of winter gloves.

"It was all over the six o'clock news." Anna gaped. *The notes. The clues in the notes.*

"What?" Ryan zipped up her coat. "It's freezing. Let me try and find you a scarf." He pointed at one of the teenagers hanging his coat. "Jason, can I use that scarf?"

"Sure, boss." Jason, a lanky kid with dark hair and glasses, passed his black scarf to Ryan.

Ryan took it and wrapped it around her neck.

"Ryan." Anna grabbed his sleeve. "A nine-year-old girl was taken three years ago from this town, and it was all over the six o'clock news."

"So? Oh." He stopped and stepped back. "Oh, the notes, I get it."

"Why didn't you tell me?"

"I never put it together." Ryan shook his head. "Why didn't you think of it?"

"I didn't know about it. It must have happened before we moved in. Those notes are—"

"Blue Team," Will bellowed into the bullhorn. "Blue Team, please report to the podium at this time. Blue team with team leader, John Adams."

Vince and Leo's father stepped onto the stage. This was the first time she had seen John not in a designer suit. He still bore the stains of money with his trim hair and manicured nails, but he camouflaged it with his puffy winter coat and snow pants.

Ryan grabbed her hand and squeezed.

Anna turned. "What?"

"I don't think you should go." Ryan's eyes were wide.

"What?" *What is he talking about? It's why we came here.* "I have to go." Anna turned.

Twenty or so people stood waving blue cards.

"Because of John?"

"Because my stomach hurts. Gut feeling." Ryan let go of her hand. "You, of all people, should understand that."

"Blue Team. Last call for the Blue Team." Will knocked on the wooden podium. "Please follow John to the buses."

"I'll see you when I get back." Anna tightened the scarf around her neck. Ryan's gut feeling or not, no way was she staying behind.

Ryan sighed. "Just promise me you'll be careful." He kissed her cheek. His unease spilled over and crashed into her. She could see it in his eyes, feel it in his touch, but she also knew, as he must, that she couldn't stay. *I have to find her.* "Promise me."

"I promise." Anna felt like the abominable snowman all bundled in winter wear. It wasn't until she followed the masses outside that she wished she had even more layers. The team loaded into the community home's vans.

"Listen up." Their driver stood in the aisle. A colossal man with plenty of weight to keep him warm. "We're heading to the fields off three sixty-eight. Stay together. Your team leader is in one of the two other vans and will give you directions when we get to the search zone. The high school lent us some snowshoes. On your way out of the van, grab a pair from the seat behind mine. Everybody know how to use them?" He raised his chin and waited. "May God bless you in your search."

"Amen," a couple of people muttered.

Some others nodded. One woman wept. Another prayed on her rosary.

The van lost then regained traction. The crunch of the ice mixed with gravel echoed through the metal floor. Anna sat behind the snowshoes and stared at the driver's navy headrest. The van was filled with people from church, or the deli, some from Ryan's store. No one spoke. The tension was palpable. The same, familiar knot developed at the base of Anna's neck.

The field off Route 368 took about ten minutes to get to in good weather. In this, it took over twenty.

When they arrived, the driver slid the handle to open the van's door, and John Adams boarded.

"Hello." He ran a hand through his wavy salt-and-pepper hair. "I'm John Adams, but I think everyone knows me." An understatement from the Prince of Subtlety.

"When we get outside, put on your snowshoes. Raise your hand if you need help, and I, or someone nearby, will assist you. Once we're all in our gear, I'll need you to form a human chain by holding hands with the people on either side of you. I'm not gonna kid you. The conditions out there are among the worst I've seen. We don't want to miss anything, and we don't want to lose anyone. With that wind and the temperature, we won't be out long, but we'll do what we can." With a somber nod, he headed out.

Anna followed the passengers down the bus steps and onto the roadside. The wind roared, and the snow whirled. Flakes stuck to her eyelashes. It hurt to breathe. The wind chill had to be below zero. Anna buckled her snowshoes and looked around for anyone needing help. No one did. She slid her gloves back on. Her fingers burned from the few moments in the frigid air.

Once everyone was finished, John Adams bellowed, "Ready?"

"Yes." Anna joined gloved hands with the men on either side of her. She had a hard time gripping their hands with the thickness of her gloves and theirs. The group trudged toward the field, the snow already knee height, with more pouring down. The wind gusted.

Someone tapped her shoulder, but when she turned, it was as if she stood in a thick cloud. Anna couldn't see anyone or anything but white. A minute or so later, someone tapped her a little harder. She turned just in time to see the person to her right let go of her hand and squish someone between them. Snow and sleet bit at her cheek. Anna looked toward her feet to avoid getting pelted.

Her new neighbor shouted toward her ear. "Hello, Anna."

Anna recognized his voice. "Hello, Leo."

Out of nowhere, John stood in front of her. He yelled something.

Anna couldn't hear over the howl. "What?" She yelled back.

"We have to go back," he screamed. The snow kicked up around him like a dust storm.

"No," She yelled back. "We just started."

"The weather's too bad," he shouted. "They're calling us back. It isn't safe. Turn around."

"I have to find her." Anna let go of the chain.

Chapter Forty-Seven

Anna plowed ahead, leaving the sea of people behind as they boarded the vans to head back to the church. She could *not* go back. They just started. *That child needs me. I have to find her.* The snow mounted, falling at least an inch, if not two, an hour. No one could see their hand in front of their face, let alone her plodding ahead toward the field. Anna headed toward the tree line. If she stayed against the trees, and only traveled left, the field would eventually spit her out by the salt mine and the main road. She could make it back home from there.

Anna used the trees to block the wind and keep her steady. The exposed skin surrounding her eyes burned like it was on fire. Her jeans were soaked and stuck to her thighs. *I should've planned better.* Anna pulled her scarf up and hat down so only her eyes were exposed. She wiggled her toes in her boots, but, after a while, she couldn't be sure if they wiggled or not.

Anna checked every branch for something, a scrap of cloth, a plastic bag, a piece of twine, anything that would make this search more than just the insane efforts of a crazed woman.

A crack overhead. Anna looked skyward. An evergreen slowly tipped toward her. *Noooo.* She froze. *It can't. Oh, God. Oh no.* Anna dove behind the tree base. Whoosh. An avalanche of snow flooded the field like raging water after a dam break. The evergreen zinged straight up, having dumped its load.

Maybe this wasn't such a good idea. The once knee-high snow now met her at her hips. The snowshoes were stuck and useless. She burrowed into the snow around her legs, and unbuckled the snowshoes, freeing her boots.

Anna glanced back over her shoulder and found nothing but white, swirling snow. *How far out am I?* Her teeth chattered. *What was I thinking? I should go back. Can I make it back? No, better to stay straight. At least I won't get lost this way.* Anna waded on. *Can't be much farther.*

Sweat beaded along her hairline. *First I'm cold, now I'm sweating.* Anna tried to wiggle her toes again but couldn't feel her legs anymore. *Am I still moving? Yes.* She leaned against a tree. *Just a second. I'll rest for just a second.* Anna sank into the snow and stared out. *Snow's an insulator. It's okay.* She could rest here. She'd be fine. Her eyelids felt heavy, and she closed them for a moment. Just a few seconds, and then she'd keep going. *One, two, three, four. On the first day of Christmas, my true love gave to me...*

Is that Jake coming for me? No. Jake is dead. Who is it? Dark hair. A man, definitely a man.

My true love gave to me a partridge in a pear tree.

Chapter Forty-Eight

The Messenger stood in the church basement as the Green Team poured in. Their search yielded nothing but red faces and frostbitten fingers and toes.

The young girl's parents looked up expectantly and deflated when no one met their gaze. Her father, a small guy with red hair and a thin beard, sat on the folding chair beside her mother and rubbed her back as she sobbed. His heart broke for them.

Each time he glanced their way, he relived what he went through a few years ago. The same search, the same basement, many of the same volunteers. The panic, fear, and frustration. All of it came back to him as if it happened yesterday. How could this have happened again?

He hoped it was a mistake. That the little girl was safe and sound and that she just wandered off somewhere, but he knew better. The monster still lived and worked and existed in town, and now the sin of his sister dug that much deeper.

Valerie had told him in his dream it wasn't over. Was this what she had meant? Signs from the dead? Insane to think, but...

Perhaps the town attracted evil the way some flowers attracted bees. Power and corruption were a fruitful soil.

He overheard many conversations but avoided being dragged into any of them.

"I guess they may call it off," one woman said. "They'll start back up after the weather calms."

The first few hours were pivotal. Who knew how long the child had been gone?

This marked the first time he'd met the little girl's parents. What a welcoming. The father had told a group of them what happened. The mother wept.

"Maggie, my wife, went into her room. A mother's intuition, right? We'd seen her just a few minutes before. Maggie went in, and our baby was gone. The window was open, and there were footprints in the snow, but, by the time the police showed up, they'd blown over like she vanished into thin air. I was watching football. Football..." The father choked up. His eyes misted, and his hands shook. He rocked. "Please let them bring her home."

The Messenger couldn't hear anymore. He excused himself and walked away like a coward.

Now, Anna was out there, searching. He stared at the clock on the wall, waiting for her group to return, and wished she hadn't gone. He knew he shouldn't have let her go. The final note would be delivered tomorrow, the day before the Feast of the Three Kings, but the notes seemed pointless in the current context.

The first Blue Team van arrived, and several people wandered down the steps. Each was quickly wrapped in a blanket and handed a cup of hot chocolate or hot coffee. Many were escorted to the space heaters to warm their hands and feet.

Cold air rushed into the basement as the second and third van loads poured in. Where was she? People pounded their boots on the throw rugs and yanked off their hats.

Moments later, John came down the stairs. He headed straight for him. *Anna. Where is she?*

"We're down one," John said.

Chapter Forty-Nine

Anna awoke on a cot. *Where am I?* A gigantic crucifix hung on the wall over the bed. Daylight streamed through a small window. Anna tried to move her arms and legs, but they were weighted down, tightly bundled under layers of blankets.

The door opened, and Father Matthew crept in. "You're up." He pulled a wooden chair over and sat.

"Where am I?" Anna forced herself up, leaning on her elbows. Dizzy and drained. She struggled to focus.

"The rectory." Something unsettling stirred in his eyes, in his voice. Her priest's normally calm demeanor had been swapped for a palpable tension.

Anna fought to remain calm, trusting her instincts while doubting her perception. "How'd I get here?"

Someone rapped on the dark, paneled door.

"Come in," Father Matthew called over his shoulder and then to Anna, "You don't remember? Leo brought you."

"Leo?" Anna flopped back, too tired to sit up. This was too much. "Did they find her? The little girl?"

Father Matthew looked toward the oak floor. "No."

Ryan stood in the doorway. "She's up?"

"Yeah." Father Matthew relinquished his seat. "Just awoke a moment ago."

"No, it's okay, Father." Ryan gestured toward the open chair. "You sit."

Father Matthew shook his head. "I have to go."

"Don't leave on my account." Ryan crutched into the bedroom and plunked down in the seat.

"I'm not, but there are things I must attend to." Father Matthew closed the door behind him as he left.

"It figures. The first time I leave your bedside, you wake up."

"What happened?" Anna kicked off the covers and sent an avalanche of blankets careening off the foot of the bed.

"What do you mean what happened? When you stepped away from the group, Leo followed you. He found you slumped against a tree. He carried you to the road and flagged down help. He brought you to the rectory since everyone in town was here, including Dr. Brennan."

What? Leo saved me? How could she not remember? "Is Leo here?"

"No. The winds calmed this morning, and he went out again to look for the little girl." Ryan used his good leg to scoot the chair closer.

"Morning? What time is it?"

"I don't know, but it's early. They gave you something so you'd sleep through the night."

"I don't remember any of it, being found, treated." Like a patient under anesthesia during surgery, time had just vanished. Would her memory come back, or had it just been erased?

"You were out of it but otherwise okay. Dr. Brennan decided to keep you here instead of sending you to the hospital. He's come by a couple times to check on you. Said you may have some blisters from the frostbite."

Anna loved their town physician. One of the few out there who would still make a house call to an elderly patient or give a free visit to a child without insurance.

Ryan picked the blankets up off the floor and set them at the foot of her bed. "By the way, I'm buying you a dictionary."

"What? Why?" Anna narrowed her gaze. Her skin felt stiff and dry, chapped by the cold. Her lips burned like a paper cut.

"Because you obviously have no idea what the word careful means."

"Either that or I don't keep promises." Anna inhaled a whiff of Ryan's cologne. She loved it—crisp and clean without overpowering. She could get used to that scent.

"It can't be that." Ryan fiddled with the edge of the top blanket. "You're still faithful to Jake, and he's been gone three years now."

She didn't know what to say. Was there anything to say?

His gaze searched her. "I thought you were gone." He hung his head and whispered, "I thought I lost you."

"I, um, I—"

"You just focus on staying warm." Using his crutch for balance, Ryan rose and hovered over her.

Anna's eyes stung. She didn't want him to leave. Not now. Maybe not ever. "Thanks for staying with me last night." *And all the other times these last three years.*

He brushed a stray hair from her cheek. "No problem." Ryan gazed at her with his crystal blue eyes and goofy, prairie dog necktie. He looked vulnerable and sexy. Something within her stirred.

Ryan leaned toward her, and an electricity rocketed through her. Time seemed to slow. She desperately wanted him to touch her, hold her. She pursed her lips. Ready. Waiting.

A knock ripped through the air, breaking the trance.

"Come in." Ryan's voice was a full octave higher.

Dora, the church secretary, peered into the room. "Ryan, Father Matthew asked me to come get you."

"Oh." A confused look crossed Ryan's face as he stood and smoothed out his khaki pants. His cheeks were as pink as a schoolboy who just got caught looking at a girly magazine. "What's up?"

"They've found a body." Dora swept a hand over her hair. "Not the child. Someone else. An adult."

Ryan shared a glance at Anna. "Who?"

Dora shook her head as tears filled her eyes. Without answering, she turned and left.

"You better go."

"I'll call as soon as I know something." Ryan lifted his crutches and headed out.

The door wafted closed, and Anna was alone again. *Why would Father Matthew ask Ryan to come? Could it be someone close to Ryan? Lord, please, help.*

Another dead body could be added to the list. At least it wasn't the little girl.

God, please help them to find her.

The fatigue was too strong and her flesh too weak. Despite wanting to stay awake, Anna sank back.

Anna didn't know how long she dozed but awoke to a neck ache. *I should get up. What time is it?* Her pillow felt like a sack of liquid concrete. She rolled on her side to fluff it. Something slipped off the side of the bed and smacked against the wood floor. Sliding her hand down the wall, Anna felt for and found an envelope. The twelfth day of Christmas. How could she have forgotten?

Chapter Fifty

"On the twelfth day of Christmas, my true love gave to me twelve flags a-flying, 11 Potrage-Bystander Rd., Ten Commandments broken, nine-year-old girl, eight ties a-binding, seven checks were written, six o'clock newscast, five golden rings, four people murdered, three years ago, two sets of books, and the reason your husband had to die."*

Holy cow. Anna flung her legs off the bed, sending the remaining comforters coiling to the floor. Her head spun. She was weak and tired but also knew darn well where the little girl was. The only place that flew twelve flags. The salt mine!

Someone had dressed her in a dry pair of sweats, or she had done it herself and the memory was lost along with the rest of last night. She spotted her jeans draped over the polished desk chair. They smelled like Murphy's Oil Soap, some transference from the too slick chair. She took off the sweats, slid the jeans on underneath, and then put the sweatpants over the top. This time she wouldn't be so stupid. She wouldn't go alone, and she'd wear layers.

Once bundled, Anna grabbed her cell phone and made her way down the maze of hallways to the adjoining church. At the windowed entryway, she glanced outside. To her surprise, the parking lot appeared empty. *What the heck?*

Anna heaved open the heavy church door and waddled down into the basement. Her legs felt like bundled cotton balls. A pair of older women cleaned the kitchen—one with stark white hair, one brunette.

"Where is everyone?" Anna's voice echoed.

"Ah!" The brunette clutched her chest. "You scared the be-gee-bees out of me." The sequins of her Christmas sweater sparkled in the dim basement light.

"Sorry." Anna spoke softer. "It's just..." The entire bingo hall was empty. The tables that once filled the floor were folded and placed on wheeled carts. The folding chairs neatly leaned in rows against the back wall. The floors looked mopped. The sterile stench of disinfectant permeated everything. "Everyone disappeared."

The woman with the white hair hung her head as she stepped toward Anna. Her sweatshirt read bingo or bust. "They found him, dear." She dabbed at the corners of her swollen eyes with a tissue. "He's dead, and he killed the little girl, too. He confessed to it all just before he died. The pig."

"Who?" Anna asked. This couldn't be right. *No. The little girl dead? No. Please. No.*

She didn't meet Anna's gaze. "Leo Adams." The poor woman seemed to deflate as she said it.

What? No. That made no sense. Leo would've had no plausible reason to save her if he were the killer. Unless she was headed to the crime scene. By bringing her back, he would've looked like a hero. No one would've suspected he... "Was there a body?"

"What?" the women asked in horrified unison.

"You said Leo confessed. Did they find the little girl's body?"

The women exchanged glances and shook their heads. "Not that we know of."

"Not yet." The woman spoke in a strangled whisper, hiding her face in the tissue.

The brunette stepped closer to her friend and rubbed her back. "I know." A tear tracked down her plump cheek. "We're happy to see you're awake. I'm Sally. This is Trudy. Ryan asked us to look after you until he came back."

"Nice to meet you both. I just wish it was under different circumstances."

"We do too." Trudy pinched her lips and pulled her shoulders back.

"This is unbelievable." Anna tried to process it all. The turn of events. Leo as rescuer. Leo as the killer. That child...

The women regarded her with sad eyes and even sadder smiles.

"I should go. Do you know where Ryan went? Did he say?"

"Hopefully, home to sleep. Poor thing was worried sick about you." Sally picked up a stray dishtowel off one of the tables.

Anna followed Sally's gaze to a wayward gum wrapper near the table's leg. Anna picked it up and tossed it in the nearby garbage can. "I don't think he would've gone home because Dora said Father Matthew was looking for him."

"I don't know. Father Matthew raced outta here a while ago. Took a big bag with him. Didn't even stop and say goodbye." Sally raised her chin, clearly in a huff.

"If you see either one, please let 'em know I'm looking for them."

The women nodded and went back to cleaning,

Anna pulled out her cell and dialed Ryan, but the call went straight to his voice mail. She couldn't bring herself to leave a message. She headed up the steps toward the exit.

Leo Adams? It can't be. Can it? Cold radiated off the glass doors. Everything outside was blanketed in snow. Anna spotted a snowmobile, and headed back toward the basement. "Any idea whose snowmobile that is?"

"Mine, dear." Sally stepped forward. She had to be at least eighty-five. "What? You surprised?" The look on Anna's face must have been uproarious because both women burst out laughing. The air itself seemed to lighten.

"I, ah—"

"Now, honey, what in the hell am I gonna do on a snowmobile?" Sally asked. "It's Will Peterson's, from Will's Restaurant."

"Oh."

"Why? You weren't thinking about going out in that stuff? Didn't you have your fill yesterday?"

"I had my fill. I'd like to check on Ryan."

"Here." Sally tossed Anna the keys. "Take it, 'cause I can tell there's no talkin' you out of it. Will left the keys in case we needed it." Sally opened her arms. "Look at us. What are we gonna do on a snowmobile?"

"Pop-a-wheelies," Trudy offered, and they chuckled again.

"You can't do a pop-a-wheelie on a snowmobile." Sally hit Trudy's arm with a dishtowel.

Anna knew this conversation would last for another twenty minutes so she nodded her thanks and excused herself.

"Helmet's on the back," one of them called to her when she reached the top of the steps.

Chapter Fifty-One

Father Matthew was nowhere to be found, and Ryan was missing too. *Are they together? And, if so, where?* Anna left voice mails for both. The battery on her phone was down to just a few percent. Hopefully, Ryan would call her back before the phone died completely.

She should've asked the women at the church where they found Leo and how he was killed. Or if he killed himself. It also would have been interesting to find out to whom Leo confessed and how many people heard him. Something didn't sit right with her. It seemed improbable that the Christmas messages and the missing child weren't connected, especially since she had been so sure she was right and the timing of it all.

Twelve flags a-flying.

Anna had to pass by the salt mine on her way home. Fool-hearted or not, she would have a look around. If nothing else, for her peace of mind. She'd come this far.

The snowmobile glided atop the wet, packed snow. Anna wasn't familiar with the many Potrage trails, so she navigated across backyards, up familiar streets, avoiding trees and the periodic above ground swimming pool or swing set. Thankfully, country lots were too big for many fences. The machine pulsed beneath her as it skated atop the snow. She gripped the handlebars and pressed forward, squeezing her legs against the seat to avoid sailing off.

When she arrived at the American Salt Company, the giant iron gates to the parking lot were closed. With Leo's passing, and the search for the missing child, she wasn't surprised to find the place deserted. She couldn't help but feel for the mine's owners, John and his wife. How awful to have to bury their son and to learn he confessed to something so horrible. One son a police officer. The other a criminal. How did that happen?

Anna checked the gate to make sure she couldn't pry it open far enough to squeeze through. Not a chance. Without a catapult, there was no way she could get into the parking lot.

On either side of the iron entry gates was a colossal ditch, like a moat without water. The drive leading to the parking lot gate parted the center of the ditch like an open drawbridge. Under normal conditions, she could never make it up that ditch's incline, no one could, but, with the several feet of packed-down snow, it was worth a shot.

She knew better than to traipse around to the sides of the property. Not too long ago, a cow got zapped and nasty editorials peppered the *Potrage Daily* for and against an electrical fence in Potrage. The cow didn't fare so well, and she wouldn't either.

Thankfully, the temperatures weren't as frigid as they had been. The morning sun warmed her cheeks as she trudged through the knee-high snow. With each step, she was able to stand on top of the packed snow for a split second before it crumpled beneath her weight. She hustled as fast as she could to avoid sinking with each step, missing the snowshoes she once wore.

At its edge, Anna realized the ditch was much deeper than she anticipated. No way would she be able to walk down. Even with packed snow, the angle was too steep. She plopped onto her butt and slid to the base of the ditch. Her feet careened against the other side. The impact jarred her ankles, knees, and hips. Getting up, she brushed the snow off the back of her pants as best she could.

The hill in front of her seemed to have swelled. The easiest part was over, and it hadn't seemed all that easy.

Anna padded her pocket, relieved to feel the cell phone, and trudged forward and upward. She used her hands, like a rock climber, for extra balance. The snow, at times, was as deep as her waist, and every time she stumbled, snow seeped into the top of her boots and the lip of her gloves.

The snow burned her skin like peroxide on an infected wound.

Breath clouds floated from her mouth as beads of sweat formed at her hairline and down the small of her back. *Just a little more, just a little...* And then she looked up. *Not even close.* Her thighs ached.

I have to help that child. Anna plodded on. *Twelve flags a-flyin. What if she's here? What if they're wrong? What if she's alive?*

Somehow, she made it to the top. Mountainous snowbanks had been plowed and pushed against the right side of the lot. The salt mounds were to her left, along with several aluminum pole barns that must have housed equipment. Outside of the plow markings, Anna didn't see anything to suggest anyone had been here later than closing time yesterday.

Anna walked over and rattled the corporate office's locked doors. Cupping her hands around her eyes, she peered inside. She spotted the receptionist's mahogany desk and the mammoth Christmas tree, but no security guard.

Oh, God. What if I'm wrong? Anna pulled off her hat and ran a hand through her sweated hair. *Twelve flags a-flying. I can't be too late. It can't be over. She can't be dead. Please, God. Please don't do this to me. To her.* Desperately, she yanked on the doors, and when they didn't give, she pounded on the glass.

Shoot. Shoot. Shoot.

Anna flopped against the building and sunk down, burying her knees in her chest, clutching her face in her hands. *Twelve flags a-flying.* This had to be it; she had to be here. *Oh, God. What if I'm wrong?*

Please. Please. Please. Help me know. Let me see.

Anna rocked back and forth. Where else could she be? It couldn't be over. She couldn't be dead.

Her cell phone chimed. *Ryan.* She slid her hand in her coat pocket, but when she pulled out the phone, she didn't recognize the number. "Hello." The phone beeped. Anna looked at the screen. Low battery.

"Hey, Priscilla." The King's resonant voice boomed. The phone beeped again. "I'm all shook up here. I got a lady standin' here sayin' she knows what those notes mean, and she says she knows who sent 'em."

Beep.

Anna's mouth felt dry. She forced herself up, leaning against the building.

Beep.

"Hello." The woman sounded timid. "I'm—"

Anna didn't have time for a long explanation. Beep. "Where is she?" Anna gripped the phone. Her heart thumped. She couldn't wait.

"Where's who?"

Anna spoke as quickly as she could. The words spilling out. "The little girl. Twelve flags a-flying. Where is the little girl the notes are about?" Beep. "Hurry. My phone is dying. The little girl. Where is she?"

"I...ah...I...I'm sorry." The woman stammered. Beep. "I didn't. I...I thought you knew. She's dead." Beep. "My daughter died a few weeks ago."

"What?" Anna almost dropped the phone. *No. No. Oh, God.* "How?" Anna choked out, barely able to breathe. Beep.

The woman's voice was hoarse, heavy with unbearable pain. "She overdosed."

Too stunned to speak, Anna's mouth hung open.

"The notes are about my daughter." Beep. "She was taken three years ago. Your husband—"

The line went dead.

"No!" Anna shook the phone and, when that didn't work, hurled it against the sidewalk. "Nooooo."

Anna tugged at the roots of her hair, trying to pry those woman's words from her thoughts. *She's dead. She was taken three years ago. Your husband. Oh, I thought you knew. The notes are about my daughter. She's dead...*

Your husband. Jake.

The little girl she dreamt of. The girl she saw at the park was just taken. Anna had been positive those notes had to do with her.

That woman in the church basement, what did she say? *This happened once before. A nine-year-old girl was taken. It was all over the six o'clock news.*

Oh, God. No. No. Oh, God. Anna was wrong. That little girl. She couldn't help her now. *I wasn't just too late. I was totally wrong.*

Anna looked to the dull, gray sky. *Why, God? Why did I see those things if I couldn't stop them? All things happen for a reason. What reason could there be for this?*

214

It felt like a sick game. *Look, look and see what I can do, and there isn't a thing you can do to stop it.* When The King called, she thought it was an answer to her prayers. The King had found answers and she'd finally know the meaning of the notes.

Now, Anna wished that prayer had gone unanswered.

Her chest tightened as life itself seemed to be torn from it. *Breathe*, Anna reminded herself, and felt dizzy and impotent. The week before last, she sat helpless and watched the very moment Daisy's heart broke. *Is Daisy somewhere taking her turn watching mine now?*

Anna wanted so badly to help that child. To help her for the many times she couldn't help the rest. Jake, Daisy, even herself. How could she let Jake go to work that day? That still, small voice said, tell him to stay, but Anna silenced it. She's had to live with that. At least with Jake, there were places to shift the blame. No seat belt, driving too fast, bad roads, black ice. Now...murdered...maybe. This child was innocent, and the only person that could've helped her was looking the wrong way.

A gust of wind smacked her face. Her ears stung, and she pulled her hat back on.

Anna glanced at the useless cell phone. Wiggly lines crisscrossed the phone's screen. The phone died before she had all the answers. *What else did this woman know? Who was she? Why would I dream of a child before she's kidnapped if I wasn't meant to help find her?* The notes and this new kidnapping had to be related. It came down to a matter of faith, and Anna had faith in what she dreamt, faith in what she felt, and faith that this wouldn't end this way. It couldn't. Could it?

Anna needed to get to a phone to call The King back. Heading back the way she came, the wind bit her cheeks. She stuck her hands in her pockets and tucked her chin in her collar. When she finally returned to the edge of the ditch she'd come through, she stopped. The canyon seemed so much bigger from this side, and Anna doubted she possessed the strength to scale it again.

Smoke rose in willowy puffs from a chimney toward the back of the property, and Anna turned and headed toward it, having no idea how she'd pass through or fly over an electrical fence. *There has to be a way. Trains full of salt get out. I will too.*

Anna never realized the enormity of the salt mine property until she walked it, and this was a small fraction of what went on underground. Several neighbors sold their mineral rights, and, while everything seemed calm on the surface, machinery gutted the ground beneath. An entire underground world existed, a world most would never see. A reality not too far from the one she was living in.

She's dead. She was taken three years ago. Oh, I thought you knew. The notes are about my daughter. Your husband.

The words like a mantra ran through her thoughts.

The woman could be wrong. She could've misunderstood. But even as she thought it, Anna knew better. *Who was she?* The King said this woman knew who sent the notes. Anna needed to find out what else this woman knew.

The even terrain ended, and Anna stumbled through the snow-covered field, the mountains of salt and towering gates behind her. Cars hummed steadily, passing along the bustling New York State Thruway below.

On the other side of the thruway, farther downhill, Anna spotted the houses. The Adams' personal property, the father's estate flanked by both sons', sat in a semicircle around what was probably some gaudy monument. The infamous Rolling Hills. The smoke signal from their home puffed gray clouds into an even grayer sky.

A phone. Anna needed a phone.

She glanced over her shoulder. *Should I go back the way I came? Would that be easier? Closer? No. That hill would be too much. This way may be farther, but she wouldn't have to scale the giant ditch.*

Anna spotted the train tracks that carted away the salt as she muddled her way down toward the thruway.

She's dead. She was taken three years ago. Oh, I thought you knew. She's dead. Your husband.

It kept her going.

As she came to the outskirts of the property, Anna thought about the

Adams family. Even from this distance, she could see their back windows and many vehicles parked in their driveway and on the street in front of their home. She imagined condolences expressed and tears shed. Today, they lost their youngest son. A tragedy no parent should ever have to face, not even the parents of a monster.

That little girl had parents as well, and their hell had just begun. Anna thought about the child and the vision, tied to eight stakes. The dream—when the little girl asked for her help, she listened and heard the sound of her soft, sweet voice. Anna listened so hard, so intently, and heard something else. Didn't she? Anna tried to recall. She hadn't remembered until this moment. Something that drowned her out, something similar to the hum of the thruway in front of her. Similar, but different. The sound of wheels rolling on metal. A car on a metal bridge or...

And then it came to her. So obvious, so encompassing, she thought the knowledge of it might swallow her whole. The sound of a car on a metal bridge or a train on a track. Anna turned, looked toward the salt mine, and saw what she had missed.

Chapter Fifty-Two

Anna followed the train tracks around the salt mine property. Running now, her clothes soaked, the layers hung like sandbags weighing her down, holding her back. The winter air singed her lungs. Snow adhered to her eyelashes, and her nose leaked. She kept going up the hill, hugging the tracks, up to the place.

Anna had spotted the dilapidated cottage countless times on her way to work. Visible from the New York State Thruway, she passed it every day without so much as a second thought. Not anymore. Now and forever, she would always be cognizant of where it was and what was in it.

Hold on. I'm coming. Not too late. Please, let me get there in time. Help me, God. Please. Help me.

Anna's right foot snagged and sank. She flung forward, tripping. Her hands, elbows, and knees flopped against the frozen ground. "Augh!" Pain tore through her, up from her ankle, burning. Unbearable. She tugged her leg, but her right foot was caught in some type of hole. Her entire leg throbbed. She looked away as her vision blurred. It had to be broken. Her whole body started to shake uncontrollably. *No. No. No.*

She hoisted herself up onto her wobbling arms and used every piece of life she had left to heave her leg out of the burrow some animal had dug. Pain rolled through her, even worse than before. Her eyes leaked, and her mouth quivered.

Anna stood and dragged forward, half-running, half-stumbling. She was close. Too close to stop.

The stench of decaying wood permeated the air. Flakes of brown paint peeled off the cottage exterior. The front porch had caved in long ago. Every window was smashed or missing and replaced with black tarp or graffitied plywood. A rotted door dangled on its hinges, a two-inch gap on one side, flush to the porch on the other. A dim light danced inside. It pulsed in sync with her pounding heart.

Her stomach fluttered as fear mixed with hope. Anna flung her body forward. She climbed the dilapidated steps, one at a time. With each stair, more pain, more tears, her right leg almost lame.

Anna burst in the doorway, fell, and smashed onto the ground. A candle that must have once lit the room sailed off the table and landed near her as the door flung shut.

Darkness. She listened and waited.

One.

Two.

Three.

Four.

Anna strained to hear, listening for something, someone. Anyone. Anything. No one moved. No one breathed.

Blood pulsed in her leg, as pain rang in her ears. It was dizzying, nauseating. Anna peeled off her sopping gloves and ran her fingertips across the floor. Sharp splinters poked her hand, but she found nothing else. Anna breathed deep. Mold. Must. Decay. Death. Sweat and urine. Sweat and tears.

The wind roared, and the walls shook in tandem. She forced herself up, half-crawling, half-dragging herself back to the door she'd come through. Anna flung the door open with the tip of her boot. The outdoor light blinded her. She had to squint to see but could hardly believe her eyes. The one-room cabin was empty. A kitchen area stripped of its cabinet doors had empty beer cans and bottles strewn everywhere. A stained and lumpy mattress lay on the floor to her left with used syringes beside it. Near the doorway, a rickety table with a rusted, folding chair.

No other rooms.

No place to hide.

No missing child.

An empty, open, rotting, wretched space.

How can this be? She has to be here. The candle that fell rolled away from the door, pushed back by the biting wind. It banged off the baseboard and stopped. The wind howled. And then, silence.

"Hello. Anybody here?" Stupid to call to an empty space, but she had been so certain. How could this be? How could she have been so wrong? Anna's chest burned as her heart broke for that child, for her family.

Chapter Fifty-Three

Anna's foot grazed a black duffel bag tucked behind the open door, blending with the shadows. She sat on the chair and yanked the bag toward her, tearing it open. Clothes: men's pants, shirts. Anna tossed them aside and kept digging. Her fingertips grazed something hard, cold, and metallic. A gun. She snatched it and set it on the floor beside her, surprised by the heaviness of it.

A soft, almost imperceptible muffle. Anna's hair stood on end. A groan. She was in an empty room but somehow wasn't alone. Goosebumps prickled her arms. It sounded like an animal, soft and high-pitched. She reached for and found the gun. Where was the noise coming from?

Anna whispered, her voice throaty. "Anybody here?" She scanned the walls for a secret doorway, even though her rational mind knew it wasn't possible. The rafters above her provided no loft, attic, or crawl space.

Thump. Thump. Faint. Outside, maybe. Anna hobbled toward the porch and stuck her head out. Thump. The sound was quieter. *What? How?* Thump. Softer now, definitely softer. Anna scooted inside. Thump.

Anna laid down and pressed her ear against the cold, wooden flooring. Wisps of her hair slid across her face, grazing her nose. Thump. Louder. Underground. Thump. Louder still. Thump. She peered between the buckling floorboards.

The child from her dreams stared back, unmoving, unyielding. A terror so real, so pure, reached up from the base of Anna's being and filled every ounce of her.

She used the butt of the gun to strike the wooden floor. Each whack reverberated up her arm all the way to her shoulder. She didn't care. She had to get to her. Bang. Bang. Bang. She smashed the rotted floor. Splinters sprayed, but the wood wouldn't give. "It's okay. You're gonna be okay. I'm coming."

Time seemed to stand still. Anna pounded and pounded, wishing she were stronger, praying she was strong enough.

Finally, the rotted plank buckled. Anna tore at the floor. She pulled and tugged the planks away. Her forearms stung. Splinters dug into her palms like thorns. "I'm coming. I'm coming. Oh, God. I'm coming." *Oh my God.* The stink of fecal matter and urine overwhelmed her.

Her shock was soon overthrown by horror.

The little girl lay tied to eight stakes—two per arm, two per leg, spread out on the dirt floor. Her mouth gagged. Her hair matted. Her clothes dirty.

Tears streamed from Anna's eyes and fell onto her chest. "It's okay." It wasn't okay. It would never be okay. Anna dove into the pit, landing hard against the dirt bottom. Her bad leg stung.

The child's gaze didn't waver.

"I'm here," Anna squeezed out. "You're safe now."

Anna scurried over, her back pressed against the underside of the floor above. She gingerly tugged on the gag until it hung around the child's neck like a perverse scarf.

The child coughed, gagged, and licked her lips.

Anna yanked the rope that bound the little girl's right arm, but it didn't give. The top of the stake was far too wide to slide the rope up over it. Anna readjusted and tried to hoist the stake out of the ground, but it didn't move. Anna's hands trembled as she fumbled with her keys, trying desperately to sever the rope, but the rope was too thick, and Anna's hands shook too hard. *I don't have time for this. Whoever left that bag will be back.* She searched for and found the gun and set it within arm's reach.

The child's legs trembled, but she still didn't speak.

Anna touched the child's cheek. "I'm getting you out of here. Do you hear me? I'm getting you out." As Anna said the words, the child began to thrash her head back and forth, back and forth. Anna grabbed her face and held it steady. A spider crawled across the little girl's forehead. Anna knocked it off. "I'm getting you out. *Now.*"

Anna squat-walked back to the gap in the floor. She stood and found herself even with the floor above. She spotted the candle and looked at the candleholder for anything sharp. Nothing. She glanced back. "I'll be right back."

"NO!"

"I have to cut the rope." Anna pressed up. Her arms barely held her. She slid back onto the floor above and looked around. Nothing. Maybe a table leg. Something outside? She couldn't leave. The floor was torn up. He'd know. If he got here first, he'd move the little girl. Or kill her.

The door slammed shut, and Anna screamed. Her fingertips stung as adrenaline rocketed through her body. Black again. The only light came from the gap under the door. Anna stopped and waited and listened. The house rattled. *The wind.* She exhaled. *Just the wind.*

Something had to hold that door open. She made her way to the table and dragged it across what was left of the floor and propped it against the door. When she did, something slid off the tabletop and landed by her boot. Matches—a whole box of them.

Thank you, Lord. Thank you. Thank you.

Anna snatched them and the duffel bag and scampered back in the hole, landing on her good leg, but her pain didn't matter anymore. She had to work fast. He was coming. She knew it. She could sense it.

Anna struck and lit the match and burned each tie, using her soaked gloves to tamp out the smoldering rope ends. Match after match lit. The smell of sulfur soon replaced everything else. She worked quickly. *Almost done. Last one.* "Can you walk?"

The little girl whispered, but Anna couldn't hear anything over her pulse thundering in her ears.

Anna leaned closer. "What?"

"We can't go." The child spoke louder and with obvious effort. "One more girl's down here."

"What?!" *Oh, God. Where? How?* Not thinking, Anna struck another match and scoured the floor bed. In the shadows, she made out a faint shape.

Anna grabbed the duffel bag and shoved it along the ground. "There are extra clothes in here. Put them on." A single unused match remained. Even if she lit the box the matches came in, it wouldn't be enough.

The candle!

Anna glanced at the little girl she had just freed. Pink marks etched the corner of her mouth. Her ankles were rubbed raw from the rope. She had slid on a worn, black sweatshirt and was peeling away what was left of the ties that had bound her wrists and ankles. "I'm gonna lift you up and into the cabin. You run to the door, get me the candle on the floor, and toss it to me. Do *not* go outside, and scream your head off if you see anyone coming, okay?"

Before Anna had an answer, she lifted the little girl out of the pit. The child raced to the open doorway, grabbed the candle, and flipped it to Anna.

Anna waited to strike the final match until she was tucked underground for fear the gusty wind would blow it out. Anna lit the candle and covered the flame with her palm as she moved toward the shape. Thump.

Anna whirled around to find the little girl had jumped back into the hole with her. Anna would've preferred to have a lookout but understood that she may be too scared to be alone.

In the warm light, Anna spotted the side of another child. Cobwebs, like feathers, swept across Anna's cheeks and forehead as she scampered closer. Anna recognized her immediately. Ashley Grey, the little girl taken from the mall a few days ago. Dried rings of blood covered her wrists and ankles. Ashley was pale. Very, very, pale. Her tiny chest rose and dropped. *She's alive.*

As Anna lit each bondage, she passed the burning candle to the little girl, who now knelt beside her. The child instinctively cupped the flames, protecting it against any draft. Anna tapped out the smoldering rope, thankful for her saturated gloves. Anna moved as fast as she could, burning rope after rope. Outside, the wind roared, and the rickety cabin door rattled.

Ashley was unconscious. Unconscious, but alive. As Anna finished tamping out the final tie, the little girl kneeling beside her stood with additional clothes for Ashley in one hand, the handgun in the other.

"Thanks." Anna quickly grabbed both. She slid the sweatshirt on Ashley, threading her limp, tiny arms through like she was dressing a doll. Anna put a pair of big, white, athletic socks on her tiny feet. The thick cuffs hid the rope still wound around her ankles. Anna stuck the gun in her pocket and tried to stand, but faltered. *We have to get out of here. Now.*

Ignoring the shooting pain from her leg, Anna stayed hunched over, her good leg shaking, her arms burning with the weight of the frail child. She was careful not to bang her head until she found the opening where the floorboards had been ripped away.

Anna hoisted the child up onto the floor above and turned back for the little girl. The very sight of her went through Anna.

The little girl looked up at Anna, and the child's eyes glistened. "It's okay. You're safe now."

The child reached out so Anna could pick her up. Her small face felt ice cold against Anna's cheek. The little girl wrapped her tiny arms around Anna's neck so tight Anna thought she'd never let go. And Anna wanted to stand there and hold this little girl and never let go, but he was coming. They had to hurry.

"Rose." The little girl whispered into Anna's collar just before Anna placed her on the floor above.

"What?" Anna stopped and clung to her a second longer.

"My name is Rose," the little girl said.

Anna pulled her away from her chest and peered into her face. "I'm Anna."

For the first time since she had found her, the little girl smiled. "I knew you would come." Rose rested her head against Anna's chest. "I dreamt of you."

Chapter Fifty-Four

"Ready to run?" Anna placed Rose on the floor above.

The child nodded as she brushed off some of the dirt and dust from her face.

Anna's arms quaked as she hoisted herself up and out of the pit. She painted on a happy front, knowing Rose watched her every move. "Ready?"

"Yeah." Rose's gaze locked on Ashley.

"Let's go." Anna nodded.

Rose waited, silhouetted in the doorway, while Anna bent and lifted Ashley. The breeze lifted the skirt of the snow behind her. Like Ashley, Rose also wore too-big, white socks without shoes. If her sneakers were somewhere underneath the cabin, they'd have to stay there.

Now that Anna stood upright, Ashley felt weightless in Anna's arms. "It's okay. You're safe now. I've got you," Anna repeated over and over as they made their way off the unsteady porch and into the uneven, snow-covered field. "It's okay. You're safe. I've got you. It'll be okay." Anna's leg no longer hurt, or if it did, she no longer noticed it.

The gun clattered against Anna's right leg with the solemn rhythm of a war drum. Anna hobbled as fast as she could down to the thruway. Rose, a few steps ahead, running, rolling, running again. *Go. Run. Go.* Every step was a step closer.

"Anna!" someone screamed behind her.

Her heart clenched. *No. No. No.* She kept hobbling.

"Stop," he screamed again.

Rose froze, a few yards in front of her, staring blankly at the thruway below. Cars zoomed past. Anna could smell their exhaust. They were close, more than halfway there. Close, but not close enough.

"Anna," the voice cried out again. "Stop."

Water ran onto the snow as feet pounded behind them. People were coming from the salt mine. Anna turned.

"Anna," Ryan called again and moved fast on his crutches, keeping pace with Father Matthew and John.

Anna looked back at Rose. The ground between her legs was yellow.

"Wait up," Ryan yelled as the three men came down the hill toward them.

In one motion, Anna shifted Ashley to her left, grabbed the gun, and wielded around to face them. "Stop!" She glared over the top of the revolver. "No one move."

John and Father Matthew threw their arms up.

Ryan just stared at her, mouth agape, eyes wide. "Anna?"

"Don't move." Anna's voice wavered; the gun didn't.

"You told me to come." Ryan stepped toward her. "You called me. You left a voice mail."

Rose stepped beside her and huddled against her leg.

"Not one more step." Anna cocked the gun, and Ryan froze. His face contorted in confusion.

She glanced down at Rose. "Let's go."

The child didn't move.

"Run."

When the child still didn't move, Anna pushed on the hammer of the gun until it clicked, stuck the gun in her pocket, and half-carried, half-dragged Rose with her other arm. They stumbled as fast as they could down to the thruway below. Nothing about running with a loaded gun, carrying kids seemed safe, but Anna had no other choice.

At the bottom of the hill, Anna positioned Rose against the guardrail as far from the busy thoroughfare as possible. "Do not move."

Rose seemed as conscious now as Ashley, entranced by whatever, or whoever, she saw on that hill. Anna glanced back. Father Matthew was speaking to John. Ryan just stared at her.

Brakes squeaked. Anna turned toward the thruway and saw taillights amidst a cloud of exhaust. A white Ford Fusion pulled off the shoulder. "You need help?" A young woman got out. She was college-age, and her tied-up, brown hair blew like a horsetail behind her.

Anna nodded and carried Ashley toward the waiting car. "We need a hospital." She glanced back at Rose. "Come on, sweetie. You're safe now."

Rose got to her feet but didn't take a step forward.

Anna loaded Ashley in the back seat and ran back for Rose. "We need to go. Your mom and dad want to see you."

Rose took Anna's extended hand and followed her.

Anna squeezed into the middle of the back seat, and Rose climbed in after her. Anna clipped both girls' seat belts. Rose stared out the windshield. The color that had drained from her face on the hillside still hadn't returned.

Anna glanced back at Ryan and was startled by a bright light. The car rocked; its windows rattled. Debris rained onto the hood and roof.

Snow slid in pockets down the hill, upheaving the ground and dragging it down too. Orange flames licked the lifeless sky. Thick black smoke danced above the fire.

The cabin they'd come from exploded.

Chapter Fifty-Five

"Holy crap!" The driver clutched her chest.

Nails dug into Anna's thigh. Rose's knuckles were white. Anna pulled her tight. "I'm here. You're safe."

Anna scanned the hillside for Ryan, Father Matthew, and John. All three lay sprawled across the ground, flung from the explosion. When she saw each man move, she yelled, "Drive!"

"But, but... There are—"

"Drive."

The woman whipped the car around in the first available median, and they headed south on the 390 toward the hospital. Every time the driver glanced in the rearview mirror, she seemed to press harder on the gas pedal. The speed limit was sixty-five; the needle hovered near ninety. "My name's Mary." The driver seemed to speak more to the kids than to Anna.

"Mary, I'm Anna. Thanks for the lift."

Mary met Anna's gaze in the rearview mirror, and Anna understood the woman's horrified expression. When Mary spoke again, her voice sounded strained. "The least I could do."

Anna looked at the goosebumps on Rose's skinny forearm. Her thin, flannel shirt and white socks were soaked. Anna leaned over the front seat. "Can you turn up the heat?"

"It's as high as it'll go." Mary adjusted the vents. It did little good.

Anna peeled off her drenched coat and sweater. She patted the sweatshirt underneath. Semi-dry, yet, still drier than anything Rose wore. Anna slid it off and covered up the little girl. Anna knew she should remove the child's wet clothes but couldn't bring herself to do it.

Ashley flopped forward, and Anna pulled her against her chest, placing an arm firmly around each of the girls.

Whoever did this was on that hill. Anna knew by Rose's reaction and by the sick pit in her stomach.

Ryan. Rose probably didn't see him. She heard him, and that was enough. *No. How? He was with me the entire time. It didn't fit. But if not Ryan, then who? John and Father Matthew both hadn't spoken, and Anna hadn't noticed Rose turn around to look at either of them.*

Besides, I called Ryan. I told him and Father Matthew where I was. They needed John to get onto the property. That's why they were there. It fit, and it didn't. John Adams? Father Matthew?

The explosion. Someone else? How else could it have happened?

Sirens sounded in the distance.

Rose's teeth chattered, and she quivered. Anna could only imagine what she'd been through—she and Ashley both. Rose knew who did this. She had the answers, but Anna couldn't ask the questions. This child has been through so much; Anna didn't want to make it worse. Although, she had to admit, she didn't know if she could.

Anna's thin T-shirt was drenched in sweat. She could smell her own stress and sweat. *It's almost over.* They made a right onto Osiano Street, the hospital dead ahead. The red lettering stood out against the brick façade. *Almost there.*

"I left that candle burning." Rose stared at the empty meadow, seemingly still hypnotized. "Underground. I left it there."

"The wind blew it out." Anna leaned as the driver made the sharp right toward the E.R. entrance.

Rose's gaze fixed forward. "He's gonna be real mad."

"He can't hurt you anymore." Anna pulled her closer and hoped it was true. "You're safe now."

The car careened into the circular drive, brakes squealing. A female nurse took one last drag before stomping out her cigarette. The locks clicked, and Anna threw open the back door.

The nurse stepped forward, as if to be sure, and whirled inside the hospital's automatic double doors. She screamed orders, and two residents in green scrubs bolted out with a stretcher. Several other nurses and a doctor followed. A security guard was already barking orders on a phone in the entryway. Another stretcher. More people. Ashley's door opened. A young man reached in and felt her neck for a pulse. "How long's she been unconscious?"

"I don't know." Anna's throat tightened. *Please, God, let her be okay.*

He unbuckled her seat belt, gingerly lifted the little girl out, and loaded her onto the first stretcher. Her arms and legs flopped like a ragdoll's. In seconds, the unconscious child was whisked into the safety of the hospital.

Rose's fingernails dug into Anna's arm. Her eyes wide, her mouth hung open in terror.

"It's okay." Anna's eyes stung. "They're here to help you."

Rose tightened her death grip.

A young doctor swung open the other door. Police sirens wailed, and flashing red and blue lights cut through the blowing snow.

"Nooooo." Rose screamed and kicked. "No! No!" Tears poured out her eyes. She reached up and clung to Anna's neck.

The doctor pried the child's hands free and lifted her to his chest. "I'm not going to hurt you."

"Anna!" Rose's guttural cry tore through the air.

"I'm coming too." Anna slid out of the back seat, and Rose dove toward her, but the security guard stepped between them. Rose screamed.

"Anna." The doctor nudged the security guard with his shoulder and nodded. "Come on." He said something to Rose, placed her on the stretcher, and motioned for Anna to follow. "She's the local girl that was taken," the doctor noted when they got into one of the triage rooms inside. The doctor was young, in his late thirties, early forties, with dark skin and hair. He checked Rose's wrists and then placed a stethoscope on her chest as he watched the wall clock. "I'm Doctor Hauper. Doctor Wilder is with the other child. Where'd you find them?"

"Cottage by the salt mine."

Rose appeared so tiny and helpless as two nurses hooked her up to monitors.

"We're having a female physician come down to examine them." He looked toward Rose and mustered a smile. "And we're giving her something to calm her nerves."

An even younger man in green scrubs stepped into the room and whispered something to the doctor.

"Excuse me." Doctor Hauper stepped out into the hall.

The medicine took effect as Rose drifted in and out. The machine beside her beeped.

Anna took her tiny hand. *Please help her.*

"Anna," the doctor returned to the room. "They need to ask you some questions." He gestured toward the hall. "I'm sure you understand."

A beautiful woman, not much older than she, with red hair and hazel eyes, looked at Anna and then at the floor. Even without the uniform, Anna knew she was a cop. She had a controlled intensity that bubbled beneath the surface. This woman had seen the worst in humanity, and Anna doubted she blinked. The investigator met her gaze, and Anna nodded.

Doctor Hauper touched Anna's shoulder. "Her parents are on their way."

"Perfect." She leaned toward Rose and whispered, "I'll be right back."

Rose opened her eyes and clutched her hand. "Don't go."

"It's okay. Your mom and dad will be here any second." Anna brushed a hair from Rose's forehead. "You're safe now."

"But you're not." Rose closed her eyes. "I told you. I dreamt about you."

Chapter Fifty-Six

Anna rested her weary head against the seatback in Jenna O' Riley's police cruiser and focused on the steady hum of the tires rolling on concrete as the cop drove her home. The clock on the dashboard read eleven, but it felt much later than that.

Together, with a few others, Officer O' Riley had asked Anna more questions about the last few days than she thought combinations possible.

"You're awfully quiet." Jenna made a left into the village of Potrage. "Tired?"

"Beat." Anna touched her leg and winced. It might not have been sore before, but it was making up for lost time now. The X-rays didn't show a break. The doctor claimed it was just a mild sprain.

"You think you're sore now. Wait 'til tomorrow." Officer O' Riley made a right onto Whispering Pines.

"It's gotta be broke. This hurts too much for a sprain."

"A sprain can be worse than a break."

"It feels like it should be amputated."

Jenna laughed. One of the few lighthearted moments they shared all night. In different circumstances, Anna could see her and Jenna being fast friends, but not now.

A Toshiba laptop sat between them. Anna spent some of the night answering questions while a different laptop told the room whether or not she was telling the truth. The computer's stress voice analyzer was similar to a polygraph, but without the wires and was admissible in New York state court, or so the officers had said.

During the CVSA part of the interrogation, she was only asked about a half dozen questions or so. Maybe a few more. The first was her name. She spoke as clearly as she could into the microphone. Then Officer O'Riley asked her to lie.

"The sky is green. True or False."

Anna said true, and the machine apparently picked up the stress in her voice. The next couple of questions verified some of the details Anna had given to the police. The final two cut right to the heart of the matter. "Did you kidnap Rose or Ashley?" "Do you know who kidnapped Rose or Ashley?"

They never asked her about the Christmas notes, and Anna opted not to tell them. First and foremost, she didn't want to get in trouble for not reporting them. She wasn't sure of the legal ramifications for withholding evidence if they were evidence. Even though she could never have been certain the notes and the kidnappings were connected, she suspected enough to follow the clues to the salt mine. That alone might be enough for her to be considered culpable.

Plus, The King said he found someone, and the notes didn't mean what Anna thought they meant. She needed to talk to the accountant about what he learned. Until she had answers, she was staying silent.

Ryan must have stayed quiet too because they never asked Anna about the notes. Not even when she was speaking to the truth machine. Luckily, the police couldn't ask what they didn't know about. So, for the moment, she was free.

Anna just wanted to get out of there and get to Ryan. The police said the men on the hill were all okay, but she had to see him to be sure. *Please, God, let him be okay.*

Anna had explained her search of the salt mine property by sharing her dream about Rose and recalling the sounds of a train on the tracks. When asked why Anna didn't call the tip line, Anna simply asked, who would have believed me?

Officer O' Riley told her afterward Rose corroborated everything Anna said, even the fact they'd dreamt of one another. It seemed everyone was so desperate to believe in a Christmas miracle faith usurped reason.

"This is it." Anna pointed toward her driveway as Jenna turned into it. Gravel crunched. The house was pitch black. *Where's Ryan?* "The men on the hill. I know they weren't hurt, but do you know if they've been released yet?"

"Yeah. They were done questioning them a while ago. Your boyfriend said you called him and said you knew where the girls were. Gave his investigators the same spiel about bad dreams or visions, and well... "

"You don't believe me?" Anna studied the officer.

Jenna had an athletic build, the demeanor of a pit bull, and the face of a weather girl—all three personalities probably coexisted in an equal rotation. Jenna's red hair was slicked back in a tight bun. Anna could tell by the flyaway wisps that Jenna shared Anna's battle with naturally curly hair.

"I don't know what I believe." Jenna slid the gear shaft into park and returned Anna's stare. "I'm just glad the girls are safe and reunited with their families."

"Me too." Anna stepped out of the car.

"Wait." Jenna got out and walked in front of the headlights. "I'm coming with you."

Anna met her at the front bumper, and they headed for the house. "I'm assuming the girls are being protected." Anna climbed the porch steps, using the railing to bear the weight her ankle could not. She unlocked the door, reached in, and flipped on the porch light and interior lights.

"Yep. We haven't got a lot out of 'em yet. Ashley's conscious but still weak. She's badly dehydrated, and they want us to wait a couple more hours. Rose is talkin', but she still hasn't given us a name. There are some prints on the gun."

"Mine." Anna flicked on the living room lamp. Surprise fluttered through her as Jenna had drawn her weapon.

"Your prints, sure, but we're hopin' maybe some of the perps too. Lab work isn't back yet." Jenna must have recognized Anna's unease. "I'm sure you're fine, but, just in case, I'm gonna check things out. We've got a car on its way."

Anna rested on the arm of the club chair. Standing on her sore leg took more out of her than she cared to admit. "I think he was on the hill."

"That's what you said." Jenna went from room to room through the main floor, turning on lights, opening doors. "We looked hard at your boyfriend and his buddies, but we just didn't see it. Everyone had an alibi, and we even showed their photos to Rose."

Where the heck is Ryan? My cell's been dead for hours. Maybe he's calling that.

"Let me check the upstairs." Jenna vanished up the steps. When she came back down, she seemed a lot more relaxed. "All clear."

"Thanks." Anna forced a halfhearted smile.

"I'm gonna head out. Like I said, we'll watch the house, but I really think you're fine." Jenna headed for the door but paused just short. "Get some rest, but we may need to talk more tomorrow."

"Yeah. Fine." Anna shook off the knot in her stomach.

"Good night. Lock this behind me."

"I will." Anna stepped closer and held the door open. "Keep me posted."

Light glinted off the side of the Potrage police patrol car that had pulled in and parked in her drive. *The cavalry has arrived.*

Jenna stepped off the porch and walked to its passenger window. Anna closed and locked the door behind her.

A chill rolled through the living room from the dose of outside air. Anna checked the thermostat—still seventy. Unable to kneel, Anna twisted up old newspapers and hunched over to shove them into the fireplace. She lit one, touched the kindling, and the fire took. No matter how tired she was, sleep would evade her, especially not knowing where Ryan was and who he was with. Maybe the warmth of the fire would begin to push out the coldness of the world.

Lights swept through the great room as Jenna pulled out of the driveway.

Anna's stomach continued to turn over. She pulled the front window's drapes closed. The Potrage P.D. sat planted in her driveway. *It'll be okay.*

She limped to the kitchen. A red light on the phone stand blinked. *Ryan.* Anna picked up the cordless and dialed her voice mail.

"You have three new messages," an automated voice said. "Message one—"

"Priscilla. It's me, The King. Your phone cut out. I keep getting your voice mail. If you get this, call me back." He rattled off the number. The King knew who sent the notes. "I'm at—"

The line went dead. She pressed the talk button again and held the phone to her ear. No dial tone. Was it plugged in? She checked. Yes. Anna replaced the phone in its cradle. *What I wouldn't give for a working cell phone.* Anna had a newer cordless phone in her bedroom. Occasionally, this older one gave her trouble, especially when she left it off its base too long, but the other always worked.

She hobbled upstairs. Thank God, the officer left all the lights on and the doors open. Once in her room, she picked up the receiver.

Nothing.

Her heart beat harder. Movement. *No. Can't be.* Anna slowly turned toward her open closet.

Suitcases. Three of them neatly stacked against the back wall.

They weren't hers.

Next, the lights went out.

Chapter Fifty-Seven

Black. Pitch black. The moon hid behind the clouds. Anna strained to hear. Nothing, but he was in the house, and Anna felt him like an arthritic man could feel the rain.

She had to get out of this...out of here.

Anna traced the outline of her bed with her palm until she met the nightstand. She peeled open the drawer and pulled out the heavy-duty, steel flashlight. As fast as she could, she raced to the bedroom window and shined the beam at the police car window. Anna flicked it on and off. S.O.S. *Please, help me.*

"The car's empty," a voice said from behind her. Anna jumped but didn't turn. Sweat prickled her hairline. Anna knew the voice, but fear thwarted recognition. She clutched the weighty flashlight. Its beam lit her feet. She froze, willing herself to face him but somehow paralyzed to do so.

He strode toward her in even, methodical steps. Closer now, against her back. His hot breath flittered against her neck.

Now.

She swung the flashlight in the direction of his face. It hit hard, and the impact reverberated up her arm into her shoulder.

He fumbled backward into her chest of drawers. Glass shattered as framed pictures careened against the ground. The flashlight sailed out of her hand and smashed against the wall, its light moving in uneven sweeps. Anna scampered over the bed. The comforter slipped beneath her hands and knees.

He dove toward her but landed to her right. His weight forced her up and out, and she rolled onto the ground. She darted up and bolted out the door, limping, then running, then limping again. Pain tore through her as something slammed against the small of her back.

She felt for and found the railing and scampered down the steps. The fire in the fireplace blanketed the downstairs in an orange, dancing light.

His footsteps pounded behind her.

Pain seared her scalp. Her head jerked back, and she saw the ceiling as he ripped a fist full of her hair. Her fingers groped the wall. She yanked a sconce from its nail. Anna flung it over her shoulder. It found its mark as her head freed. She raced down the remaining steps into the living room.

"Stop!" His feet pounded behind her.

Pain rang through her shin as Anna's calf clipped something. "Ah." Her legs sailed out from under her. She flew arm over arm, stumbling forward. She crashed onto the floor. Stingers bit her elbow and hip. Momentum flung her, sliding on her side, across the floor. Her ears exploded as her head collided with the bookcase. Her vision blurred, and a copper taste filled her mouth.

"It wasn't supposed to be this way." The dim, orange glow of the fire made him look like both demon and man.

Vince Adams lumbered toward her. The badge on his Potrage P.D. uniform flickered in the fire's twitching light. His right cheek was swollen and discolored, and a thin line of blood ran from his temple to his chin.

Her mind could hardly wrap around it. She almost didn't believe it, but it made sense. Sick, eerie sense. Vince kidnapped the girls. Leo's older brother. The man who was supposed to protect and serve.

The tip of the black gun pointed at her face. "You surprised?"

"Not surprised, Vince." Anna forced herself to a seated position, feeling nothing but a terrible sense of foreboding. "Just disgusted."

"Did you find the bags I packed for you?" He smiled a sick, sadistic smile. "You should have left them in the cabin." He lowered the gun and stepped toward her. "Now, you have to *leave*. You ran to escape justice. Clearly, you knew where the girls were… Of course, your trip's ticket is one way, but only you and I know that."

"Kind of like your brother Leo." Anna willed herself to stop trembling but couldn't. She met his gaze.

He was close now, towering over her. She gritted her teeth and stayed focused, unwilling to give him the satisfaction of turning away.

"Just like my brother, Leo. The evidence we'll find against him will be heartbreaking for our family." He took her chin in his hands and yanked her up.

Anna thought her head might pop off like a dandelion top.

Once she was on her feet, his moist lips pressed against her cheek. "Don't you see, Anna?" he whispered. "She was my redemption. You took that from me." He let go of her face.

She cringed. "She's a child. You sick pig." Her neck snapped, and her face stung. Instinctively, Anna stepped backward, clutching her cheek in her hand. Blood pooled in her mouth. Her ankle throbbed.

The fireplace warmed the back of her legs. "Where's Ryan? What did you do to him?"

Vince sneered but said nothing as waves of grief and anger washed over her.

No, God, no. Please. No.

Her expressions must have betrayed her.

"Poor Anna. They say to love and to lose is better than to never have loved at all. Tell me. Is it true?"

Fury consumed her. "I will kill you, you animal." Anna glanced over her shoulder.

There. A log, balanced on the burn pile, half in the fire, and half out.

Flickering lights danced around the front draperies. Someone may have pulled in. Vince must have noticed too and stepped toward the window to check it out. His gun trained on her. He peeked around the drapery.

Anna lunged and grabbed the burning log. She thrust it at him like a spear.

Vince screamed as the blazing end of the wood log rammed against his gut. His clothes caught fire, and Anna swung for his face. Vince flung his arms and knocked the wood from her hand. It rolled onto the carpet, tiny flecks flying like a pinwheel.

Anna tried to reach for the log, but both sides blazed now. Small flames sprang up all around it. The sofa lit. The drapes caught.

Vince charged at her and snatched the sleeve of her unbuttoned sweater. Anna twisted fast and slipped free. She stumbled into the end table, grabbed the lamp, and hurled it toward him. She missed.

The stench of burnt clothes, flesh, and fibers mixed as smoke and flames filled the room. Anna hobbled for the door, dragging her leg, moving as fast as she could.

"Stop!" Vince screamed, and she knew without turning he had drawn his gun.

Chapter Fifty-Eight

The front door flung open and smashed against the wall. Anna hit the floor. Her ears rang as gunshots exploded through her living room. Anna curled in a ball on the floor, covering her head. *No. No. No.* More gunfire. Sirens in the distance. Her house burned around her. The heat was dizzying. So loud. It was so loud. Anna buried her head. Too afraid to think, to pray.

"Get out." Somebody pulled her up by her shirt. "Get out," Jenna O' Riley said again. "Let's go."

Anna looked back at the living room. Vince lay on the ground. Gray matter spilled around his head. The stench of death was squelched by the smells of the fire. Anna dry-heaved, her home ablaze around her.

She made her way to the door, looked, and doubled back.

"What are you doing?" Jenna O'Riley yelled and bolted after her.

With all her strength, Anna dragged her grandma's desk away from the flames. She had to get it out. Had to save it. Jenna raced over and lifted the other end. Together, they carried it out of the house, off the porch, and into the driveway.

A cat meowed. The cat. *Oh, God. I forgot the cat.* Anna moved toward the house, but Jenna stopped her. "Your cat's there." Jenna had to yell to be heard over the roaring fire. She gestured toward the flower bed. The cat crept out. It meowed again, apparently annoyed that it had wasted one of its nine lives.

Anna ran over, picked it up, and buried her face in its fur. "Thank God you're okay."

The fire took everything else.

Chapter Fifty-Nine

Anna read somewhere that it took a long time for a house to burn. She guessed her home was the exception to the rule.

"How'd you know?" she asked Jenna as the Potrage Fire Department doused what was left. Jenna's face and clothes were covered in soot. Anna followed her away from the house, where it was slightly quieter but no less chaotic. The sirens fell silent, apparently giving up. Anna had done that fifteen minutes ago.

Another sheriff came and took the cat, put him in a neighbor's carrier, and set the carrier by the tree behind them. Another draped her in a blanket. An EMT shined a light in her eyes and listened to her chest with a stethoscope.

"Really." Anna forced a smile. "I'm fine."

Jenna touched the young man's shoulder. "We're all set."

The medic took the hint and his bag and stepped away.

"How'd you know?" Anna tugged the blanket tighter. Her breath wafted in the bitter, winter air. "The prints?"

"No. We put a uniformed guard outside Rose's room. Her reaction was... Let's just say there was no misinterpreting it. I started to think. The gun he could have snagged at any arrest and kept it. Leo died today, but his brother was back at work tonight? Come on. And it's not like coming from that family he needs the money."

Anna shook her head. "Of course."

Another sheriff's car pulled in her driveway.

Ryan slid out of the passenger's seat. "Anna," he screamed.

Anna dropped the blankets and raced into Ryan's open arms. Tears leaked from her eyes as a sob burst from her chest. "You're all right. I thought you were gone. I thought he killed you."

For a while, neither of them spoke. They just stood in her driveway and clung to each other. Anna promised herself she would never let go.

Ryan softly kissed the top of her head over and over. "Thank God you're safe."

Eventually, Ryan's grip on her eased. "I love you so much."

Anna took a half-step back and had to look up to meet his gaze. "I love you, too."

Ryan's face and chest were covered in grime, and it took Anna a moment to realize the filth had smudged off of her. Ryan crooked a hand under her chin and gently kissed her lips. She balanced on her tippy toes and kissed him back. The heat between them was hotter than any fire.

Chapter Sixty

O fficer Jenna O' Riley cleared her throat. Anna peeled herself from Ryan's embrace, even though she didn't want to. Ryan draped an arm over Anna's shoulders as she nestled against his chest. Safe. Loved. Grateful.

"Sorry." Officer O' Riley's smug grin said she was anything but.

Anna couldn't help but like Jenna, with her fire-red hair. The same color as the peppers on the Chinese menu that marked the spicy dishes. Fitting.

A walkie crackled, dragging Anna back to her circumstance. "I can't believe Vince did this. I don't know why. I just...I guess because I thought for sure the kidnapper was on that hill, based on Rose's reaction. She literally peed where she stood."

"Vince was on the hillside, but he wasn't standing behind you. He was tucked inside the bushes to your right. That reminds me, I wanted to ask. Rose mentioned a door in that cellar. From what I could decipher, it sounded like a walkout. Did you notice anything like that?"

"I didn't, but it was dark, and I was focused solely on getting those girls out of there. I don't know that it was high enough, though."

"From what I could piece together, Vince blew up the cabin with the evidence and hid until he could blend in with the investigators on the scene."

Ryan exhaled. "Of course. I bet that's how he cold clocked me at the store that night. He beat the paramedics to the scene."

"It could've been so much worse than a headache and a broken ankle." Anna glanced up at Ryan. *Thank you, God.*

Ryan pulled her to his chest and kissed the top of her head. "It's over now."

To Jenna, Ryan said, "I can never thank you enough for coming back tonight. You saved her."

"Oh, gosh," Anna gushed. "You did. Thank you." Anna's cheeks burned. How could she not have thought to say thank you?

Jenna shook his head. "Listen, I've got a lot to do. I'm going to let you guys get back to…*reconnecting*." Jenna's smirk returned. "I'll give you a call in a day or so." Jenna looked toward what remained of Anna's house. "Do you have your cell?"

Anna shook her head and motioned toward the house. "Just one more thing I'll need to replace. Time for an upgrade anyway."

"She'll be at my place." Ryan rattled off his home and cell phone numbers. Jenna jotted them down.

"I'll be in touch." Jenna slipped away.

"Good night," Ryan and Anna said in unison.

Anna looked at Ryan. "You don't mind putting me up for a while?"

"Well," Ryan grinned. "There's only one rule."

"What's that?"

"No firearms." He beamed. "You looked mighty tough on that hill, pointing that gun at me."

"Oh. Sorry about that. I…I… Rose was so—"

"Anna." Ryan stepped back. "I'm kidding."

"Look at the bright side." She shrugged. "I don't have a lot of stuff. Just a desk." The cat meowed in the carrier behind her. "And I'm keeping your cat. We've sort of bonded."

"Sounds good to me."

"You don't mind?"

"No. I hate that freakin' cat. All it does is complain. I couldn't understand why you brought it in the first place."

Anna laughed.

"O'Riley said you guys are gonna need a ride." A sheriff, who looked like he should be asking someone to the prom not protecting the citizenry, came over. "Your place, right?" The officer nodded at Ryan.

"Yep."

The sheriff gestured toward his police cruiser. "If you two will follow me. Oh, and they're making arrangements now to bring you your desk."

"Oh." Anna sighed. "Thanks. It was my grandmother's. I just…I guess it meant a lot more to me than I realized."

"No problem, ma'am. You saved those girls. It's the least we can do."

Anna bent and picked up the cat carrier. "You ready?" she asked the cat. It meowed.

Ryan was a step ahead.

"Hey, Ryan," she called out.

He stopped and turned, balancing on his crutches.

"What's its name?"

"What?" Ryan asked.

"The cat." Anna hobbled toward him. Ryan on crutches, her limping, they had to look like quite the match. "I just thought of it. You never told me the cat's name."

"Mickey." He beamed.

Anna halted. "You named your cat after the world's most famous mouse?"

"I thought it would be…ironic."

The cat peered out the gate of the carrier.

Anna lifted the carrier to her face. "I get it. No wonder you complain so much."

She sat in the squad car and stared at what was left of her house. The house she and Jake had built. The home which had been her sanctuary, her hiding place.

Anna squeezed closed her eyes and leaned her head against the seat. An entire spectrum of emotions drummed through her, but one beat louder than the rest. More than anything, she felt free. Free to start over, free to live, free to just be.

Free from everything, but the notes, and that freedom, was just a phone call away. She needed to call The King.

Chapter Sixty-One

A s soon as Ryan slipped into the shower the following morning, Anna picked up his phone and dialed.

The King answered after the first ring. "Hey, Rye. Good timing."

"It's Anna. I'm borrowing Ryan's phone. Mine's sort of out of commission."

"I figured 'cause I've been callin' and you didn't answer and didn't call back." The King sounded winded. "I didn't know if you weren't gettin' my messages or what. But if I didn't hear back today, I was just gonna head home. What happened?"

Too anxious to learn the answers, Anna didn't want to explain the whole saga. Not yet anyway. "My phone's shot. I need a new one. But...hey...you said you know what all the notes mean and who sent them. I figured some of them out. Like twelve flags a-flyin' meant the salt mine. And...well...I found the girls."

"Look it. There's a lady here. She let me camp out on her couch last night while we waited for you to call me back. Your timing couldn't be better 'cause I was just about to walk out the door."

"Your message said she knows what the notes mean."

"Yeah. Let me let her tell you so I don't screw it up. She says she knows who sent you those notes. You're gonna flip. Just wait. Here."

Shuffling came from the other end of the phone.

"Hello." A woman's voice filled the line. "This is Bonnie. We got cut off yesterday."

Anna clutched the phone. "I found them. I found the girls that were missing."

"What missing girls?"

Anna fished through her soot-covered clothes, piled in the laundry basket, and pried the twelfth day of Christmas note out of her jeans pocket. "The ones that the notes were about."

"No. I'm sorry. I think you're mistaken. They weren't about any missing girls." Bonnie sighed. "They were about my daughter."

"I don't know about that."

Bonnie inhaled and made a wheezing sound. "If I could go back. I would've never... You have to believe me."

The women's tone was filled with a regret so heavy, Anna could almost feel the weight of it. She wasn't sure what this lady was going to tell her but already recognized this call would be one she wouldn't soon forget. "Maybe you should start at the beginning." Anna plucked a pen out of the pencil can and took a seat on one of the chairs at the kitchen table.

Ryan came into view, his hair wet and messy. He wore jeans and a white T-shirt. "Who's on the phone?"

Anna flagged him away.

Bonnie started to cough. The sound made Anna shutter. Some people were so ill you could hear it. It seeped out of them like puss from an infected wound.

"Are you okay?"

When Bonnie spoke again, her voice was phlegmy. "Yeah. Fine." She cleared her throat. "I'm not proud of what I've done. If I could go back... But. I can't. Three years ago, my daughter, Valerie, was walking home from school. She...she was jumped by four guys, Vince and Leo Adams, Tommy Peters, and Darrell Hartman. She knew Vince. He was her crossing guard and got in the car with 'em." Bonnie coughed again. She sounded weak, as if retelling the tale sucked the life out of her. "They took her to a field off Route 368. Teasing and taunting her, that sort of thing, but then Vince started tying her up. I guess the Hartman boy got upset and left. Tommy went after him. But they both left her there. Vince tore her clothes and started to..." Bonnie's voice cracked. "He took horrific photos of her. Bad. And left her there. Tied eight ways. We searched for days. The story of her

There was an official speaking with the merchant at the head of the line. These border officials received a new title every few years, but last Alexander remembered they were called Trade Custodians.

There was a table by the gate with a large book on it. The custodian on duty was a tiny ball of a man, who bounced up and down on his heels as he argued with the merchant before him. The subject of their disagreement was…

Alexander leaned in to listen…

…Arabian brewing beans? Alexander furrowed his brow. What on Earth were Arabian brewing beans?

"I'm sorry," the official was saying. "But here we've readopted the religion of our ancestors and are now worshiping the twin gods Dythis and Areti. We do not drink the brew of Islam."

"I'm a Christian and I drink the brew of Islam!" the trader objected. "Everyone should be drinking the brew of Islam! Muslims make good brew!"

In the end, the trader was refused passage and walked back along the road swearing under his breath.

The second trader was caught smuggling a skeletal hand. He claimed it was the hand of Saint Valerian, a priceless relic. The custodian was a bit skeptical because he had already confiscated at least eight hands belonging to St. Valerian from other travelers. So the second trader was also denied passage.

It seemed the Kalatheans were not admitting many visitors today. Fortunately, Alexander's cart neither contained suspicious Islamic beverages nor the skeletal remains of saints. Two Kalts and a fugitive were all he had to be concerned about.

One of the guards motioned for Alexander to come forward. When the trade custodian saw Filbert and Florian he sighed deeply.

"More Kalts?" he grumbled, and then looking at Alexander he asked, "And where are you from?"

"Where am I coming from now, or where am I from originally?" Alexander asked.

"Both," the man answered.

21

The Brew of Islam

Alexander should have been terrified. The stronghold that marked the Kalathean border was in sight. It was an impenetrable fortress that arched across the roadway. Guards patrolled all around it, and archers watched from the towers to make sure no one slipped past.

It was forbidden to bring weapons of war into the country. At least, it had been when Alexander was king. All blades had to be shorter than the traveler's forearm.

Alexander and his two companions each had a broadsword hidden in a secret compartment built into the bottom of the wagon.

The border guards weren't likely to do a thorough search unless they had reason to be suspicious. Of course, if they recognized Alexander as a wanted murderer that would be plenty of reason.

So much could go wrong. Alexander was on the threshold of certain doom, yet he felt a sense of peace and purpose. As strange as it was, he was also excited. This was his home and these were his people.

They took their place in the line of merchants waiting for admittance. There were only two carts ahead of them. Under the circumstances, Alexander shouldn't have been surprised by this, but he was used to seeing long lines of visitors waiting at these checkpoints.

20

Bite-y Sting-y Things

Three days later, they rendezvoused with Filbert. His castle was only half the size of Erkscrim, really more of a manor house with a wall around it. Alexander couldn't help but wonder how Filbert agreed to such an arrangement.

They stayed there two nights, resting and preparing themselves for the journey ahead. Filbert's wife was a soft spoken person—an odd contrast to Filbert. Despite Florian's story, she didn't seem to bear any ill-will toward him. In fact, the few times they interacted, it was almost like the incident that pained Florian so deeply in the retelling never happened at all.

Alexander was eager to continue. Now that he'd made up his mind to return, he didn't want to delay. They traveled all through the summer and into the fall. Though it was a wearisome journey, Alexander found it fascinating seeing the changing landscapes and exploring the villages they passed through.

The twins, though foolish when it came to philosophy, were wise in the ways of the world. When they encountered others, on the roads and in the villages, they instinctively knew who was trustworthy and who wasn't. When they sensed a change in weather, they knew whether to chance proceeding or not. Though they drove Alexander to the brink of insanity on more than one occasion, he had to admit that he would have been lost without them.

The weeks dragged on as they pressed forward. Alexander began to think they would never arrive. But as they moved farther south, the landscape changed. The lush forests gave way to rocky hillsides dotted with shorter greenery. The sun grew brighter and Alexander felt a strange nostalgic happiness wash over him.

One morning, he woke to the sensation of something crawling across his blanket directly over his chest. They were camping a short distance from the road.

He opened his eyes to see Filbert and Florian both standing over him with horrified expressions. Filbert had his blade raised and Florian was holding his arm whispering: "Don't, you'll kill Alexander."

"What's crawling on me?" Alexander grumbled, though he suspected he already knew.

"It's a crab demon with a catapult stinger on its rear!" Florian hissed. "Don't move!"

Alexander rolled his eyes. He gripped his blanket and sat up slowly, allowing the enemy to slide into his lap. Then he took the lamp from beside him and crushed the crab-demon to oblivion. Filbert and Florian made a horrified gasp with each blow.

Alexander took the flattened remains by the tail and held it up for the twins to see. He couldn't help but smile as they shrunk backward.

"This is a scorpion," he explained. Considering the twins were somewhat well traveled, he was surprised they hadn't encountered one before. Then again, scorpions avoided humans when possible.

"What happens if it stings you?" Filbert asked.

Alexander widened his eyes in mock horror.

"Heaven forbid!" he exclaimed. "You might end up with an itchy swelling on your arm! Even warriors such as yourselves couldn't bear it!"

The horror faded from their faces. Filbert lowered his blade.

"You're hilarious," Florian remarked. "Any other demon creatures you forgot to warn us about?"

"Let me think," Alexander began. "Lots in the sea, on land just the scorpion. Oh, and the rock viper. Hides in the brush, the bite is lethal. So don't step on it." He yawned, tossed the scorpion aside, and pulled the blanket over his head. "Other bugs I think... I dunno."

"Why on Earth do you want this kingdom?" Filbert complained. "It's full of bite-y sting-y things!"

"Don't bother them, they won't bother you," was Alexander's muffled response.

Though it was a warm day, Filbert and Florian both decided to wear their boots. (Several villages back, Alexander traded his for a pair of sandals.)

As they packed their things and started on their journey, Alexander warned, "There is a creature in Kalathea far more lethal than the rock viper."

Filbert and Florian glanced at each other apprehensively.

"It won't wait until you step on it to strike. When it's made up its mind to kill you, it will hunt you down, pursuing you with an endurance only hatred can supply. It has killed more Kalatheans than all other beasts combined. I, myself, barely escaped it as I made my way to Kaltehafen for the first time."

Filbert and Florian's expressions were of both horror and intrigue.

"What is this creature?" Florian asked. "When we are through with reclaiming your kingdom, we should hunt these animals and bring their heads back with us to Kaltehafen."

"I'd rather you didn't," Alexander replied. "If you are going to hunt humans, hunt your own subjects, not mine."

Alexander's point did not ease the twin's fears of the various "bite-y sting-y" things that lurked in the wilderness around them. They became the subject of his endless mockery as they carefully scanned the road and double-checked their campsites before lying down. It was nice to be the instigator of mockery for once as opposed to being the subject.

Alexander had the good fortune of stumbling upon a harmless rat snake one day, which he slipped into Florian's blanket while he was sleeping. He might have felt guilty about the anxiety that he induced, if Florian hadn't taken vengeance by seizing him, and throwing him into a lake.

After several more weeks of travel, the twins began to realize that nature did not have a personal vendetta against them and their precautions became more sensible and less paranoid.

Then, one wonderful day, as they passed through a village, Alexander heard voices speaking Greek. Alexander, who hated to talk, was suddenly talking to anyone and everyone he encountered. He commented on the weather, asked for the news, and made all manner of chatter he normally found pointless and dull.

Filbert and Florian knew a little Greek, enough to ask directions and purchase supplies, but they didn't have the patience to take lessons from Alexander. At times, he would try speaking to them in his native tongue. They could usually understand him, but would always answer in Kaltic.

The twins let him do the talking for them most of the time. He learned a number of interesting things in his conversations. For example, Kalatheans were leaving the kingdom in droves. He encountered several in the village, all of whom warned him sternly not to continue his journey. They told him that the old gods had returned, taken control of the capital, and were subjecting the people to all kinds of cruelty.

As if tyrannical gods weren't bad enough, a few months ago, barbarians started immigrating to the kingdom in massive numbers. They were Kalts mostly, loud, rowdy, and probably carrying diseases. The people petitioned the Senate and their gods to deport them all. Unfortunately, with so many Kalatheans fleeing, there was a labor shortage and the Senate couldn't afford to lose them. The gods responded, by forbidding Kalatheans from leaving. The borders were heavily guarded. If Alexander chose to return, he would have to stay.

missing ran on every local news network. She was only nine. Darrell and Tommy knew about it so, that very night, Vince ran over Darrell and framed Tommy for it. Easy to do when you're the only cop in town. Tommy was afraid and took off."

Had Anna not seen what she had, the last twenty-four hours, she might have been skeptical. Now, she was just sick. Anna looked at the twelfth day of Christmas note and started to cross stuff off, nine-year-old girl, eight ties a-binding, six o'clock newscast, three years ago.

Bonnie inhaled loudly. "My brother finally found my baby." Bonnie's voice faltered. "Val was in bad shape. Later that same night, I got a call from John Adams. He offered me one hundred thousand dollars to keep quiet and move out of town." Bonnie started crying harder. "I was poor. I knew I couldn't beat them. That power, that money. We lived in a rundown trailer. One hundred thousand dollars was ten times the value of our home. That's a lot of zeros on a check."

Yeah, five of them. Five golden rings. Gold. Money. Anna crossed off another clue. "Your trailer—was it on Potrage-Bystander Road?" Anna thought of the powder-blue mobile home. She had never made it past the utility pole.

"Yeah. Number eleven." The woman sobbed. Anna gave her a second to compose herself. "We were broke, and the damage was done."

"How was my husband involved?" Anna's chest felt heavy enough to crush her lungs.

Bonnie's guilt weighed on Anna as tangible as an anchor. The poor woman.

"We were paid with seven checks out of the salt mine account and listed on their books as an independent contractor. Your husband was their accountant and found, when he looked at the previous year's books, that we only consulted for one year. A hundred thousand dollars is a lot of money for someone to get for just a year's worth of consulting in Potrage. Your husband was a smart guy. He knew something was off but wasn't sure what. Rather than ask his client, and upset the apple cart, he showed up at my door."

"When?"

"Few months after it happened. I told him the whole story, and he hunted out Tommy through Daisy and, together, Jake and Tommy were going to come forward. Next thing I heard, your husband was dead and Tommy was long gone."

I looked at the list. The money came out of the salt mine. Twelve flags. They lived at 11 Potrage-Bystander Rd. Ten Commandments broken when a nine-year-old girl was bound in eight places. Seven checks cashed. The abduction all over the six o'clock news. Five golden zeros in a hundred thousand dollars. The four people murdered were Daisy, Darrell Hartman, Jake, and Daisy's son, Tommy. It all started three years ago. Jake cross-referenced two sets of books and died for what he knew.

"The whole community looked for Valerie when she went missing. Back then, we played it off like she had run away but came home after she saw her face on the news. Vince was more than happy to oblige in the cover-up."

"I bet."

Bonnie coughed. "Tommy kept in touch with me here and there. He was as scared as I was of the Adams folks. Thought they'd kill his momma if he showed his face again. But when he learned Valerie committed..."

It was as if she couldn't bring herself to say the word.

"When he found out Valerie had taken all those pills, he got in his car and drove straight to Potrage. Was gonna spill everything. I guess Vince got to him first. Him and Daisy. Then, I heard Vince framed his brother, Leo, 'cause Leo was the only other person who knew what happened."

"Vince killed Leo."

"Figured that was coming sooner or later," Bonnie said.

Anna wanted to ask what drove Valerie to commit suicide so many years later but didn't know how to frame the question. *How do you ask something like that?* "Do you know how Old Man Baker fits in?"

"No," she said. "I don't know who that is."

"When did your daughter..." *How do I ask this?* "Pass away?"

"December twenty-second."

"A few days before Christmas." Compassion welled anew in Anna's chest. This poor family. This poor mother.

"Right before you started getting those notes."

252

CHAPTER SIXTY-ONE

"Did something else happen to Valerie, or was it just too much to bear?"

"The photos came out. Some boys in her class somehow got some pictures from some internet website. They were passing them around school."

Anna ran a hand over her face. *Poor Valerie.*

"Valerie was only hanging on by a thread. After everything that had happened, she was never the same. We tried counselors and therapists. Once she got into middle school, she got into drugs and alcohol."

Middle school? Oh Lord.

Bonnie continued, "One afternoon she came home ranting and raving about these pictures. I called the school, but...Valerie stormed out the door that day and never came home."

Anna's eyes stung. "I am so sorry." The words felt inadequate but were the only ones Anna could muster. *Middle school.*

"They found her in some drug house downtown. I don't even know how she got herself down there. She'd taken a bunch of pills. I know my brother took it hard. I don't know how he could live and work in Potrage and see these people day in and day out, all these years, and not crack. He was the only other person who knew what really happened back then."

"I see." Anna didn't. *If you knew the truth, how could you not expose it?*

"That's actually why I agreed to talk to you. I know he's a friend of yours, and I was hoping you would talk to him for me. I know he hates me, but if he could just listen to me. Just once. I want to tell him how sorry I am. How much I regret what I've done. I have cancer, and I...I don't have much time left. I'm hoping to talk to him just one more time. Besides." She waited. "Valerie left something for him, and, under the circumstances....Oh...he's just got to see this." She broke into sobs.

"Who's your brother?" Anna nearly dropped the phone when Bonnie told her.

Chapter Sixty-Two

I didn't know what to say. *How could he keep this from me? I had my suspicions, but...*

"Anna, is everything okay?"

Anna nodded but couldn't meet his gaze. Fatigue drained her strength. She was so tired of the deception. Nothing made sense. She used those notes to find the girls, but they didn't mean what she thought they did. She had no idea what she was going to say, but she had to say something.

"What is it? What's wrong?"

Anna took a deep breath. "I know you sent me the Christmas notes."

"Oh my gosh. Come in." Father Matthew moved aside and gestured for her to step into the rectory.

Anna's ears stung from the bitter winter air. She stepped inside as a gush of warm air flooded her.

The rectory smelled like stale cigarettes, although it had been years since anyone smoked there. Dark oak tongue and groove paneled the lower half of the walls. Anna took a seat on one of the orange vinyl visitor's chairs in front of the dark walnut desk. The shag carpet looked the color of clown hair. Bookshelves lined the back wall, filled with gigantic texts. Books about faith. Books about forgiveness.

Can I forgive this?

Father Matthew and Anna had one of those relationships that had seamed together. It felt like she'd known him for three decades, instead of three years. Anna understood his isolation, and she thought he understood hers. Anna never knew why he became a priest, but his infinite compassion for the poor, the sick, and the grieving made him a perfect fit.

Father Matthew sank into his desk chair. "I'm so ashamed. I didn't mean to bring this to your door, to your home." He took off his glasses and ran a hand over his face. "You, my dear friend, were almost killed. And my niece... " He looked at her, and his eyes shimmered. "My niece is dead."

"I know. Your sister told me."

"Valerie was only..." His gaze fell to his cluttered desk. "She overdosed," he whispered. "I loved her so much. She was so beautiful."

"I'm so sorry." *Lord, if you can hear me, please give me wisdom.* Her gaze fixed on the wooden crucifix that hung over her priest's shoulder. Jesus hung there with His hands and feet nailed to the cross, his head wrapped in the crown of thorns.

The crucifix. A Catholic priest. A confession. It wasn't a pact with his sister Father Matthew couldn't break; it was much deeper than that. One Anna could understand. One Anna could forgive. Forgiveness flooded her spirit. Father Matthew lived with so many secrets. Anna stared at his trembling hands and knew she could live with this one. It was a matter of faith, and she had faith in him. He wouldn't hurt anyone. He wasn't capable of it. Why the notes? It didn't matter. It was over now.

"We've known each other a long time, Father." Anna reached out and held his folded hands. "Whatever your reason for those notes, you don't have to tell me. I trust that whatever it is, it's one I would understand."

He studied her through swollen eyes.

"I'd just like to know how Old Man Baker fits in." Anna let go of his hands and rested her back against the chair. "That is," Anna nodded toward the cross, "if you can tell me."

Father Matthew closed his eyes and exhaled. "Vince told Mr. Baker that he would be sent away, locked up for being crazy, if he didn't stay quiet about what he saw that night. The night Jake died. Poor Mr. Baker believed him. Did or said whatever was needed to stay out of an institution. I've been funneling Mr. Baker money so he's less dependent on the Adamses, but the emotional stronghold they have on him is, well, as you've seen, unbelievable. My best guess is Jake's wasn't the only car on that road."

"And someone forced him off." Anna nodded. *Old Man Baker. I not crazy. You the widow.*

She just shook her head and let the comfortable silence fill the space between them. So much pain. So much loss. For she and Father Matthew both.

She studied Father Matthew and, for a moment, tried to imagine the sacrifices he had made to live the life he did. A life of isolation, dedicated to serving others. No children, no wife, hardly any true friends. The dirty jokes stopped and the silly pranks ended when a priest came into the room.

Father Matthew was just a man, a man who had given up everything. Now, he had the never-ending Catholic Church sex scandal to contend with and the people who scowled at the collar he wore. The sins of the few had forever stained the souls of the many.

"I had no idea this was going to happen again. Vince was dormant, like a tumor in remission for years. By the time I'd found out another child had been taken from Potrage... Oh, God. It all happened so fast. And I never would've thought that the little girl in Rochester could be connected to him."

"This isn't your fault. It's the opposite. I saved those girls because of those notes."

"What?" His brow furrowed. "How?"

"I spoke to your sister. She had an explanation for every note, but what you meant to tell me, and what I thought you meant, were two different things. The notes each had a dual meaning. I thought the nine-year-old girl was Rose, the little girl I pulled from the cabin. I was working in current time, and you were referring to the past. You were telling me about your niece, but I thought you were leading me to the missing girls. I watched the six o'clock news. That was the day Ashley Grey was taken."

"The other child you—"

"Yes. And on the utility pole right in front of 11 Potrage-Bystander Road, there was a poster of the missing girl, and when I got the note about twelve flags a-flying, I went to the salt mine." As she told him, goosebumps prickled her arms. "I *knew* they were there. I knew it because of those notes."

"That can't be." He closed his eyes and slowly shook his head. "It can't—"

"It is. It's just like the urban legend of 'The Twelve Days of Christmas' song. Each verse has a dual meaning, just like your notes." Anna leaned forward and touched his forearm. "I never believe in coincidences, Father."

Father Matthew's gaze returned to his cluttered desk.

"Neither should you." Anna let go and sat back. "Your sister wants to talk to you. She has cancer, and there's not much time. She's really sick." Anna got up and moved toward the door, knowing he would need some time alone. "You need to forgive her, for both of you. Oh." Anna opened the door but paused in the doorway. Paint chips flaked off into her palm. "Your niece left something for you."

Chapter Sixty-Three

Valerie left something for him? Now, he had to call his sister. Father Matthew watched Anna through the paned window as she walked down the walkway. She tucked her chin in her fuzzy, gray coat, and her curly hair flapped in the breeze behind her. Would their relationship ever be the same? *No, it would be different...deeper.* Secrets did that, silent bands that forever bonded souls.

Can it be true? The dual meaning of the Christmas notes. He didn't know. Odd, however, Anna never asked him why he sent her the notes. Almost as if she knew and didn't have to.

He remembered it like it was yesterday. The conversation replayed in his head over and over for the last three years.

"Bless me, Father, for I have sinned, and it's been six months since my last confession." John Adams hung his head, and Father Matthew knew he didn't want to hear what the man had to say, but John had started, and it was too late. John had known, as Father Matthew did, that this exchange would be bound by the Seal of Confession, and Father Matthew would never be allowed to speak the sins of the penitent. A crime had been committed, but everyone was safe. No one was in danger. The Adamses' secret would be safe.

Father Matthew stared at the phone on his desk. No sense putting off the inevitable. Was his sister really sick? He hoped not but feared it to be true. How could he not notice how gray her skin looked at Valerie's funeral? How much weight she'd lost. Father Matthew thought it was the sadness and the stress. But, no, it was something more.

258

He picked up the phone and dialed, surprised that after all this time he still knew the number.

"Hello, Bonnie," he choked out. The breath seemed to be sucked from his lungs. "It's Matt."

"I'm glad you called."

He heard it in her voice. No, his sister hadn't lied to get him to call her. She'd be with Valerie soon enough. He hated his sister but somehow found he loved her at the same time.

"I guess you heard about the girls that were taken." She started to weep.

"I did."

"If I'd...I wouldn't of...I never thought it would happen again. You have to believe me."

"I do." He let out the breath he was holding. "I never thought it would happen again either."

"I loved her, Matt. I loved my daughter, too." She was frantic now. The words pouring out like an avalanche. "If I could go back, I would. If I had known. I don't know how she found out about the money... I never... I wouldn't have. We were leaving anyway. We were so poor. It was so much. We had to start over." She sobbed, and his heart squeezed in his chest, and he knew his sister's did the same. "I didn't take that money to sell her out. I took it to protect her. I was afraid of what they'd do to her if I didn't take it."

He listened to her crying, and his heart cried, too.

He thought about Anna and the dual meaning of the notes. "It's okay." The room seemed to spin. "It's okay." He couldn't hold it back. "I understand." To protect Valerie. Yes, it made sense. Why hadn't he thought of that?

"I'm so sorry I made you live with this secret all this time. Can you ever forgive me?"

"It wasn't your fault." He wanted to tell her about John's confession but couldn't. Would he have kept silent solely at his sister's urging? He couldn't say. It didn't matter. "I'm sorry too. I shouldn't have thought... "

"No. No. It's okay."

His sister was all he had left and soon, she'd leave him too. *Please don't take her from me. Please.*

Bonnie coughed.

"Are you okay?" He gripped the phone. He had vacation time. He should go there, be with her.

"She left something for you." Bonnie cleared her throat.

"What?"

"Valerie left a note for you. I'll mail it, but I want to read it to you, because, well, with everything that's happened. It's...well...here...I'll read it."

When she read the words aloud, his sister somehow sounded just like his niece. Father Matthew closed his eyes and imagined Valerie before him in the field that was neither too hot nor too cold that smelled like lilacs. He could see her standing there, beautiful; her long hair floating around her in a white dress that seemed to glow.

"'Hello, Uncle. If you're reading this, I'm already gone. I know you're going to be upset. Upset with me, my mom, maybe God, but I have to go.

"'I just wanted to tell you I know you loved me and you were always there for me.

"'If I can, I'll send you a sign I'm okay. A dozen of them, if need be, and I won't stop until you know for sure. I love you. Valerie.'"

He heard papers rustle and his sister returned to the line.

"I... I mean, can you believe it?" His sister stuttered. "Like she...I mean...I can't. When I found it just after the funeral, I didn't make the connection, but the notes...twelve Christmas notes. Anna said she saved those children because of those twelve notes. A dozen signs—twelve notes. Do you think Valerie could've...I mean...It's just... "

"I don't know," he said. *Oh, God, can it be? No.* Father Matthew rested his back against the desk chair and tried to take it all in. "There's no way she could've..."

"That's what I thought at first, too. But now... Now, after everything that's happened. Oh, God. Do you think? I mean..."

"Yes." He sighed. He knew it was what his sister needed to hear. "Yes, I do. It seems impossible, but... "

"Me too." Life itself seemed to fade from her. "I have to go. I'm so tired. I'll mail this to you. I just had to tell you."

"I'll call you soon." He suddenly didn't want her to hang up. "Maybe I'll come see you."

"That would be nice," she said dreamily.

Oh, God. "I love you," he said.

"I love you, too," she said. "Pray for me."

"I will," he said. *I will. Please help her.*

Father Matthew hung up the phone and stared at the cross on the wall. He thought about the events of the last few days. The notes, the missing children. He looked heavenward. *No. There was no way.*

Please help my sister. Oh, God. Father Matthew hung his head. "Forgive me, Father." He held his face in his hands. *What have I done? Oh, Lord, what have I done?* "Oh, God. What have I done? Please. Oh, please forgive me." He didn't want to give up the priesthood. He couldn't. It was the only path he had ever known. The only place he fit in. Now, he needed to. *What kind of priest sends notes about a confession? Surely, that would violate every rule.* His anger drove him to do it, and, in that rage, he'd drafted silly notes, like a coward, telling himself he wasn't leaking the secret but wanting someone to find out the truth.

He didn't confirm anything for Anna, never said the words aloud. But the notes broke the Seal of Confession. Would God forgive him? Could God forgive him? He had to tell the Bishop; he knew that. It was over. The church would never allow him to remain. With all that had gone on in the church, no transgression could or should be overlooked. *Oh, God.* He reached for the phone but was stopped by a knock on the door.

"Father. Father. Open up." Someone pounded. "Hurry. Quick. Father."

He stood and caught his reflection in the glass window. Dressed in black with his collar on—it defined him. For he was more fit to be a priest now than any time in the last three years. It was who he was and all he had. Could he live with another secret? Another to answer for when his time came.

Rap. Rap. Rap. More knocking. He tugged open the door.

"Father, you have to see this." One of the altar girls stood on the step, her eyes wide in wonder, a giant smile across her face. "Come look. Come on." She jumped down off the step and raced into the yard.

Father Matthew threw on his long, black coat and followed her. A few other kids from the neighborhood had gathered.

There, in the middle of the snow-covered lawn, was a perfect circle of green grass. In the center of the circle was a lilac bush—the bush his niece had given him on his birthday. Each branch was covered in spectacular purple blooms. A single band of sunlight enveloped the bush as wisps of snow whirled around the rest of the yard.

"Father." A boy, no older than twelve, tugged on his long black coat. "What does it mean?"

Father Matthew looked down at the child—a chubby boy with blond hair and giant dimples.

If I can, I will send you a sign that I'm okay. A dozen of them, if need be. The twelve Christmas notes. Anna was right. There was no such thing as coincidence. He looked at the lilac bush. *I won't stop until you know for sure.*

"Does it mean something?" the boy asked again.

"It means," Father Matthew pushed out the words, "sometimes things happen we cannot understand. But that's okay. It's not our job to understand." Father Matthew's gaze swept over each of the children's faces and relished their awe and wonder. Standing there, in the freezing cold, he saw the blooming bush as they did. And through their eyes, he found his faith. "We only need to believe."

Acknowledgements

There are too many people to thank and I know I will leave many off this list. First and foremost, thank you to my friend and mentor, Vonnie Davis, who passed away way too soon. I wish she was here to celebrate with me. Thank you to my agent, Dawn Dowdle—a friend, cheerleader, and literary counselor all rolled into one. Thank you to the team at Level Best Books, especially my editor, Shawn Simmons. Thanks to Jeff Szczesniak for his expertise, the HCW gang for their tough but constructive critiques, and to my friends and family who never let me give up on my dream. Finally, thank you Jesus for Your love, grace, and mercy. I hope I have answered the call.

About the Author

Jennifer Bee resides near the Blue Ridge Mountains of Virginia with her husband, two kids, and a house full of pets. Prior to becoming a full-time author, she worked in marketing and owned her own advertising agency. In her spare time, Jennifer loves to swim, read, and spend time outdoors. She is the author of the Anna Greenan Mystery Series.